W9-BVJ-478

THE WILD HEART

'I'll be back, Morna...' To Jared it was a foolish promise he had never expected to keep. Now the girl whose heart he had captured was a passionate young woman – and he was a man haunted by bitterness, desperately struggling to save his family's estate. His desire for revenge set him on a dangerous course which was to lead him to a cruel destiny. Condemned to exile, he vented his fury on the woman who loved him – the one woman who could save him from himself. Did Morna have the courage to follow him halfway round the world?

THE WILD HEART

The Wild Heart

by

Anne Herries

Magna Large Print Books
Long Preston, North Yorkshire
BD23 4ND, England.

British Library Cataloguing in Publication Data.

Herries, Anne
    The wild heart.

    A catalogue record of this book is
    available from the British Library

    ISBN   0-7505-2275-5

First published in Great Britain 1986 by Mills & Boon Ltd.

Copyright © Anne Herries 1986

Cover illustration © André Leonard by arrangement with
P.W.A. International Ltd.

The moral right of the author has been asserted

Published in Large Print 2005 by arrangement with
Linda Sole

Magna Large Print is an imprint of Library Magna Books Ltd.

Printed and bound in Great Britain by
T.J. (International) Ltd., Cornwall, PL28 8RW

CHAPTER ONE

The girl on her horse might have been a part of the windswept landscape as she sat motionless, intent on the scene below. From her vantage point at the peak of the cliff, she could clearly see the tragic consequences of what had been the worst storm of the winter.

The wind had blown strongly all night, whipping the sea into a frenzy about the treacherous coastline and lashing the stunted trees in its path as it coursed inland across the lonely moors. As happened all too often along the Cornish coast, a ship had been driven into the small cove and had foundered on the rocks. Wreckage from the unfortunate vessel lay scattered on the beach, and was being picked over by the villagers. Women wrapped in thick shawls against the bitter cold, barefoot children, and men who had been thrown out of work by the recent failure of the local tin mine, hunted feverishly for anything of value in the débris littering the sands. Some of the bolder men had gone out to the wreck, climbing over the rocks which had been exposed by the receding tide, thick ropes tied round their waists so that they could be hauled back to safety if they fell into the swirling water.

Morna Hamilton watched as several casks were snatched from the deck of the listing vessel, which was already more than half submerged. The next high tide would take it to the bottom, together with the cargo that remained in its holds. Suddenly her eyes strained towards the figures clambering on the wreck, picking out the long dark locks of one man in particular.

Her heart gave a lurch as she saw him pointing towards a dozen or more casks still secured to the deck and partially below water. She might have known he would be here, the girl thought bitterly, his promise to meet her forgotten in the excitement of salvaging whatever he could from the doomed ship.

Anger glinted in her blue eyes. He must know how difficult it was for her to get away now that she had company in the house, yet he had ignored the arrangements they had made for Morna to see the stallion he was proposing to sell, preferring instead to join the crowd on the beach and risk his life for a few barrels.

'You wretch, Jared Trenwith!' she cried, her full sensuous lips tight with temper. 'I hope you drown...'

The moment the words left her mouth she

was regretting them as Jared dived beneath the water washing over the deck. It was obvious even from this distance that he was struggling to free the ropes binding the remaining casks to the ship, and Morna caught her breath as a huge wave crashed over the wreck, sweeping the men still above the waterline off their feet. She could hear the frantic screams of women waiting on the shore as the men on the rocks began to haul their companions in. It was a scene of utter confusion as men fought the elements, desperately trying to save their comrades from being smashed against the jagged spurs.

Morna watched breathlessly, her hands clenching unconsciously on the reins as she waited for that head to surface. Where was he? she wondered, torn between anxiety and fury that he should hazard his life for so little.

'If you die, Jared, I'll swear you'll never rest in peace,' she muttered, a surge of panic spreading through her as she saw another huge wave crash against the ship. If Fate were cruel enough to rob her of him now she would die, she thought, feeling a sharp pain crushing her breast so that she could scarcely breathe. 'Oh, please don't die...'

A burst of cheering from the beach sent relief coursing through her tense body. The casks were floating free of the deck now, and the dark-haired giant lay across them, clinging on as his eager helpers caught the rope he had secured to his little raft. Morna's lips twisted in a wry smile as he and his prize were hauled to safety even as the wreck began to shudder and heave violently.

Silence gripped those on shore as the ship finally slipped beneath the waves. It was too late to recover anything more, though wood and other débris might be washed up on shore over the next few days. The men were making their way back to the beach, shouldering the precious barrels they had snatched from the sea. There was much laughter and shouting as the hero of the hour was surrounded by his triumphant companions.

Morna scowled, anger reasserting itself now that the danger was past. So Jared was once again the darling of the villagers, with whom he seemed to spend most of his time since his return from India after the scandal of his father's death. When she had heard that he was returning, her excitement had kept her awake for nights on end. She had been so certain that he was coming back to her – coming back to keep the promise he had made her the night before he went away, when as a skinny child of thirteen she had wound her arms about his neck, clinging to him and weeping as she begged him not to go.

'Don't go away, Jared,' she had pleaded,

her face red and blotchy with crying. 'I shall die if you do. I can't bear it. I can't...'

She remembered so clearly the indulgent smile on his face as he looked down at her, and his teasing, careless reply. 'You've a lot of growing-up to do yet, princess, and I'm bored with being the son of a country squire. I want some excitement – but when I come back I'll take you with me, and we'll explore the world together.' He ruffled her hair then in a lordly way. 'That's if you haven't forgotten me and married some wealthy marquis – or a duke perhaps?'

His teasing had brought a watery smile, but she had clung to him even more fiercely as she vowed, 'I'll never marry anyone but you, Jared. Never, never, never!'

He had laughed then, with the confidence and arrogance of a man who had pride in himself and faith in his own ability to conquer the world. 'I'm not sure that anyone else would want a minx like you, Morna! But maybe I'll have you, if you're still as wild and wilful as you are now. I expect you'll be one of those prissy little society girls...'

His teasing had finally roused her from the depths of despair and she had flown at him with her fists, beating against his chest in a rage. He had caught her wrists, holding her and grinning as she vainly pitted herself against his superior strength. Her rage had turned to frustration and then to helpless laughter as he tossed her over his shoulder and carried her home, depositing her at her door with a grin.

'I'll be back, Morna,' he had promised, giving her a careless wave as he turned and walked away.

She had waited and waited throughout five long years, sometimes despairing that she would ever see him again, for he had not written to her once in all that time, and the only news she had had of him was when his father occasionally rode over to dine with hers. Yet she had never forgotten his promise to come back for her, though she knew it had been given on the spur of the moment to comfort her – but he must have meant it or he would not have said it. There had always been something special between them. She knew it! Now Jared was back, and had been for several months, but she had scarcely seen him. Because of their long-standing relationship she had expected him to visit her home, if only because they had both lost their fathers this past year, but he had stayed away, just as he had avoided all his old friends. It was almost as if he had chosen to cut himself off from his own class, and his odd behaviour had set the tongues wagging. When they did happen to meet it was only because she had gone out of her way to arrange it. And now he had broken his promise to meet her today. The girl wanted to scream her protest aloud. What devil had prompted him to hazard his life for such a paltry reward?

Perhaps her feelings were so intense at that moment that they communicated themselves to the man below. He glanced up suddenly, seeing the girl and horse outlined against the glowering sky. Waving, he moved towards the cliff path, obviously intending to scale it and join her.

As she watched him begin the climb, warring emotions inside her made Morna's chest feel tight. Her longing to see him was mixed with anger, fear of rejection and jealousy that he should prefer the company of the villagers to hers. Finally, pride won.

'Oh no, I'll not be second best for you or any man,' she muttered. 'You broke your word, Jared Trenwith, now you can pay for it!'

She waited until he had almost reached the top of the steep incline, then wheeled her horse about and rode furiously across the great sweep of open grassland, laughing out loud as she imagined his annoyance when he reached the top and found her gone.

Jared stared after the girl, now only a tiny figure in the distance, a look of amusement mixed with annoyance in his grey eyes. So the Hamilton minx had decided to teach him a lesson, had she? Well, maybe he'd deserved it. Common politeness demanded that he should call and offer his condolences on the death of her father, and he knew he owed her more than that. He had made her a foolish promise, never thinking that she would expect him to keep it, especially now. The smile faded, leaving a bleak look in his eyes. He was too much a man of the world not to be aware of Morna's interest, but he wanted no entanglements there. There was no room in his life for a woman now. Besides, the girl was a skinny scrap of a thing with eyes too large for her face and a violent temper. It was a strange thing about those eyes, though. It was the look of despair she had given him that made him promise to return that night, and despite himself those eyes had haunted him throughout the years in India.

Jared shook his head, mocking his own thoughts. It wasn't even as if she was the type of woman who appealed to his strongly sensual nature. Danielle with her tempting curves and compliant nature was his idea of a pleasing companion in bed. For a while he had toyed vaguely with the idea of marrying her, but she had recently wed another. A frown passed fleetingly across his brow. Danielle had dented his pride, but it did not matter. No woman had the power to reach him these days. Although the tan he had acquired in India had long since faded, his features had the sculptured look of a man inured to the hardships of military campaigns. There was something about the honed steel of his physique that warned the world to be a little wary of this man, and his eyes were cold, as if they had seen too much.

As a youth, Jared's spirit of adventure had led him into many a scrape, but it was his own restlessness that prompted him to seek service in India rather than any real scandal. He had been bored with country life, and since his father had warned him against running up gambling debts in town, he had decided to find some excitement. Military life had suited him, and he rose quickly to the rank of Captain. He believed he would have continued to rise in the army had it not been for the sudden death of his father and a letter that brought him hurrying home. What he discovered on his return forced him to resign his commission and throw himself into the struggle to save his family's estate – a struggle that had appeared hopeless from the start.

It was the desperate state of his finances that had caused Jared to consider selling the stallion, a course he was reluctant to take. He had cherished hopes of establishing a stud with that animal, but it seemed now that his plans were doomed to failure. Unless…

A shout from below broke the train of his

thoughts. The men on the beach had opened a cask of rum and were signalling to him to join in their celebration. Waving to acknowledge the summons, Jared felt his mood lighten. Compared to those unfortunate wretches, he was a lucky man. He still had a roof over his head, even if there were a few holes in it, and he had Devil Lad. If he could find a way of stopping the bank foreclosing on the mortgage next month, perhaps there was still a chance of making his dream come true. Though, if he must sell the horse, he would rather it went to Morna – but not if she wanted it as a present for her younger brother Philip. He supposed he ought to have kept his appointment with her, but the news of the wreck had put it out of his head.

'Come on, Captain, there'll be none left for you if you tarry!'

Grinning, Jared began to scramble back down the cliff face. He would share in the rum, but he'd take nothing more from the prize they had captured that morning. To the men on the beach, their triumph against the sea meant that their families would not starve this winter. His own need could not be satisfied by the profit from a few barrels, nor would he have accepted his share if it could. If the Trenwith land was to be saved, it would be by his own efforts. There might just be a way, if he cared to take it...

Morna reined in as the red brick walls of her home came into view, not wanting to go indoors just yet. She sat for a moment, drinking in the beauty of the old house, feeling the familiar ache deep inside her. Hamilton Towers had been built towards the end of the Elizabethan era and was a solid manor house, evidence of the huge fortune then enjoyed by her ancestors. A fortune that had grown over the years, buying a baronetcy for Henry Hamilton when King James I needed his coffers replenishing. Although the baronet of the time had lost a part of his fortune in the South Sea Bubble in 1720, and the more recent failure of the Hamilton tin mine had depleted the family resources still further, Morna's brother had inherited a sizeable sum on their father's death nine months ago.

The thought of her brother brought a frown to Morna's brow. It was because of Philip, rather because of the friend he had invited to stay – that Morna was reluctant to enter the house. She had disliked Sir Richard Stainton on sight, and only her own pride had prevented her from betraying it.

Sighing, she dismounted as she saw her brother leave the house and walk purpose-fully across the lawns towards her. From the look on Philip's face, it was clear there was trouble brewing. The two of them were apt to quarrel violently, and he had departed for

London several weeks ago with their last furious row still unsettled between them.

'Where have you been, Morna?' he demanded as she gave her reins to a groom and went to meet him. 'Don't you realise it is discourteous to our guest for you to be absent all morning?'

A quick flush stained her cheeks. She realised only too well that her freedom must be curtailed for a while. She could not ride all over the countryside whenever she pleased during Sir Richard's visit. Yet, despite the difficulties involved, she had been determined to keep her appointment with Jared.

'I had a meeting I could not cancel,' she said defensively. 'Had you told me you were bringing a guest home, Philip, I could have made other arrangements.'

'I am not accountable to you.'

'Nor I to you.'

Brother and sister faced each other angrily. They were much alike in looks; both black-haired and with startlingly blue eyes and high cheekbones. In childhood they had been almost inseparable, although Morna was the elder by a year, the bond between them surviving their frequent and noisy quarrels. Neglected by their father, they had been allowed to run wild after their mother died. The pair had succeeded in terrifying a string of tutors and governesses, none of whom stayed more than a few months. Consequently, both had grown used to having their own way.

'You've been to see Trenwith,' Philip accused suddenly. 'I told you you were not to speak to him again.'

'I'll speak to him if I wish!' Morna's lips set stubbornly. 'I don't know why you quarrelled with him, Philip, and I don't care what you say.'

For a moment Philip's eyes narrowed dangerously, then he shrugged. 'Please yourself then, but never ask him to this house while I'm in it.'

'I doubt he would come, if that's your attitude.'

Morna looked at him uncertainly. She had never known what had caused the quarrel between Philip and their neighbour. As a boy he had idolised Jared, following his hero everywhere. Jared had accepted his homage, treating him with a careless affection and tolerating his presence, as he had Morna's whenever she tagged along.

It was true that Jared had changed since those days. The first time she had seen him after his return from India, he had stared right through her and she had thought him a hard-eyed stranger. Then he had smiled, and she glimpsed the youth who had stolen her heart.

'Don't let's quarrel again, Morna.' Philip gave her a winning smile. 'I've come home so that we can give a dance for your birthday…'

'A dance?' Morna looked at him in surprise. 'We haven't had a ball for years – not since before mother died.'

'Then it's time we did.' Philip slipped his arm through hers. 'You'll be nineteen next month – it's time you came out, Morna.'

A peal of laughter broke from her, lighting up the blue eyes and giving her the appearance of beauty. 'Oh, Phil! You can't be serious...' She stared at him, the laughter leaving her face. 'You don't expect me to go through all that nonsense?'

Philip frowned, his mouth firming. 'You're not a child any more. You're a young lady and my sister: it's time you started to behave in a manner befitting your birth.'

His own manner was slightly pompous, and the girl looked at him defiantly. 'I believe I have done nothing to make you ashamed of me?' She might have added that his own behaviour before he left for town had left much to be desired.

Realising he had upset her, Philip squeezed her arm. 'You must know I didn't mean that the way it sounded – but surely you don't wish to stay here alone all your life? Haven't you thought of marriage, Morna?'

'No!' A rueful smile crept over her lips. 'Well, perhaps I have thought of it occasionally.'

Her brother grinned. 'You would be unnatural if you hadn't! Father should have done something about it a couple of years ago.'

'He did speak to me once,' Morna admitted. 'It was when he asked Cousin Jane to come and live with us. I think he intended Jane to chaperon me.'

Laughter lurked in her eyes once more, and Philip snorted his disgust. 'A fine chaperon our cousin would be. She does exactly as you tell her!'

A picture of their timid, plain-faced cousin came into Morna's mind. 'Jane is so grateful to us for giving her a home, Phil. She wouldn't dare to argue with either of us – I think that's why father gave up the idea of sending me to London for a season.'

'I doubt he even considered it seriously.' Philip sounded bitter. 'When did he ever bother about either of us?'

'Don't, Phil,' Morna begged, laying her hand on his arm. 'He was so alone after mother died. That last year when you were at university...'

Her brother's face hardened. 'I hated every moment of it. He knew I was no scholar, Morna, yet he forced me to go – so that I would be humiliated.'

'You can't think he meant to hurt you!'

'Can't I?' Philip's expression was grim. 'I don't know why you're defending him: he never cared for you.'

Morna's eyes slid away from her brother's

23

stony gaze. It was true that their father had neglected them other years, yet during the last months of his life, his illness had made him seem vulnerable. Perhaps because she had helped Cousin Jane to nurse him, Morna had lost any feeling of bitterness towards him that she might have harboured. Philip had come home only a few hours before their father's death, and so did not know how much he had suffered. It saddened Morna that he should still feel such a deep hurt and she hugged his arm, wanting to drive the shadows from his face.

'Who shall we invite to the dance, Phil?'

Philip flicked her cheek with his finger. 'Everyone! All our worthy neighbours – and a few of my friends from London. Richard has promised to stay on for it.'

Was she imagining that slight hint of nervousness in his voice? Morna wondered. She had noticed something when he introduced Sir Richard the previous evening. Yet she could see no reason why he should be afraid of his friend.

Almost as if he had read her thoughts, Philip looked down at her. 'Richard has been a good friend to me, Morna. Without his support, I could not have gained entrance to the exclusive clubs in town. One has to be put up for them, you know.'

'Would that matter so very much?'

Philip gave a hoot of laughter. 'Now I

24

know it's time you stopped living like a hermit down here, my girl! You sound like a plebeian.'

They had reached the main hall. Morna shivered as the cold struck into her. Even in summer it was always cool in this room, and the huge fire burning in the open grate today was making little impression. She moved towards a smaller room to her left, pausing on the threshold as she saw Sir Richard relaxing by the hearth in what had once been her father's favourite chair.

He had been reading, but he laid the book down and got to his feet at once. 'Miss Hamilton, you must be frozen. Please, you must come to the fire immediately.'

Morna stiffened, resenting the note of familiarity in his voice. 'Thank you, Sir Richard, but I prefer to change my gown before joining you.'

'You have been riding, I see. Had I known you meant to venture out this morning, I would have come with you.'

Her eyes snapped with anger. Sir Richard was undoubtedly a striking man with his dark eyes and thick, almost wiry hair. Above average height and of medium build, he wore his clothes with an air of distinction... Yet there was something about him that sent a shiver of revulsion through her. He might be a gentleman by birth, but there was an underlying coarseness in his character that

25

displeased her.

'It is my habit to ride alone, Sir Richard.' Her tone was a reproof but he ignored it, his smile unwavering as he touched her arm.

'Ah yes, you must often have felt the isolation of this place, Miss Hamilton. It was unkind of Philip to desert you. I have chided him for it, I promise you.'

'I do not find it lonely, sir. I have lived here all my life, and...' Her protest died as she saw the mockery in his eyes.

'Of course, I meant no disrespect. There is much to recommend your home to me, Miss Hamilton. However, I feel that you would enjoy the pleasures and diversions to be found in London. I shall insist that Philip uses his influence to persuade you to accompany us when we return.'

Something in his words sent a chill through her. It was almost as if he were dictating to her, as if he believed he had the power to control her life – and Philip's.

Glancing at her brother's subdued expression, Morna frowned. Was it possible that this man had some hold over Philip? The thought worried her, and she moved sharply away from him.

'You will excuse me now,' she said coldly. 'I shall return in a little while.'

Walking quickly from the room before either of the men could find some reason to delay her, Morna chewed her lower lip as she made her way upstairs and along the open gallery. Philip was acting very strangely, and she was certain it was because of Sir Richard. She wished fervently that her brother had not brought the stranger into their home, but she knew that he had every right to do so. Hamilton Towers belonged to him, not to her. She herself had inherited only her mother's jewels and the sum of ten thousand pounds. It was a respectable dowry, but nothing compared with her brother's inheritance.

As yet she had scarcely touched even the income from her own money, though she had very definite plans about what she wanted to do with at least a part of it. For the moment those plans had been frustrated, and already Morna was regretting the impulse which had caused her to ride away before Jared reached the top of the cliff. It had taken considerable courage to arrange the meeting in the first instance, and she did not know when she would be free to make other arrangements.

Guessing that Jared must be desperate to consider selling the stallion, she had hoped to purchase the animal and leave it in Jared's stables, thereby becoming his business partner. It was a bold move, and one that many would consider both unwise and unladylike; but such considerations meant little to Morna. Besides, a partnership could lead to other things...

27

Sighing, she began to tug at the fastenings of her bodice. Despite going out of her way to meet Captain Trenwith as he exercised the stallion on the moors, she had managed no more than an exchange of compliments with him whenever their paths crossed. It was almost as if he were determined to keep a distance between them, allowing none of the intimacy that they had once enjoyed.

It was only when she had heard that Jared was considering selling the stallion that Morna had dared to send a servant to his home with a message inviting him to the Towers. The Captain had declined, saying in his letter that he would be pleased to welcome her to his house if she wished to inspect the horse. She had agreed at once, never dreaming of cancelling the appointment even when her brother arrived home unexpectedly. So it was not surprising she had been so angry to find him on the beach instead of at his house.

Tossing her riding-gown to the floor, Morna looked at her reflection in the mirror, pulling a face at what she saw. Her face, like her body, was too thin, though her eyes were large and brilliant. There was, however, no way she could ever be thought beautiful, the girl decided at last. No, if she were ever to achieve her heart's desire, it must be through her material assets and not her looks.

Living in the country as she did, it was impossible to remain in ignorance of Jared's circumstances. If she had needed confirmation of her beliefs, one glance at the Trenwith estate must have told her all. The barns and cottages were falling down, and the house itself was crumbling away from lack of attention. Unless Jared did something soon, it would be too late.

Ten thousand pounds was not a great sum, but it would repair much of the neglect suffered over the years, and her mother's jewels must be worth as much again. Most men in Jared's circumstances would be glad of the chance to wed an heiress who, if she were not beautiful, was far from ugly. Unfortunately, Jared Trenwith was not most men. He had an obstinate, proud nature and a way of keeping one at a distance when he chose – but he had made her a promise, and Morna was determined to remind him of it.

She sighed again as she pulled on a plain grey gown that did nothing to improve her looks. Somehow she must find a way of meeting Jared again soon, but how? In the act of twisting her heavy dark hair into a severe knot at the nape of her neck, the thought suddenly struck her and her eyes began to sparkle. The impish grin transformed her face, bringing it to sudden, glowing life. Did she dare? Why not? After

all, Philip had told her to invite everyone...
And it would serve him right!

'You look very pretty, my dear.' Cousin
Jane's tone was full of approval as she
smiled at Morna. 'Indeed, I do not know
when I have seen you look so well.'

Morna pulled a face as she glanced at her
own reflection. It was true that her dress of
deep blue velvet was more becoming than
her mourning gowns, but Jane's opinion was
distinctly biased. There was a warm affection
between the two despite the differences in
their characters, and it was Jane's gentle
persuasion that had decided the girl to put
off her blacks for this evening at least.

'I suppose we should go down now,' she
said, slipping an arm through Jane's. 'Our
guests will be arriving soon.'

Jane's hand trembled, but she made an
effort to control it. 'I am always so nervous
on these occasions, my love. I fear I shall say
something foolish and disgrace you.'

'You could never do that!' Morna gave her
a wicked smile. 'I am much more likely to say
something outrageous and shock our worthy
neighbours – except that they must be
beyond being shocked by anything I do now.'

'Oh no,' Jane protested loyally. 'You can be
a little ... headstrong at times, but you never
go beyond what is perfectly acceptable to a
sensible mind.'

'Jane! How can you tell such untruths?' Morna laughed at her cousin's expression. 'I know I have shocked you only too often.'

Jane smiled and shook her head. The girl's liveliness worried her at times, but she could never have found it in her heart to condemn anything Morna did. Before coming to the Towers, she had lived in a large, cold rectory with a father who had stifled every natural urge she had ever known. Morna's kindness in welcoming her, after the loss of both her father and her home, had tapped a deep well of love within her. She wanted nothing more of life than to stay on at the Towers and serve her young cousin in any way she could.

As they walked along the gallery together, she saw Sir Richard approaching and her whole body tensed. Although she had spoken to no one of her feelings, Jane instinctively sensed danger to the girl she loved from this man. There was something predatory in the way he looked at Morna sometimes that frightened her cousin.

Morna felt her companion stiffen and smiled at her reassuringly. Sir Richard's continued presence in the house was an annoyance that must be accepted. She had not changed her opinion of him these past two weeks, despite all his flattering attentions to her, but she was not afraid of him.

They met at the head of the stairs, and the girl raised her chin defiantly. 'Our guests will be arriving soon, sir. I hope you will not find this evening's entertainment a little slow for your taste.'

'How could I be bored when you will be present, Morna?'

A small frown creased her brow. He had begun to address her by her first name recently, claiming that his intimacy with her brother made him almost one of the family. She had been about to rebuke him for his familiarity when a look from Philip stopped her. Each succeeding day had convinced Morna that this man did have some kind of a hold over her brother, and because of her conviction she held back the angry retorts that often sprang to her lips. For Philip's sake, she must be polite to his guest.

Accordingly, she did not refuse him now when he claimed the honour of the first dance of the evening. Nor did she object when he stood by her side to welcome their visitors, though his proprietary manner towards her was irritating.

Philip had invited two gentlemen from London for the dance. They had arrived some hours earlier and were changing in their rooms. Neither of them had made a favourable impression on Morna, and she was not surprised to find that they kept very much to themselves when they finally came downstairs. Their clothes were too fashionable for a country affair, and it was obvious they felt themselves superior to the assembled company, though both remembered their manners sufficiently to ask their hostess for a dance. Afterwards, they disappeared in the direction of the library, where several card tables had been set up, and were not to be seen again for the rest of the night.

Their absence affected Morna's enjoyment of the evening not at all. A little to her surprise, she found herself much in demand by the local gentlemen. Young men, who had hardly glanced at her when they met in church or on market days at Bodmin, were suddenly paying her attention. Their compliments made her laugh, bringing a mischievous sparkle to eyes that were almost as blue as the velvet of her gown. For she had little doubt that it was her inheritance which had made her so attractive in their eyes.

Nevertheless, it was a heady experience for a girl who had rarely been in company, and who had been until recently accustomed to dine only with the vicar and a few of her father's oldest friends. Her pleasure was dimmed simply by the absence of Captain Trenwith. She had sent his invitation herself, and though he had not replied, she had confidently expected he would come. As the evening wore on, however, she was forced to accept that he was not going to arrive. His total lack of response puzzled her. Why had he neither accepted nor refused her invitation? Despite her annoyance at his rudeness, she continued to look for him until late in the evening, her eyes constantly straying towards the door.

'You seem a little tired, Miss Hamilton. Would you like to rest for a while?'

Realising she had allowed her attention to wander from her partner, Morna blushed. 'I am thirsty,' she admitted. 'Shall we find some refreshment?'

The young man agreed instantly, offering his arm. They walked together from the dance floor, conversing easily as they made their way towards the buffet tables.

Henry Jackson was the younger son of one of her father's closest friends. They had known each other all their lives, though neither had ever been very interested in the other. Morna was glad that Henry had refrained from showering her with compliments this evening.

'It was quite a storm last month,' Henry said as they sipped a cup of cold punch. 'A terrible thing that ship going down the way she did.'

'Yes.' Morna shuddered. 'I saw her actually go under – did you?'

'Good lord no!' Henry ejaculated. 'Father would cut me off without a penny if I had anything to do with that nonsense. You know what people are saying, of course?'

'No?' Morna looked up at him question-ingly.

'They say the vessel was deliberately lured on to the rocks.'

'Oh no!' Morna was shocked. 'I can't believe that. She was driven in by the storm. No one in the village would do anything so wicked! This is the nineteenth century, Henry. The wreckers haven't been active for years.'

'Maybe not – but things have got pretty bad here recently. When children are going hungry, their parents can be tempted back to the old ways.' His eyes slid away from her steady gaze. 'Philip's decision to close the mine put a lot of men out of work, you know.'

'Philip had no choice,' Morna said defensively. 'The mine was losing money.'

'Your father had agreed to fund further exploration at a new level. It is the general opinion locally that he would not have closed the mine without at least trying to find a new lode.'

Morna was silent. She had quarrelled violently with her brother over his decision, but she had no intention of betraying him to an outsider.

'Even if many of the villagers did lose their jobs, I don't believe they would deliberately lure a ship on to the rocks – that would be murder.'

'As you say,' Henry agreed. 'And it's whispered that Trenwith is their leader.'

'That is a scandalous accusation!' Morna cried, her eyes sparking with anger. 'How dare you say such a thing?'

'You can't deny he's behaved very oddly since he came back,' Henry said awkwardly. 'Besides, I'm not the only one...' He broke off as Morna walked swiftly away from him. 'Please, I did not mean to offend you.'

Morna did not glance back as she left the room. Her heart was beating so rapidly that she felt ill. Henry Jackson's accusations were nothing but lies, of course, but even so she found them distressing. If the villagers had been driven to such a terrible act it was partly her fault; she should have found a way of helping them after the mine failed. Indeed she had tried giving food and money to a few individuals, but had found her offer brusquely rebuffed. It simply had not occurred to her that the closure would have such terrible results. She sought sanctuary in a little room at the back of the house. She closed the door behind her, shutting her eyes to hold back her tears. It could not be true that Jared had encouraged the villagers to do such a terrible thing! It could not!

'Morna, are you ill?'

The room was lit only by the firelight; and in her distress, Morna had not noticed Sir Richard sitting in a chair by the window.

She stiffened as he rose and came towards her, her hand instinctively groping for the door handle.

'You must not go on my account,' Sir Richard said softly. 'Something has upset you, I think?'

'I must return to my guests...' Morna retreated a few steps and found the door at her back. 'I thought the room was empty.'

'Please, do not be afraid of me.' Sir Richard laid his hand on her arm. 'Surely you are aware of my deep regard for you?'

She felt the moistness of his palm on her bare flesh, and shivered. Since his arrival, she had taken good care not to be alone with him, and she mentally chastised herself for her carelessness this evening.

'I know of no reason why you should have a regard for me, Sir Richard. We hardly know each other.'

'It is true that we met only recently, but I felt drawn to you from the first moment, Morna. There is something about you which intrigues me.' His fingers caressed her wrist. 'You have a certain wildness of spirit I find exciting...'

Morna jerked away from him. 'You have no right to speak to me thus, sir! My brother would not approve of such familiarity.'

'Philip would not deny me the right to speak my feelings.' His soft laughter sent chills down her spine. 'Surely you have seen how eager he is to please me? Have you never wondered at it, my dear Miss Hamilton?'

'What do you mean?' She stared at him, her eyes wide. 'Are you threatening me, Sir Richard?'

'Threatening you? Now why should you think that? I have been trying to tell you how much I admire you.' He raised her hand to his lips, kissing it. 'It may be that I shall ask you something very soon, Morna – but Philip shall give his consent first, since you will have it so.'

'If you are suggesting that you wish to marry me...' Morna broke off as the pressure of his fingers became painful on her wrist.

'You would not want me to insult you by suggesting a less honourable relationship?' Sir Richard's voice held a soft menace. 'No, no, my dear girl, I am convinced you will be sensible when the time comes.'

Every nerve in her body was screaming a protest, but she held them in check. She could scarcely believe that this man had dared to speak to her so openly, and she knew something must be terribly wrong. She had sensed his underlying arrogance from the beginning, but until tonight he had hidden it behind a veil of politeness. Now he was suddenly sure of his power, so much so that he had let her glimpse what behind his habitual mask.

Lifting her eyes to his, Morna saw the

triumph there. 'What has happened tonight?' she whispered. 'Have you some mysterious hold over Philip?'

His features assumed a look of reproach. 'Your brother is my friend. He has already made his wishes concerning you, known to me – but I will leave him to tell you himself.'

He released her wrist at last. 'Go back to your guests, Morna. We shall talk of this again another day. I am a patient man, and I shall allow you time to collect your thoughts.'

Morna smoothed her flesh where his fingers had bruised it. 'If you imagine Philip has the power to change my mind about … about anything, you will find you are mistaken.'

'I do hope you are wrong,' he said, a cold smile on his lips. 'For then I should be forced to a less pleasant course of action – but, as I said, I am sure that a little talk with Philip will set your mind at rest.'

'I shall speak to him immediately.'

'You might be wiser to wait until the morning. Philip is not quite himself at the moment. I left him sleeping in the library.'

'Sleeping? You mean he's drunk, I suppose?'

'I fear it may be so. Oh, do not look at me so accusingly. You must have heard me reproach him for drinking too much on several occasions?'

She hesitated but was too honest to dis-
agree. 'Yes. His drinking is a habit he
acquired at college. I cannot blame you for
that.'

'Indeed not! You will have noticed that I
drink little wine?'

'Yes.'

'I have always found that too much wine
muddles the brain. Philip will tell you
himself that I have tried many times to
break him of this foolish habit.'

'Yes, he has told me.' Morna bit her lip.
'Until this evening I believed your influence
on him was helping him to stop drinking so
heavily.'

'An understandable lapse in the circumstances.' Sir Richard shrugged. 'I am fond of
Philip. I attempted to warn him, but... Ah
well, perhaps it might have been worse.'

Morna looked up in bewilderment. 'You
are speaking in riddles, sir. What are you
trying to tell me?'

'I would prefer you to hear the story from
Philip's own lips.'

Sir Richard opened the door for her.
'Believe me, Morna, I know you will understand when your brother explains. Now –
should you not return to your guests? It will
not do for people to wonder where you have
gone.'

Morna gazed into his face for a long
moment, searching for the clue to all her

unanswered questions, then she turned and walked from the room. Terrible suspicions were filling her mind – suspicions that just could not be true!

CHAPTER TWO

'Philip – how could you?' Morna stared at her brother across the library table the next morning. 'This is our home! No, I can't believe it!'

Philip's face was sullen. 'Before we came down, I already owed Richard more than I could pay without mortgaging the land. He has been very decent about it, Morna. He could have demanded settlement weeks ago.'

She tossed her head angrily. 'No decent man would allow you to gamble your home away – especially when you had been drinking! I think his behaviour has been despicable.'

Now Philip's eyes were sparking. with anger. 'I hadn't been drinking when I lost the estate – well, only a glass or two anyway. I was on a winning streak – Harland and Burrows can confirm that. Richard had been going down heavily all night; Burrows won several thousand from him.'

Morna frowned. She had no intention of asking the two London gentlemen for their opinion, as Philip must know. Besides, she was inclined to blame them as much as Sir Richard for Philip's foolishness. She looked at him reproachfully.

'So why did you gamble our home, Philip?'

'I began to go down...' The anger died from his face, to be replaced by a mixture of fear and humiliation. 'I don't know why I did it. Richard warned me to stop before I lost everything, but somehow I couldn't. It would have seemed ... cowardly...'

'He made you feel that way.' Morna's hands clenched into tight fists. 'Oh, I don't know how – but I sense his power over you whenever you are together.'

'That's nonsense! I'm not a child.'

'Are you not? Then why did you behave like one? Throwing your inheritance away as if it were a broken toy!'

'I haven't thrown it away! At least, there may be a way out of this mess.' Philip avoided her angry gaze, a deep colour creeping up his neck. 'Richard's very taken with you...'

'No!' She stamped her foot, her eyes glittering with outrage. 'If you are suggesting that I should marry him, Philip, you may as well save your breath. I would rather be thrown on the parish.'

'I probably shall be if you turn him down.'

'You should have thought of that last night!'

'Morna, why won't you at least consider it? Richard must be a wealthy man; you could live in town and have everything you wanted.'

She looked at him scornfully, seeing his weakness clearly for the first time. Outwardly, he was the charming, selfish brother she had always adored, but he had changed somehow – unless the weakness had simply been hidden from her until now. Thinking about it, Morna realised that all too often it had been she who had taken the lead in their childish escapades, and she who had accepted her punishment without tears. Philip had wriggled out of a whipping whenever he could, complaining bitterly when he was forced to take his beating. He had wept on her shoulder the night before he was sent away to college, but she, too, had been crying, her heart broken because they must part. She had not thought of Philip's tears as weakness then, but now she realised it had been fear that made him seek comfort from her, not the pain of parting. Yet weak as she now saw he was, she loved him still, and she could not desert him.

'I still have mother's jewels and the ten thousand, Phil. Perhaps we can buy back the house?'

He looked at her with shame in his eyes.

'The house would be too expensive to keep up without the land, Morna.'

'Then we'll buy that back, too – or as much of it as we can.'

Philip shook his head. 'You don't understand. I – I owe him more – more than you could hope to pay.'

'You owe more?' Morna's face went white. 'Oh, Phil, you must have been mad!'

His expression turned sour. 'Don't look at me like that. I'll find some way of paying him.'

'Well, don't expect me to honour a gambling debt. I still think Sir Richard should never have accepted such a bet from you.'

'You have no idea of what you're talking about. How could you, when you've never been in a card game in your life?'

His scorn stung her. 'No – and I shall never be foolish enough to throw my inheritance away.'

'There's no need to be so damned prudish!'

'I am not a prude. Nor am I quite the country oaf you seem to imagine!'

'I've never called you that.'

'No, but you've implied it several times since you came home, laughing at my country ways and acting so high and mighty...'

'At least I haven't spent the past several weeks chasing all over the countryside after a man who doesn't want me!'

Morna recoiled as though he had struck

her. 'What do you mean by that? Who has been telling you spiteful tales?' She glared at him. 'Who has been whispering these lies behind my back?'

Philip's gaze dropped. 'I'm sorry, I shouldn't have said that. Where are you going?'

Morna was halfway to the door. She halted and threw him a haughty glance. 'I'm going for a ride. I need to be alone – to think what I shall do when your honourable friend throws us out of the house!'

'Morna, wait...' Philip cried as she stormed out of the room. 'I didn't mean to hurt you. I didn't mean to lose everything!'

His words fell into the empty room, mocking him. For a moment he stared despairingly at the door she had slammed behind her; then he turned to the wine decanter on the buffet behind him, picking it up with hands that were not quite steady.

Morna touched her heel to her horse's flank, urging it on to a pace that suited her mood. The wind stung her eyes, and her hair flamed out like a banner behind her. The stark winter landscape was a blur of brown fields and leafless trees touched with white, and the ground was hard beneath the flying hooves. She was numbed with the cold and the ache inside her. Philip had betrayed her. He had gambled away the home she loved so dearly, tossing it on the card table as if it meant nothing. Bitterly, she realised the estate could mean little to him if he had carelessly let it slip through his fingers.

'It was that man,' she muttered through tight lips. 'He stole it from Philip. I know he did!'

Tears were blinding her eyes as she rode. How could Philip do it? she asked herself over and over again. How could he throw it all away?

Her wild ride had carried her in the direction of the Trenwith estate, which was divided from Philip's by a small wood. Realising where she was, Morna eased her mount to a steadier pace, threading her way through the trees and dashing the tears from her face with the back of her hand. She halted as the house came into view, her heart beginning to pound against her ribs as she held the horse in check. It was the first time she had dared to come there uninvited, and she was uncertain of her reception. Would Jared still be angry because of her petulant behaviour on the morning after the storm? Was that why he hadn't answered her invitation to the dance? Philip's taunts were still ringing in her ears, and for a moment she considered turning back. Perhaps she had been stupid to read too much into the promise Jared had made her, after all.

Morna could remember clearly the day she had first known that her love for Jared was something special. She had been six years old that day when they were all playing on the beach, the Hamilton children tagging on behind the youth they both admired for his fearlessness. At fourteen Jared had already been taller than any other local boy, his well-developed body showing signs of manhood. Morna had run on ahead of the others, climbing over the spur of jagged rocks that protruded into the sea. It was as she turned to laugh and wave her triumph at them that her foot slipped and she went tumbling into the surf that boiled around the dangerous rocks. Jared had plunged in straight after her, grabbing her as she went under for the second time and hauling her back to the safety of the beach. He had pummelled her chest violently until she was sick. She lay there feeling wretched, opening her eyes at last to find Jared bending over her. As she looked into his eyes she had felt a sudden overwhelming surge of love for him. In that moment she had known that she loved him more than anyone else: more than Philip, more than her mother, more than her father...

Tears stung Morna's eyes as she stared at the house, but she dashed them away angrily. She had every right to demand an explanation. Jared could at least have sent her a letter, telling her why he could not come to her dance. Besides, it was even more important now that she should make him an offer for his horse and advance him whatever he needed to set his affairs in order. If Philip was in danger of losing the estate, she might be forced into marriage with a rich man simply to save her brother from ruin, and she could not bear that. She had carried the dream of being Jared's wife in her heart for so long now that she had never imagined being married to anyone else – and certainly not to Sir Richard! Somehow she must make Jared see what a sensible arrangement it would be.

Remembering the gossip concerning him the previous evening, Morna frowned. It was all malicious nonsense. She would not let her mind be poisoned by such foul slander. It just wasn't possible that Jared was a murderer!

Making up her mind at last, she eased her grip on the reins, allowing her horse to move forward at a slow walk. Now she was actually on Jared's land, and as she passed a row of labourers' cottages, she noticed that the roofs were being re-thatched. Only two weeks ago, when she had come here to meet Jared, she had seen gaping holes in the thatch and wondered at her neighbour for letting his property become derelict. She had assumed that it was because of financial difficulties, but it seemed she must have been mistaken.

Riding into the courtyard at the front of the house, Morna was startled to find it strewn with building materials. From the activity all round her, it was obvious that major repairs were under way. She glanced at the gracious building of buff-coloured stone, seeing it with new eyes. Parts of it dated back long before her own home, and it was these wings which were in need of urgent restoration. The central structure had been torn down at the beginning of the last century, however, and was comparatively new, being no more than a hundred years old.

Dismounting, Morna gave her horse into the care of an astonished groom and picked her way between piles of timber, scaffolding and large blocks of stone, towards the main wing. The front door was set back under a portico of white stone and presented a solid buffer against intruders. Her courage almost failed as she stared at the cast-iron bell pull, then she reached for it determinedly. The bell pealed lone and loud within the house, echoing hollowly until it faded away. She was reaching for it again, when the door was opened.

'Yes? What can I do for you?'

Morna stared at the woman who stood in the hall, momentarily struck dumb. On her last visit, one of the grooms had told her that Captain Trenwith was out, and she had not got as far as the house. Somehow she had not expected Naomi still to be here. She had imagined the housekeeper would have left after all the scandal of William Trenwith's death. Everyone knew she had been his mistress for years – even, some said, before his wife had died. The local people had shunned her long before her master's shocking death. It was she, of course, who had discovered him with the pistol still in his hand.

'I am Morna Hamilton,' the girl said, recovering her power of speech. 'Is Captain Trenwith at home?'

'Is he expecting you?'

Morna blinked, surprised by the older woman's haughty tone. It was a little unusual for an unmarried girl to come calling on a bachelor gentleman, it was true, but that did not give Naomi the right to look at her like that. She was behaving almost as if she were the mistress of the house.

An unworthy suspicion crossed Morna's mind. Naomi was no longer young, but she was still a handsome woman. She had been Jared's father's mistress – could she possibly be...? No, it was a stupid thought, and Morna was shamed by it. She smiled pleasantly at the older woman.

'No, Captain Trenwith is not expecting me, but I have come on a business matter and I am sure he will see me if you tell him I am here.'

Naomi's lips thinned. 'He's not at home...'

She attempted to close the door, but Morna placed her foot against it. 'Please tell him: it's important.'

'He's not...' Naomi broke off suddenly as she heard the scrape of a boot in the hall behind her. She moved back reluctantly. 'Very well, come in. I shall enquire if Captain Trenwith wishes to see you.'

'Thank you. Oh!'

The reason for Naomi's change of heart was apparent as Jared strode into the hall. He was dressed for riding, and it was clear he had been on his way out. He stopped abruptly as he saw Morna, his brow creasing.

'Miss Hamilton. To what do I owe this unexpected honour?'

Morna's heart began to beat rapidly and a hot flush stained her cheeks. 'We had an appointment, sir – which you broke.'

Jared stared at her in silence for a moment, and then his frown cleared. Her hair had blown into wild tangles and there was a smudge of dirt on her cheek. She had grown a few inches taller and her body had lost its childish awkwardness, but in every other way she was exactly as he had remembered. A hint of amusement crept into his eyes and his lips twitched at the corners.

'Ah yes, how could I have forgotten? I believe you wanted to see Devil Lad?'

Morna eyed him uneasily. Was he laughing at her? The Jared she had known was always teasing her, but his mockery had never been cruel. She was not certain about this new Jared. He was a stranger to her, and yet the mere sight of him was enough to make her knees go wobbly.

'I was angry with you that morning,' she said now, her eyes oddly appealing as she gazed up at him. 'I know I should have waited for you to reach me. May I see the stallion now, please?'

Jared stared into her eyes, watching them change colour and sensing the emotion inside her. He experienced a tiny shock as he realised that there was a subtle change in her: the girl he had remembered as a wilful, headstrong child was now a passionate woman. His first instinct was to send her away instantly, but then he realised he wanted to be with her for a while.

'We'll talk about the horse later,' he said, recovering himself. 'First, I must offer you some refreshment. Naomi, bring whatever is suitable to the morning-room, please.'

'The morning-room? But...' Naomi met his eyes for a moment as if to challenge the order, then dropped them. 'Yes, sir.' She walked softly away, reminding Morna of a sleek black cat.

Jared turned to the girl, smiling now, his manner more friendly that it had been since his return. 'I must ask you to forgive the state of my house. It has been neglected for far too long, though Naomi does what she can. Soon, now, I hope to make things easier for her.'

Morna glanced at his profile as he led the way through the house, feeling a little shiver of excitement run through her now that they were actually together. His features were relaxed at this moment, reminding her strongly of the young man who had set out to conquer the world only five years before, and she thought that perhaps the years had not really changed him so very much after all. He was still the bold, handsome hero who had rescued her from many a disaster, capturing her girlish heart as he bound bloodied knees and made her laugh despite her pain. Except that now there was something more – something that made her feel breathless when his eyes looked into hers.

She had been surprised to find the house-keeper still here, but now that she thought about it, she realised that Jared would not care how much gossip her continued presence in the house caused. He had shown his contempt for the local gentry only too plainly.

Jared opened a door and stood back for her

to enter. She gave him a shy smile, blushing as she saw his brow arch. Glancing round the small salon, she could not help noticing the faded curtains and sagging cushions. No doubt it had once been a very pretty sitting-room, but years of neglect had taken their toll.

'This was my mother's favourite room,' Jared said, obviously feeling the need to explain. 'I intend to restore it to its former elegance very soon.'

'Have you sold the stallion?' Morna looked at him in sudden alarm.

'No. What makes you think I might have done so?' She felt her cheeks growing warm as he looked at her, and knew that she had spoken too plainly. She had thought his situation was near desperate, but she had obviously been misled. 'Oh, I just wondered,' she said, embarrassed by his piercing look. 'May I sit down?'

'Of course.' She heard his harsh, mirthless laugh, and flinched. 'You've noticed the builders, and you're wondering where I found the money for improvements after all this time – aren't you?'

He was angry; she could hear it in his voice, and she knew she had made a mistake. Yet all her hopes rested on her information being correct and she realised that the moment to speak had arrived. Drawing a deep breath, she gazed up at him.

'I had heard – I believed you were in some financial difficulty?'

'I was. Temporarily.'

'I see...' She was taken aback for a moment, then she realised that there was only one possible source for his new-found wealth. 'You must know what everyone will say?'

Jared's eyes flashed with cold fury, and she gasped, taking a defensive step backwards. This was something new: she had never seen him look like this before!

'Please enlighten me, Miss Hamilton,' he said coldly.

'I don't believe it, of course.' Her hands trembled, and she hid them behind her as he seemed to tower over her menacingly. 'Why didn't you come to my dance last night?' Her voice squeaked as she saw his nostrils flare with temper.

'You are trying to change the subject.'

'No...' Morna drew a sharp breath as he frowned. 'No, I promise you I am not. Had you been there, you could have refuted a scandalous charge made against you.'

'What charge?'

His curt tone made her blink and she wished passionately that she had not begun this, but it was too late now. He would have the truth from her.

'They... People are saying that that ship was deliberately lured on to the rocks during the storm...' she faltered as his mouth hardened.

'And?'

His expression was murderous, and the girl shivered. 'I – I think I should leave...' He moved swiftly to stop her, his hand grasping her wrist as she turned away. She raised her eyes to his, feeling her head swim as she met the accusation in his steady gaze. 'Please let me go! I ought not to have come here, but I wanted...'

Watching the changing play of emotions on her face, Jared felt a surge of rage and bitterness rise up inside him. So she believed the lies they were telling, did she? Disappointment added fuel to the blaze, making him want to lash out at her.

'No, you should not have come – but considerations of propriety have never bothered you, have they Morna? You were always a wilful, inconsiderate brat. You always had to have your own way, didn't you?' His grip tightened on her wrist as she gasped and tried to wrench away from him. 'Why did you come – to buy the stallion? Or was it because you had been listening to gossip and your curiosity got the better of you? Oh, I know what they've been saying! Naomi told me when I came back last night.'

For the moment, the impact of his stinging words was lost as she grasped at a straw of information. 'Have you been away?' She struggled with her thoughts, trying to make sense of all her conflicting emotions. 'Was that why you didn't answer my invitation?'

'Yes.' His eyes veered away briefly. 'I went to London to arrange a loan from a friend, if you must know.'

'Then you are not ... You have not...?'

'That ship was driven in by the storm. I had nothing to do with it! Nor, I'll swear, did any man in this village.'

Morna stared at him, not quite able to hide her doubts. She wanted desperately to believe him, but somehow she knew he was hiding something from her. Besides, Jared was not the kind of man who borrowed from his friends. He was too proud to ask for anything. But why should he lie to her?'

Jared's eyes were flinty as he looked at her and saw the doubts. He did not know why it should matter to him that the girl should believe the gossip, but he was suddenly aware that it did. When he had cut himself off from all those who had been his friends before he left for India, he had thought himself invulnerable. He had shunned everyone who had come calling in the first few weeks of his homecoming, rejecting their expressions of sympathy with a cold indifference, and believing that they came out of idle curiosity. He had thought for a while that the Hamilton girl was different.

57

'You don't believe me, do you?' he asked, a sick spasm clutching at him as he glared down at her. He had thought that she would accept his word without question. Releasing his hold on her wrist, he gave her a savage push away from him. 'Go on then, leave. Run away, Miss Hamilton! After all, I'm a murderer – a heartless wrecker who lures men to a terrible death. I might decide to take that pretty neck of yours and break it with my bare hands.'

Her lips moved, but no sound came out. Gazing up at him, Morna swallowed with difficulty. At this moment he looked capable of anything – including murder!

His nostrils flared as she stood there, obviously unable to move or speak, and he clutched his hands into tight fists, fighting the sudden hot surge of rage that flared in him. 'You think that of me? You really believe that, Morna?'

The tone of his voice as he said her name brought a sigh from her. It had a kind of appeal and disbelief that sent a tingle of pain through her. She saw that he was looking at her intently now, really seeing her, without the barriers he had seemed to erect between them since his return from India. She lifted her eyes to his, blinking back the tears.

'Jared, I...' she whispered. 'No...'

Something stirred in Jared then. Memories

crowded into his mind, raising long-for-
gotten pictures of a child he had cradled in
his arms after he had dragged her from the
sea. She had clung to him in her fear and
pain, and he had felt a protective urge to
wipe away the tears and make her smile
again. She had come to him when her
mother died, too, and he had held her while
she wept. He recalled the way she had clung
so fiercely to him the night before he left for
India, begging him not to leave. Without
understanding why he did so, he reached out
and grasped her by the shoulders, experienc-
ing an odd grinding ache deep within him.
She shouldn't be afraid of him... Not she...

Morna trembled, sensing the charged
emotion, knowing she had somehow touched
a deep chord. She could hardly breathe as he
gazed down into her face, fearing what he
might do and yet powerless to prevent it. Her
mouth parted in surprise as he slowly
lowered his head to hers, his breath warm
and sweet on her skin. There was an instant
when he seemed to hesitate and she moved
instinctively towards him, wanting his kiss.
Her action seemed to fuel the flame of his
anger once more, and she saw his expression
harden. Then his lips were on hers, grinding
cruelly in a punishing kiss that bruised her
soft flesh.

She felt his anger and began to struggle,
pressing her palms flat against his chest as a

sensation of terror swept through her. Somehow she had unleashed a savagery in him that sought to punish her. He wanted to hurt her, to humiliate her for daring to doubt him.

She twisted her head violently, breaking free at last. He was breathing heavily, his face contorted by passion and an ugly expression that she dimly recognised as lust. She caught her breath, wondering what she had done to make him look at her like that. She shivered, half afraid that he meant to attack her again; then the hot glow died out of his eyes and he turned away with a harsh laugh.

'You deserved that, Morna. Go home and leave me alone. I've no room for a woman in my life – even one with a considerable fortune!' He turned round then, his eyes meeting hers deliberately. 'I made you a promise once, but it was only to stop your tears. I don't want you – or your money. Do you understand?'

Morna flinched as though he had struck her. She could hardly fail to understand when he had spoken so plainly. He had guessed what was in her mind, and this was his answer! For a moment she was too shocked to move, her eyes mirroring the pain he had inflicted as she stared at him; then she saw a change come over his face as he witnessed her hurt.

'Morna, I...' he began.

'Stay away from me!' she cried, holding up her hand to ward him off. 'You disgust me, Jared Trenwith. You are a liar and a cheat – and I hate you!'

Feeling the sickness rise in her throat, she turned and rushed from the room, almost bumping into Naomi in the passage. For a moment their eyes met, and she saw triumph in the housekeeper's face. Pushing past her, Morna fled towards the door.

'Aren't you staying for some tea, Miss Hamilton?' Naomi's mockery followed her as she wrenched open the front door. 'What a shame...'

Morna thought she heard Jared call her name as the groom helped her to mount her horse, but she would not look back. She was hurting so badly that she thought she would die. Nothing would induce her to stay and see that expression of pity in Jared's eyes. He had never meant to keep his promise to her. He had rejected her, and he had dared – he had dared to feel sorry for her! It was that that hurt more than all the rest! She should never have come here. She should never have let him guess what was in her mind...

Riding furiously across the moors, Morna felt the pain tear through her. She had carried a false image of Jared in her heart for so long. She had idolised him ... worshipped him from afar... She had loved him for most of her life, and he cared nothing for her. She was just a child he had indulged while it suited him, making her a lying promise just to be rid of her. He was cold, cruel and unfeeling, not worth one of her tears!

So why was she crying?

Jared stared after the girl as she galloped out of the stable yard. For a moment he was tempted to go after her, yet he knew it was the worst thing he could do. She would hate him if he offered her kindness, but what more had he to offer? A bleak look came into his eyes and his fists curled at his sides as he cursed himself and the world. He had not meant to speak to her like that, but something in her eyes had made him strike out in self-defence, wanting to wound her.

'Damn,' he muttered harshly. 'Damn everything to Hell!'

He was angry with Morna for breaking down the defences he had built so carefully these past months. She had no right to force herself into his life, no right to look at him with those haunting eyes, stirring up memories he did not want to remember. He had thought of her as being still a child, refusing to look at her when they met, but today she had made him aware of her as a woman. How he wanted her in that moment when he felt her mouth open beneath his, her body moulding itself pliantly against his. It was the realisation of his desire for her that made him lash out so cruelly. He couldn't afford to get involved with a woman now, especially a woman like that. He had to be free – free to make what he would of his own life. And yet there had been a moment when he held her... Jared shook his head, his mouth twisting with mockery.

'Don't be a damned fool, Trenwith,' he said softly. 'She's the same as all the rest...'

It was nearly dark when Morna slipped into the house through a little-used door at the side and went straight up to her room. After her wild flight from Jared, she had tethered her horse and spent a long time walking on the moors, trying desperately to unravel the confusion of her thoughts.

All her fine plans had come to nothing. She felt shamed and humiliated by Jared's rejection. It was clear he had long ago guessed what was in her mind. She must have shown her feelings too plainly, and he must have been laughing at her behind her back all this time. Philip had heard gossip, and she thought now that it could have come from only one source.

'Oh, how could he?' she whispered, barely aware of the cold as she wandered, alone with her bitter thoughts. 'How could he be so cruel? There was something between us once... I know there was!'

It was her own fault for reading too much into the careless affection of a young man for an amusing child who idolised him, but in all those months it had never occurred to Morna that Jared knew what she was thinking. She had believed that she could lead him gently towards a deeper relationship, never doubting that he would finally discover the benefits of a marriage between them. Of course he would not love her as she loved him, but love must come when he realised what a good wife she was. And she would have been the perfect wife – she would have taught him to love her!

Morna's teeth were chattering as she hurriedly changed her gown. She had stayed on the moors for too long, and she would be lucky if she did not take a chill. Washing the tear-stains from her face, she pinched her cheeks to bring back some colour. She was much too pale, and her eyes were red-rimmed. Something must be done, or Jane would be asking questions.

Half an hour later a transformation had taken place. Wearing a gown of dusky pink velvet, with her long, heavy hair brushed in a sleek swirl on one bare shoulder, Morna felt she was looking her best. It was important to her that she should look well this evening, important that no one should guess how she was hurting inside. Philip's London friends were still here, and she still had some pride left, even though it was badly dented.

Morna's efforts were rewarded by the startled look on Charles Harland's face. The previous evening he had scarcely glanced her way, thinking her a rather plain little thing. Tonight there was something different about her, and he could not be sure whether it was the way she had dressed her hair or the new sparkle in her eyes. He got quickly to his feet as she moved towards the little group by the fire, offering her his chair.

'You're late, Morna,' Philip said irritably. 'We've been waiting dinner for you.'

'My apologies, gentlemen. Jane, I'm sorry.' Morna smiled at the young man hovering by her side. 'I'm afraid I've been very rude, neglecting you all today. Please forgive me.'

'Oh no,' Harland said swiftly. 'It is a lady's privilege to keep her unworthy minions waiting – especially a beautiful lady.'

Morna accepted the compliment with a little flutter of her lashes. His flattery was balm to her wounded pride. Tonight it suited her to flirt with such a willing gallant, and she took his arm as everyone moved towards the dining-room.

'I was out riding, and I didn't realise how late it was,' she said, catching her breath as she saw Sir Richard glance at them. His expression was so plainly jealous that it made her laugh.

'Why do you laugh?' her companion asked.

'Nothing – just a private thought.'

Morna met Sir Richard's eyes, her lips curving provocatively. She saw surprise and then satisfaction in his face. He had understood her message. She might be flirting with the young man at her side, but the considerable effort she had made with her appearance this evening was for him. She was inviting him to approach her with the question she had prevented him from asking the previous evening. She was prepared now to listen to his proposal of marriage.

Morna had come to a decision during her long, cold vigil on the moors. Since she could not have the man she loved – a man, she realised now, who had existed only in her own mind – she would save her brother from ruin by marrying Sir Richard.

Her dislike of him did not seem important any more. Her heart was broken, her pride in tatters. What did it matter who she married now?

A welcome break had come to the gloom of winter, and bright sunshine heralded the arrival of a not-too-distant spring. Feeling the warmth through her bedroom window, Morna was tempted to snatch a cloak and slip out of the house before anyone could stop her. After two weeks of enforced confinement with a chill, a mood of restlessness had seized her and she longed for some time alone. Since she had accepted Sir Richard's offer of marriage he had scarcely left her side, and though he was considerate of her comfort, she found his constant attentions suffocating.

For once there was no sign of either Sir Richard or Philip as she made good her escape. Morna felt her spirits lifting as she walked swiftly through the gardens. A long, solitary walk was exactly what she needed to clear the cobwebs from her head. Everything had happened so quickly after she had agreed to marry Sir Richard. An announcement of their engagement had been sent to the *Gazette*, plans for a spring wedding were already in motion, and tomorrow they were all to travel to London so that Morna could buy her bride clothes.

Richard had been more than generous now that she had consented to be his wife. He had agreed to settle Hamilton Towers and all its land on her as a wedding gift, and she could do with it as she pleased. She was wearing a large diamond ring on her left hand, and her future husband had promised her all the clothes and jewels she desired.

'When you are dressed as befits your standing as my wife, you will be a leader of

Society, Morna,' he said, kissing her hand. 'You have made me very happy, my dear. With you at my side, no door will be closed to me.'

· The hint of passion in his voice made Morna shiver. When he looked at her in that way, she wondered if she could bear all that their marriage would entail. Yet the very fact that he wanted her was helping to restore her pride. She told herself that she had misjudged him from the start. His behaviour of late had been perfectly proper, and he had even managed to control Philip's drinking. So how could she object to his influence over her brother when it was so obviously beneficial? It was an advantageous match, and she was fortunate that he had fallen in love with her.

Something deep in Morna's subconscious warned her that Sir Richard loved only himself, and that he had his own reasons for pressing his suit, but she blocked all such thoughts from her awareness. He had nothing to gain by marrying her, so it followed that he must be in love with her. And a man in love would do almost anything to please the object of his affections. Besides, she could always console herself with the knowledge that she had saved her brother from ruin.

Such was the state of Morna's mind as she walked enjoying the fresh air and the sound of birdsong all round her. There were signs everywhere that the long winter was drawing to its close ... and then she would be the wife of Sir Richard. It was so peaceful in this quiet corner of the world, and she was apprehensive of the future. Richard had made it clear he intended their home to be in London...

The sound of a gun-shot broke the pattern of her thoughts. She frowned, realising it had come from the wood which bordered her family's estate. Could Philip or Richard have taken a gun out? She did not believe either of them cared much for shooting as a sport. Another shot made her decide to investigate. Someone must be trespassing on Hamilton land.

It was curiosity, not outrage, that carried Morna into the wood, though poaching was a serious offence. They had always employed a gamekeeper until a few months ago when old Tom Harvey died. Philip had not bothered to replace him, having little interest in such matters. He seldom ate game, preferring a plump chicken or beef on his table.

It was colder in the wood. Morna walked slowly in what she hoped was the right direction, hugging her cloak to her body. If one of the villagers was stealing game from her estate, she wanted to know who it was. She had no intention of persecuting the culprit, but she knew that many of her neighbours would take a very different view. The local magistrates considered poaching a serious offence, and anyone convicted of it could be transported to the colonies for a period of seven years.

Hearing odd, rustling sounds behind her, she halted, listening intently. The sharp crack of a twig being trodden on made her jump, but even as she turned, something struck her temple and she fell to the ground, stunned.

She regained her senses to find a man kneeling on the ground beside her. Looking into his face, she experienced a sharp, lancing pain and gave a cry of alarm as his hand reached out to touch her.

'No! Don't you dare to lay a finger on me. You've done enough harm already!'

'Lie still, Morna,' Jared said, frowning as she tried to rise. He had seen the look in her face as she recognised him, and it was all he could do to stop himself taking her into his arms. 'You have a nasty bruise on your temple. You must have hit your head when you fell.'

'When I fell?' she stared at him, angry now. 'I was struck from behind by someone – probably you!'

'You don't really believe that?' His brows lifted, and she dropped her gaze, feeling ashamed.

Seeing she was determined to rise, Jared took her hands and pulled her to her feet, steadying her for a moment as she swayed. She flinched as she felt his touch and he let her go, watching her while she struggled to control her emotions. At last she managed to look at him again, thanking him in a low voice that he could hardly hear.

'You don't believe I would attack you, Morna?' he asked again.

'I shouldn't have said that,' she admitted at last, realising that it was important to him. 'It was a poacher. I heard shots, and came to investigate.'

'That was unwise in the circumstances.'

'You mean we Hamiltons are not popular because of the closure?' Morna sighed as she saw the confirmation in his face. 'I have tried to help some of the families, but they all refused my money.'

'What the men need is work, not charity.' Jared frowned as he saw her touch the back of her head and wince. 'I'll find out who did this, Morna. The punishment will fit the crime, believe me!'

She bit her lips as she heard the menacing note in his voice, guessing at the punishment he would administer. 'No, I'd rather you didn't. Please forget it happened. It was my own fault. I shouldn't have tried to find out who it was, but – but I was going to offer him a job.' She looked up suddenly, a hint of mischief in her eyes. 'We need a gamekeeper, you see.'

Jared saw the look, remembering it of old. He threw back his head, laughing loud and long. 'I believe I may have misjudged you, Morna! You're not like the others, after all. If it was who I suspect it might have been, he would be a good choice. I'll put out the word that you're looking for someone...'

The smile left him and a tiny nerve flicked in his neck. 'I shouldn't have said those cruel things to you the other day. I wasn't myself. I'm sorry – and I want to apologise...'

'There's no need!' Morna turned away from him swiftly. She had forgotten their last meeting for a moment, but now it all came back to her and she felt the sting of humiliation once more.

'There is a need, Morna.' He felt a sudden urgency to explain, and she looked up at him. 'I behaved badly, and I've regretted it ever since. I wanted to speak to you before this, but I was afraid you would not receive me if I called on you.'

Something in his tone told her that he was serious and she felt a sudden rush of tears. He was looking at her in such a way ... and she could not bear it. She moved away from him as she fought to control her emotions. She must not lose control. She must not let him see how much it meant to her. His hands touched her shoulder, moving up to turn her cheek towards him, and a deep shudder went through her.

'Please forgive me, Morna. I have not known what I was doing these past months...'

His words almost tore the heart from her breast. She looked at him in helpless longing, her lips parting as her breath came faster. He reached out for her in silence and she felt the little shudder that went through him as their lips met.

'Morna...' he whispered hoarsely. 'I didn't know what I was saying…'

'Oh, Jared...' she half sobbed, her hand going up to touch his face. 'Jared, I...'

He caught her hand, pressing it to his mouth. 'It was my fault...' he began, then stopped and looked at her left hand. The words froze on his tongue, and Morna felt a wild desire to laugh as she saw the accusing look in his eyes. How dare he look at her like that when he had rejected her so coldly only two weeks ago?'

On the verge of hysteria, she lifted her chin defiantly. 'Will you not congratulate me, Jared? I am engaged to be married.'

Her desire for laughter left her as she saw his face twist with anger and disgust. 'This was a little sudden, I think?' The pressure of his fingers was painful as the ring cut into her flesh.

She tried to look away, but found her chin caught as he forced her to look at him. 'Sir Richard asked me to marry him at my dance,' she whispered miserably. 'I considered his offer carefully and – and I decided that it would suit me to be his wife.'

'You are engaged to Richard Stainton?' Jared ejaculated in disbelief. 'Have you lost your mind, Morna? Surely you can see what kind of a man he is?'

'Sir Richard is my brother's friend...'

'Philip is a fool! I could scarcely believe it when I heard he brought that man to your house.' Jared flung her hand away angrily. 'I tried to knock some sense into that brother of yours months ago, but he was feeling too damned sorry for himself. I had hoped that time would...'

'You have no right to criticise Philip,' Morna snapped, beginning to feel angry now. 'Besides, what do you know of Sir Richard?'

'Enough.' Jared's eyes glittered. 'Philip is a young idiot, but I should have thought you would have had more sense than to be taken in by a man of his stamp!'

She glared at him. What was he talking about? What did he mean – and why wouldn't he tell her? 'If you are accusing Richard of something, I demand to know what you mean.'

Jared's eyes glinted with temper. He stared at her, seeing the wilful pride in her face, wanting to shake her. Why wouldn't she simply take his word for it that Stainton was no good? She had always been proud and heedless, but in the old days she would have listened to him. He felt a surge of frustration as he looked into her angry eyes, and he was on the verge of blurting out all the bitterness he had held inside him for so long – but what good would it do? Maybe he could make her understand why she should not marry Stainton, but where did that leave him? His situation would remain unchanged. He shook his head, holding back the torrent of bitter words.

'Forgive me,' he said coldly, in control of himself now. 'As you said, I have no right to criticise Philip, nor to tell you what you should do with your life. You will naturally marry whomever you wish.'

Morna struggled for words but was unable to speak. She sensed that just as he had been about to tell her something important, he had changed his mind. Now he had assumed the expressionless mask of the stranger who had returned from India after his father's death, and she did not know how to reach him.

'I shall discover the name of the man who attacked you, Miss Hamilton, and he will be punished,' Jared said with a slight nod of his head; then he turned and strode away, leaving her to stare after him in stunned dismay.

'Jared...' she whispered at last. 'I'm sorry...' But it was too late. He had gone.

CHAPTER THREE

'Are you warm enough, Morna?' Sir Richard reached across to tuck the travelling rug more securely round her knees. 'You look a little pale.'

'I have a headache,' Morna replied with a sigh. 'I expect it is merely the journey. I shall feel better when we stop for the night.'

Jane fumbled in her reticule and brought out a small glass scent-bottle. Unscrewing the silver cap to shake a few drops of cologne on to a lace kerchief, she offered it to the girl with a solicitous gesture.

'Hold this to your head, my love, it will help you. To be sure, Sir Richard's carriage is very comfortable, but travelling does tire one so. It is no wonder you have a headache; I myself have experienced similar discomfort on long journeys.'

Morna thanked her and took the kerchief, noticing the flash of annoyance in Sir Richard's eyes. She knew he was displeased because she had insisted on bringing her cousin with her. He had offered to find her a companion more used to Society, saying that he knew of a highly suitable lady who would be delighted to chaperon her. Even

Jane had begged to be allowed to remain at the Towers, but Morna had been adamant. She would not go at all if Jane would not go with her.

For the first time in her life, Morna was feeling nervous and uncertain of what she ought to do. She had promised to marry Sir Richard and their engagement had been announced; it would cause a scandal if she were to break that promise now. Besides, he would be very angry and might demand immediate payment of all the money Philip owed him. Yet her encounter with Jared the previous day had upset her more than she cared to admit.

Injured pride had pushed Morna into making a hasty decision. Looking back, she realised the doubts had begun almost immediately after she had agreed to the marriage, but she had managed to subdue them until her meeting with Jared forced her to think deeply about what she had done. His forthright condemnation of Sir Richard had made her very uneasy, and she had recalled her own feelings at their first introduction.

Ever since the journey to London had begun early that morning, it had become more and more clear to the girl that she had made a terrible mistake. Her hurt and humiliation had blinded her to the truth. No matter what Jared said or did, she was still in love with him – and she could never love Sir Richard! She longed to call out to her brother, who had chosen to ride beside the coachman on the box, and ask him to turn the carriage round, but she knew she could not. It was too late to change her mind. She was caught in a web of her own weaving, and there was no way out unless she could persuade Sir Richard to let her go...

'Hold, there!' The voice rang out loudly in the darkness. 'Hold your horses, man, or I'll fire.'

The carriage came to a sudden, shuddering halt, throwing the occupants together as they lost their balance. Jane's cries of alarm, and Sir Richard's furious cursing, obscured the sounds from outside, and it was not until they sorted themselves out that anyone really knew what was going on.

'That fool of a driver,' Sir Richard muttered. 'What does he think he's doing?'

'There was a shout,' Morna said. 'I'm sure I heard someone tell him to stop.'

'Then it's time he learned his orders come from me. I'll soon see what this is...' The words died on his lips as he opened the carriage door and found himself staring down the barrel of a gun. He looked up at the man holding it in evident disbelief. 'Who the devil are you?'

A fleeting smile passed across the highwayman's mouth. His face was partially covered by a black velvet mask, and the collar of his coat was turned up to touch the brim of his large hat.

'Old Nick himself, perhaps?' The highwayman's eyes glittered behind the slits in his mask. 'Yet since you yourself can claim some acquaintance with the Devil, perhaps not. Oblige me by handing me your purse, sir – and that fine ring on your hand.'

'I'll see you in Hell first!'

'Indeed, we may well meet there – but not before you have given me your purse, Sir Richard.'

Jane gave a little scream, and crossed herself. 'For mercy's sake give him your purse, Sir Richard, or he'll kill us all.'

'Be quiet, you foolish woman!' Sir Richard glared at her.

Morna sat forward, staring up at the shadowed face of the highwayman. 'My cousin meant no harm, sir. She has nothing of value – but I have a ring and a little money…'

'Keep your trinkets, lady.' The robber's voice was harsh. 'I do not steal from women. I take only from those who can afford to pay my toll. Come, sir, give me your purse, and I will let you go on.'

Sir Richard hesitated, his face registering the suppressed fury he was barely control-ling. The highwayman's request had been made in a calm, reasonable manner, but there was a hint of steel beneath the silk and a definite menace in those glittering eyes.

Jane had started to weep noisily into her kerchief. Morna slipped an arm around her shoulders, looking at her fiancé accusingly as he hesitated.

'I think you should give him what he wants, Richard,' she said quietly.

An impatient jerk of the highwayman's gun gave point to her words. Scowling, Sir Richard tore the ring from his finger and slipped it inside a bulging leather pouch. It made an interesting clink against the gold coins as he tossed it to the highwayman, who caught it deftly with his left hand.

'My thanks to you, sir – and to you, fair lady, for your good sense.' His smile sent a little shiver through Morna. 'Pray continue your journey in peace.' He looked up at the coachman and Philip, who had sat silently watching the little drama. 'Drive on, man.'

'You will pay for this, rogue!' Sir Richard shook his fist as the carriage lurched forward, almost throwing him through the open door. 'I'll see you hang for this night's work!'

His threat brought another smile from the highwayman and a cry of alarm from Jane. 'Oh, please do not,' she begged as Sir Richard continued to hurl insults through the open door. 'He may yet decide to murder us all!'

Morna had been watching the highway-man from her window. He sat motionless, staring after them for a moment; then he turned his horse and rode swiftly in the opposite direction.

Feeling a sudden, irrational irritation with her cousin, Morna withdrew her protecting arm. 'Pray do not be so foolish, Jane,' she snapped. 'It was quite obvious that he meant you no harm. It was only Richard who stood in any danger from him.'

Jane stared at her, surprise and reproach in her eyes. 'How can you be so calm? I swear my nerves are all a twitter.'

'Cease your foolish chattering, woman,' Sir Richard said, his face tight with anger. 'Had you not distracted me, I might have got the better of that scoundrel.'

Seeing Jane flinch as if she had been struck, Morna was sorry for her own flash of temper. 'I am sorry, Jane,' she said. 'I shouldn't have snapped at you – and it wasn't your fault. Richard had no choice but to hand over his purse.'

'I think the man was bluffing…'

Morna cut him short with a lift of her brows. 'Then you must thank Jane for saving your life,' she said. 'Had you not obeyed his orders, I believe he would have shot you.'

Sir Richard's face twisted with spite. 'I was at a disadvantage. If that damned fool of a coachman or your brother had had an ounce of courage, they might have done something.'

'They might very well have made things much worse. Besides, Philip never carries a gun. You must know he dislikes them.'

Since Sir Richard himself was not in the habit of carrying a pistol, he was left with little to say on the subject of Philip's inaction, but he continued to grumble and curse about the incident until they finally reached the inn where they were to rest for the night.

Morna was silent, bearing his tirade in patience. She was seeing a side of Sir Richard that she could not but find distasteful, and it made her realise again just how foolish she had been in agreeing to be his wife. Once they had alighted from the carriage, he turned his venom on the hapless coachman, and to a lesser degree on Philip, sneering at them both for their cowardly behaviour.

Morna sighed wearily. She would have attempted to defend her brother from Sir Richard's spite, but her head was aching badly now and she was feeling very confused. Something was bothering her – something so worrying that she was unwilling to think about it just yet. There had been a certain moment when she thought she knew who the highwayman was, despite his mask. Yet it was impossible. It could not be...

'You look quite ill.' Jane was at her side. 'Take my arm, dearest. I am sorry if my nervousness made you cross.'

Morna saw the hurt in her eyes and squeezed her arm. 'It was not your fault. I expect I was upset, too – and my head is very painful.'

'Then you must go straight up to your room,' Jane said, her good humour restored. 'I shall tuck you into bed myself, my love, and then I shall bring a light supper up to you on a tray.'

For once in her life, Morna was only too willing to allow her cousin to take charge. It was a welcome relief to be fussed over and cosseted like a child. After eating the delicious chicken broth Jane had brought her, she settled down into the warmth of a comfortable feather-bed and closed her eyes. She would not think about any of her problems tonight ... not even the smile on the highwayman's lips that had reminded her so vividly of Jared...

'You must have that hat, Jane,' Morna insisted as soon as she saw her cousin in the fetching bonnet of blond straw; with its confection of pink silk roses draped at one side. 'It really suits you.'

'Yes, it does,' Jane agreed with a sigh. She lowered her voice so that the milliner's assistant could not hear. 'Only I'm not sure that I can afford it. They are so expensive here!'

'It is a present, of course. I want you to wear it to my wedding.'

Morna's cheerful manner gave no indication of the true state of her emotions. She had been in London for two weeks, and every passing day seemed to make it more and more impossible for her to extricate herself from the net she had become entangled in. Richard had lost no time in introducing her to several important hostesses, and she had been inundated with invitations to dinners, dances and musical evenings. As the clothes she had brought with her were hopelessly inadequate, she had had no choice but to plunge into a mad spending spree. Being a very natural young woman, she found it all exciting and had it not been for the shadow hanging over her, must have enjoyed her first visit to town immensely.

Jane protested over the expense of the bonnet, the latest of a string of gifts pressed on her by her cousin, but Morna prevailed as usual. She ordered several pretty trifles for herself, and the two ladies left the exclusive establishment together, well pleased with their morning's work.

'You really should not be so extravagant, Morna,' Jane said, her cheeks pink with pleasure. 'I did not need that hat.'

'No, but you look so well in it. Besides, Richard has settled a generous allowance on me, and I shall never spend the half of it.'

'You must not spend Sir Richard's money on me!'

Morna laughed at her cousin's shocked expression. 'Don't worry, dearest. I haven't touched a penny of Richard's money. Nor shall I, until...' her voice caught slightly. 'Until we are married.'

Jane looked at her anxiously. 'You must not be cross with me, Morna, but – but are you sure all this is what you really want?'

'You mean those hats? I thought they were so pretty I couldn't resist having all of them...'

'You know I did not mean the hats.' Jane sighed as she saw the closed expression on the girl's face. 'Very well, I shall not pry. I know it is not my place to question...'

Morna pressed her arm. 'Now don't be miffy, Jane. I would rather not talk about it, that's all.'

'Your happiness is all that matters to me, my dear. I would stand by you if – if you needed me.'

'I know.' Morna smiled at her. 'You are a comfort to me always. I...'

The smile died from her face as she saw a man on the opposite side of the street and stopped walking just for an instant. He was striding out as if he were in a hurry and his back was turned to her, so that she could not be certain it was Jared Trenwith. Except that she would know him anywhere! He had a certain, masterful way of holding himself – and no one else had dark hair with quite those reddish glints. Her heart thumped madly and her fingers clutched involuntarily at the sleeve of Jane's pelisse.

'What is the matter?'

'Nothing. I – I saw someone. At least, I think it was him...'

'Who?' Jane glanced at her white face. 'You look pale, my love. Are you ill?'

'No. No, I expect I was wrong. It cannot have been him after all.'

Morna knew she was not mistaken. Every nerve in her body was tingling from the shock of seeing so unexpectedly the man who had occupied her thoughts so often these past weeks. What was Jared doing in London?

The night when Richard's carriage had been waylaid by a highwayman was still fresh in her mind. She could not rid herself of the suspicion that Jared's face had been behind that velvet mask. The possibility haunted her dreams, waking her often with a start as she saw again that mocking smile. Yet she did not want to believe he could have done such a terrible thing. She had heard the menace in the highwayman's voice and sensed a deep, cold anger in him. She had not exaggerated when she told Richard she really believed his life had hung in the balance for a time – but that would mean that Jared had contemplated murder!

No, she must have imagined she had seen a resemblance to Jared's smile on the lips of that desperate robber! Morna resolutely pushed the doubts from her mind. She had quite enough troubles of her own without worrying about the dangerous masquerade that Jared might or might not be involved in. Squeezing her cousin's arm, she made a determined effort to be cheerful.

'Are you looking forward to Lady Alexander's ball tomorrow, Jane? They say it is to be one of the major events of the season. I think it will be exciting, don't you?'

It was the biggest and grandest affair Morna had so far attended. Having been greeted kindly by Lady Alexander, an impressive, handsome woman in purple silk – Morna danced first with Sir Richard and then with her brother. After these two dances, she was besieged with eager partners, and it did not surprise her to see both her male escorts disappearing in the direction of the card room, though she wondered at Philip's foolishness.

He was still in debt to her future husband and managing on the proceeds of a diamond necklace she had sold for his benefit. Giving him the money to cover his expenses during their visit to town, Morna had warned that she would not sell more of their mother's jewellery to pay his gambling debts. He must learn to live on the revenues of the estate, which would once more be his on her wedding day. However, there was no way she could stop him gambling, and she could only pray he would behave sensibly.

Although she had been in London such a short time, Morna had already made several friends. Her lively, unaffected manner had brought her many admiring glances, and she was always surrounded by a little group of gentlemen. This evening was no exception, so she scarcely missed the attendance of the man who would shortly be her husband. Indeed, she was secretly relieved that he had taken himself off to the card tables.

The evening passed swiftly in an enjoyable haze. Even Jane had found a comfortable niche amongst the matrons, her usually pale face flushed with pleasure as she watched Morna's success. The girl had not sat down all evening!

'Have you ever thought of visiting the colonies, Miss Hamilton?'

Morna looked up in surprise at the face of the rather earnest young man she was dancing with. 'I am not perfectly certain what you mean, Mr Robson?'

Most of her partners so far had confined their conversation to fulsome compliments on her appearance or to titbits of gossip about their mutual acquaintances. There was, however, something different about her present companion.

'My cousin Harry has just come back from New South Wales,' he explained with a shy smile. 'He has been telling me what a fine place it is for anyone with sufficient courage to make a new start in life.'

Morna wrinkled her brow. 'I thought it was raw and savage, fit only for convicts and the like?'

Jack Robson laughed, looking much less earnest now. 'You are not the only one who thinks that way, Miss Hamilton. Indeed, it must have been just as you say a few years ago, but the country is beginning to open up. Harry was telling me about the proposed new Swan River settlement on the western coast...' He broke off apologetically. 'But I must be boring you – you cannot wish to hear about such things?'

'No, indeed, you are not boring me,' Morna assured him with a smile. 'Do you intend to return to New South Wales with your cousin, sir?'

'I should like it above all things, but...' he shook his head regretfully. 'Father expects me to manage the estate, of course. I am his only son and it is getting too much for him these days.'

'Perhaps you will visit your cousin one day,' she suggested, seeing his very real disappointment. 'Please tell me more about your cousin's adventures, Mr Robson. I really would like to hear what you have to say. It is true that, out there, there is a bird that laughs and a creature that hops about with its young in a pouch at the front of its body?'

'Yes – and many more wonderful creatures.'

The young man's face lit up. He obliged her by giving her a vivid description of Sydney Town and the surrounding country-side, his enthusiasm for the country he had never visited evident in every word. Nor was he content to leave her after their dance had finished, insisting on escorting her into the supper-room so that he could continue his stories.

When she was eventually claimed by a new partner, Morna knew exactly how many sheep Harry Robson owned, the extent of his considerable holding of land, and the advantages of the merino flocks over lesser breeds. She was genuinely entertained by his tales, and would have liked to hear more if her next partner had not been anxious to return to the ballroom for the dance she had promised him earlier.

'Mr Robson was telling me about New South Wales,' she said as they began to dance.'

'How boring for you,' her companion replied with a lift of his brows. 'Tell me, Miss Hamilton, have you read Alfred Tennyson's poems?'

'Yes, one or two. I purchased a copy only yesterday.'

'And what did you think of them?'

Morna knew that many people were criticising the poet's first published work, but she had enjoyed what she had read so far and she refused to be pushed into a hasty judgment.

'I have not yet made up my mind. I think perhaps, in time...' The words froze on Morna's lips as she caught sight of a man who had just entered the room. 'In time he may be a great poet,' she finished, recovering her composure.

'I fear I cannot agree with you. His work is sentimental – too namby-pamby by far.'

Morna was scarcely listening to his pompous pronouncement. Captain Trenwith had entered the room a moment ago. She watched as he paused on the threshold, letting his gaze wander round the assembled company. It seemed to dwell on her for one second before he turned and went out again.

'I am feeling a little faint,' Morna lied. 'Would you be kind enough to take me back to my cousin, sir?'

Her companion could do nothing but comply with her wishes, though he was obviously displeased. Morna sat by Jane for a few moments, fanning herself agitatedly before making an excuse to leave. She walked unhurriedly in the direction Jared had taken, her heart racing wildly. She must find him and ask him the question that had been haunting her for days. It was no good, she had to know the truth! She could not bear the uncertainty any longer. A quick glance round the supper-room was enough to ascertain that her quarry was not there. Feeling sure that she would find him at the card tables, Morna continued her search, only to draw another blank. It seemed that she was too late: Jared must have left the house immediately after quitting the ballroom.

On her way to rejoin Jane, she decided to slip into the gardens for a breath of fresh air. Taking a short cut through a pagoda-like orangery, she paused to examine some of the delicate blooms growing in the tropical atmosphere of the hot-house. Her curiosity caught by one exotic plant she had never seen before, Morna bent her head to see if it had any scent. Then, hearing a slight sound, she raised her eyes to find herself staring into the face of the man she had sought in vain.

'So it was you,' he said, his voice bitter. 'I was not sure. You look somehow different this evening, Morna. Obviously you are enjoying your stay in town. I hear you have taken very well.'

The note of sarcasm in his voice flicked

her on the raw, bringing a glint of anger to her eyes. 'Why shouldn't I enjoy myself?'

For a moment Jared did not reply. He seemed to be labouring under an excess of emotion, his jaw hardening as he glared down at her. Morna followed the direct line of his gaze and found it riveted to the third finger of her left hand.

'So you are still determined to marry Stainton?'

For a moment she had thought there was a flicker of pain in his eyes, but the scornful twist of his lips sent a surge of fury through her. He had made it clear he did not want to marry her, so why should he care whom she chose as her husband?

'Why do you ask? It can mean nothing to you!'

'It would not, if it were any other man...'

His words were like a knife thrust through her heart. He did not care that she was marrying another man, only that the man was someone he considered an enemy. Emotion rushed into her throat, making her want to vomit. In her despair she lashed out at him, blurting out the suspicions in her mind.

'At least Richard is not a highwayman,' she cried shrilly. 'I know it was you who held up our carriage the other night!'

Her words stunned him for a moment. She saw shock wipe the colour from his face, then his hand shot out, gripping her wrist as he looked at her intently.

'You guessed the truth, then?' he said harshly. 'I was afraid you might, even though I tried to disguise my voice. Have you told Stainton?'

Morna shook her head, her eyes dark with misery. She had hoped that he would deny her accusations, and now she felt confused by his admission of guilt.

'No,' she whispered. 'I had hoped I was wrong. Why did you do it, Jared?'

She gazed up at him as though expecting to see some sign of guilt or shame, but there was none. Instead she witnessed a mixture of anger and curiosity as he in his turn studied her face.

'Why did you tell Stainton to give me his purse?' he asked after what seemed an eternity, but was in reality only a moment. 'Were you afraid I might kill him?'

Was that a note of jealousy in his voice? Morna wondered, puzzled by his attitude. Why were there no denials – no explanations?

'Would you have done so?' she asked, holding her breath.

There was a pause as Jared stared at her, his inclination to brush her question aside with anger. Something held him back as he realised that she deserved honesty from him.

'I was tempted,' he admitted, his eyes wintry as he recalled the moment when his finger had moved on the trigger in response to the intense hatred he felt for his enemy. 'It might have been easier if I had simply made an end of him then. However, I have other plans for that particular gentleman.' The menacing note in his voice sent a tremor shooting through Morna.

As he relaxed his grip on her wrist, she rubbed at her bruised flesh, puzzled. 'Why do you hate Richard so much?' she murmured, raising her troubled gaze to meet his. 'There must be a reason. Please tell me? I have the right to know, haven't I?'

'Perhaps,' he said reluctantly. He hesitated, watching her rub her wrist and feeling a stab of remorse. It seemed he had hurt her again without meaning to. 'I'm sorry if I've bruised your wrist. You made me angry, and I didn't realise what I was doing. Yes, perhaps you should know the truth about the man you intend to marry.'

Morna sensed that for the moment he had lowered the barriers. Wanting to reach him, she laid her hand on his arm. 'Before you say anything more, I should like to tell you why I decided to accept Richard's offer...'

'Philip owes him money. You can tell me nothing about that man that I don't already know!'

His harsh words silenced her. Philip's debt had been only a small part of her reasons for accepting the offer, but how could she explain that his own rejection had driven her to make her hasty decision? It would simply expose her to his scorn once more.

'Philip lost his estate at the card table. The land, the house – everything. I had no choice.'

'Your brother is a rash fool, but do not judge him too harshly. It may not have been entirely his fault.'

'What do you mean?' She looked at him, surprised. 'I did think that Richard might have influenced him in some way, but...'

'Stainton is a ruthless devil, and a cheat!'

'A cheat?' Morna was shocked by the accusation, despite her own forebodings. 'You think he actually cheated Philip out of the estate?'

'I should imagine it's certain.' Jared's eyes glittered with anger as the bitterness poured out of him. 'He cheated my father out of thousands of pounds. I believe he was the cause of the shame and misery that drove father to take his own life. Indeed, I know it for a fact.'

His face was ravaged with pain, and Morna was shocked by this glimpse of his suffering. Until this moment she had not understood how badly he had been hurt by his father's suicide.

'Oh, Jared, no!' she cried, feeling a surge of love and pity for him. 'How can you be so certain?'

For a moment the mask had slipped and she saw raw emotion in his eyes. 'Father was ashamed of wasting my inheritance. He wrote to me of his suspicions just before he ... he died. Naomi found the letter under his hand, and she sent it to me, begging me to come home and seek revenge for his death. I hardly believed her at first, but when I realised it was true I had no alternative but to sell out. I've been fighting ever since to save what I can from the ruins.'

Morna nodded, understanding so much that had puzzled her before. 'But if your father suspected Richard, why did he not expose him publicly?'

'He could not prove anything. Stainton was too clever for him, and father was ill – but unlike Philip, he came to his senses and stopped just in time. Instead of signing over the estate, he took a mortgage out on the land to pay his debts and he wrote to me, asking me to come. Then he killed himself.'

Morna saw the pain in his eyes and her throat caught with emotion. 'I'm so sorry, Jared. I – I had no idea! No one knew why your father shot himself, though there were rumours...'

His mouth twisted bitterly. 'I've heard them – including the most ridiculous of all, that Naomi killed him herself.' His laughter was harsh. 'She was the one good thing in his life. My mother hated being a wife, and after I was born she decided to have no more children. She used her illnesses to avoid those duties she found so distasteful. I believe she was grateful to Naomi for taking her place in Father's bed. Oddly enough, he adored her. He never ceased to grieve for her after she died.'

Morna could not speak. She moved towards him involuntarily, wanting to ease the terrible agony inside him, her eyes moving to his.

'Jared, I...'

For an instant she thought he would take her in his arms, then a closed expression came over his face as though he was deliberately shutting her out. 'It was all a long time ago, Morna, but you know now why I stopped Stainton's carriage that night. I intend to use his own money to ruin him at the card table.'

'How? How can you hope to win if he is such an accomplished cheat?'

'I've met his type before, and I've been observing him for some time now. I shall watch and wait until I know how to beat him, then I'll take back every penny he stole from my father. After that...' His eyes narrowed dangerously. 'After that, I shall expose him for what he is. I shall do it in such a way that no hostess will receive him. He will be a social outcast.'

Morna heard dedication in his voice and

knew that nothing would sway him from his chosen path. 'You can't be sure of winning,' she said at last. 'You will need a deal of money to take him on. Will you let me help you? I have perhaps twenty thousand pounds...'

'No! I don't need anyone's help. I told you that I shall use his own money. Every time he wins at the card tables, I shall find a way to relieve him of it.' Jared's face was fiercely proud.

'You'll stop his carriage again?' Morna looked at him in horror. 'You cannot – you must not!'

'I shall do what I have to do. There is only one way to expose Stainton, and that is at the card table – for that I need money. It will be justice that it is his own gold that destroys him.'

'But it is so dangerous...' Morna whispered, her fear for him making her eyes dark with anxiety. 'Richard was furious! I know he intends to carry a pistol in future when he travels.'

'Are you afraid for me or for him, Morna?' An odd smile flickered across his face. 'Are you worried that I might kill him before you can marry him?'

He was clearly insinuating that she was a mercenary wretch who cared only about getting her hands on Richard's fortune. Morna flinched at the mockery in his tone,

remembering his heartless rejection of her –
the cruel words which had sent her flying
from his house to weep bitterly on the
moors.

'Highway robbery is wrong, Jared. No
matter how right your cause is, the way you
have chosen is wrong. My cousin was very
frightened that night, and it could have
turned out so much worse. Supposing Philip
had been carrying a gun, would you have
shot him?' He was silent, and her eyes chal-
lenged him. 'Well, would you?'

Jared looked at her, a deep anger
throbbing in his brain. She should not need
to ask such a question of him, and the fact
that she had was a kind of betrayal.

'What do you think? Am I a murderer,
Morna?'

'I – I don't know,' she faltered, confused
and miserable. 'I don't know you any
more...'

'So there's nothing more to say. You've
condemned me without a trial.'

Jared scowled and turned away, but as he
did so something exploded in his head and
an uncontrollable fury swept through him.
That she could stand there and silently
accuse him with her eyes was beyond bearing! He swung round, wanting to hit out in
his despair, needing some way of taking his
revenge for her denial of him. Then he
looked into her face and his heart felt a stab

of agony. Suddenly he knew that he wanted her more than he had ever wanted any other woman. He reached out for her, jerking her hard against him so that she was pressed against the steel of his chest in a crushing embrace.

'Is this the kiss of a man who would murder your own brother in cold blood?'

His lips came down to cover hers, possessing them in a surge of fierce desire. Shocked, she struggled, pushing at his body in a vain attempt to stop this ravaging of her mouth; but even as she fought him, his kiss changed, becoming softer and yet at the same time more demanding. Sensing the difference, Morna's lips opened beneath his, surrendering to his passionate entreaty. Her hands slid up, over his shoulders, into the thick hair curling at the nape of his neck. She felt herself sliding, sliding into a warm, sensuous void where she had no will of her own, no power to resist the responses he evoked from deep inside her. Then, just as suddenly as he had taken her into his arms, he released her.

'Well...' he muttered thickly, his nostrils flaring with the extent of his desire for her. 'Could you kiss a murderer like that – could you?'

Morna closed her eyes, unable to look at him, her throat too choked with emotion to reply. She was in a daze, still too drugged by the power of his kisses over her senses to think clearly. He took her silence for accusation, and when she at last managed to look at him again, she saw that he was furious.

'Perhaps you could,' he said coldly. 'I had forgotton for a moment. A woman who would marry a viper like Stainton for the sake of money could do anything, even make love to a murderer.'

His vicious attack made her lose her head. 'How dare you?' Her hand snaked out, slapping him hard across the face. 'Oh, how I hate you! Go away! Leave me alone. I never want to see you again. Never…'

She looked up at him despairingly. Then she gave a little sob, catching it in her throat before it could become a cry of pain. She would not let him see that his insinuation had destroyed her. Turning, she walked away with her head held high, out of the hot-house. Her eyes were blinded with unshed tears as she walked, looking neither to the left or right.

After she had gone, a man stepped out from behind a tropical shrub. Richard Stainton's face was a mask of cold fury as he watched Morna return to the ballroom.

'You'll pay for that little episode, my sweet,' he hissed between white lips. 'That kiss you gave so willingly has just sealed our brave highwayman's death-warrant. I promise you that. Oh, yes, I promise you that – and when you are my wife, you will learn to regret you ever knew he existed...'

Lounging negligently in his chair by the fireplace, Jared watched the four men at the card table in the middle of the room. It was a select group gathered here this evening at Lord Edward Marston's house. Most of the men were wealthy young bucks with more money than skill; and only his long-standing friendship with Teddy Marston had secured Jared the desired invitation to dine among such company.

'Your luck out then, old chap?' Lord Marston refilled Jared's brandy glass and sat heavily in the chair opposite, his slightly fleshy face relaxed into its usual good humour. 'The devil's in the cards tonight. I lost a packet to Stainton's last hand. He seems to be on a winning streak.'

'So I have observed,' Jared murmured drily, his brow lifting. 'Young Millington's a careless player, don't you think? I haven't seen him win yet.'

Teddy Marston frowned. 'The young idiot won't be warned. Stainton advised him to give it up for the evening an hour ago. He immediately doubled the stakes. I know he inherited a colossal fortune from the General, but he'll run through it at this rate.'

'I have often observed that a certain type

of young man does exactly the opposite of what his elders advise.'

'I know what you mean!' Teddy laughed. 'We had a few in the regiment, didn't we?' He sipped his brandy, easing his large frame into a more comfortable position. 'Those were the days, old fellow. Don't know about you, but I find myself wishing I were back there more and more.'

'Poor old Teddy.' Jared grinned. 'Finding life a bit tame now that you're the Lord of the Manor, eh?'

'Come off it!' Marston growled. 'You know damned well I never wanted all this nonsense. Sold out because it was my duty, what? Family to think of, and all that. Did the same yourself.'

'It was a matter of necessity in my case.'

'You know I'm ready to help at any time...' Teddy's face was pink. 'No, don't fire up, old fellow, I'm well aware you won't touch a penny of my wretched money – though what use it is to me I can't say. Wouldn't be here at all if it weren't for you, you know. Those native fellas would have done for me pretty quick if you hadn't been there to save the old neck, what?'

'You'd have done the same for me.' Jared frowned. 'Do you remember Crawford at all?'

'Yes... Why?'

'A month or so back, he paid me the sum

I won from him that last night in India. I got the feeling he's pretty tight for money. I wouldn't have taken my winnings if I hadn't needed it to stave off the bank for a while. You might lose a hundred or so to him if you can manage to do it without his realising it, Teddy.'

'Glad to help a friend, you know me, Jared.'

'I'll pay you it back as soon as I can. By the way, I shouldn't play with Stainton too often if were you.' Jared's gaze slid towards the card table, noticing that the game was over. He stood up unhurriedly, apparently uninterested in what was going on around him. 'I must be on my way now. My thanks for this evening, Teddy.'

'Any time. Dine with me at my club one night soon? We can talk over old times.'

Jared nodded absently, his attention wandering as he caught a snatch of the conversation going on among the card players. It was obvious that Stainton had risen a substantial winner. He was consoling young Millington, offering to give him a chance at revenge when his luck changed.

'I'll walk back to your club with you, Stainton,' one of the players offered. 'It's on my way.'

'I'm not staying at the club tonight,' Sir Richard replied carelessly. 'Going out of town for a couple of weeks with a friend of mine, so I said I'd sleep at his house at Hampstead tonight. Get an early start, eh? My carriage is waiting. May I give you a lift somewhere?'

'No, thank you. I wouldn't fancy crossing the Heath at this hour myself. Still, that's up to you. Goodnight, then.'

Jared left the house while the others were still thanking their host. He walked swiftly in the direction of the hostelry where he had left his horse in anticipation of a chance such as this. He had been watching Stainton for several weeks now, and he was certain he knew how Sir Richard had managed to fool everyone for so long. He was very clever, leading his chosen victim of the evening into a skilful trap, often losing large amounts himself until the trap was sprung. From players of equal skill, he was careful to win only reasonable amounts, sometimes rising from the table after going down quite heavily; but his young, wealthy opponents were taken for every guinea he could goad them into staking.

Jared had listened to Stainton's conversations with gullible young men often enough to understand what went on. The man seemed to have an uncanny insight into their minds, as if he knew exactly how they would respond to certain suggestions, and he used his knowledge against the weak, vain or unhappy to cheat them out of their fortunes. It was obvious to Jared that he chose his victims with care, probably studying them for weeks to learn their weaknesses before moving in for the kill. He was a vulture, living on prey too feeble to defend itself.

Now it was Stainton's turn to feel the net closing in. Jared's face was grim as he paid the ostler for taking care of his horse. He was not riding Devil Lad this evening; the stallion was too distinctive and might be recognised. Everything had been planned down to the last detail, and this horse would go back to the posting house from which he had hired it that morning.

A slight smile lit the narrowed grey eyes as Jared mounted, nudging his horse out into the quiet streets. If things went well, he would soon be in a position to challenge Stainton at the tables. This time it would be the baronet who fell into a trap – and the cream of the jest was that it would be baited with the gold he had won this evening! The smile faded, and Jared's mouth thinned. Stainton would be stripped of everything he had stolen from his victims before the game was done.

The opportunity presented to him tonight was almost too good to be true. There had been other nights when Stainton had won, but he had usually been on foot. It might have been easy enough to attack him in the streets, but the role of highwayman suited Jared's notion of fair play better than that of a common thief. If Morna was right, Stainton carried a pistol now. Well, that made them even. It would be a test of nerve. A preview of the contest to come...

For a moment, Jared's thoughts turned to the last time he had seen Morna. Once again he found himself dwelling on the moment when she had responded so willingly to his kiss. For an instant then he had been tempted to give it all up; to gather her in his arms and carry her away with him. After all, what would he really gain from wreaking his revenge on Richard Stainton? If Morna's answer had been different, he believed he might have been able to put the past behind him. The realisation that she still believed he was capable of murder had hardened his heart.

Women were not to be trusted. Danielle had not broken his heart when she married another man; Jared knew it now, remembering with wonder the anger he had felt then.

'The Comte is neither as handsome nor as satisfying a lover as you, *mon chéri*,' she had whispered as they lay together in the bed after making love. 'But he wishes to marry me, and he is wealthy. I must think of the future, no?'

His anger had been merely dented pride,

he saw that now, just as he saw that Danielle's clinging ways would have soon become tiresome. He preferred a woman with a will of her own and fire in her eyes. Realising how his tastes had changed in a few short weeks, Jared cursed softly. His path was chosen.

There was no room for Morna in his life now. Yet, if she had smiled at him in her old way and told him that she still believed in him…

Cursing, he made an effort to shut the picture of her out of his mind. 'She's not for you, Trenwith,' he muttered fiercely. 'Forget her. You've work to do this night – and you'll need all your wits about you!'

He spurred his horse to a gallop. Stainton's casual conversation with his companion had revealed what was clearly the best place for the robbery to take place. There was a certain spot on the Heath that the baronet must pass on his way to his friend's house at Hampstead, but to get there first he would have to ride like the damned.

Sighing, Morna put down the book she had been reading and got up to take a turn about the room. It was the first evening she had spent quietly at home since their arrival in London, and she had been looking forward to it. Now, however, she was seized by a mood of restlessness.

'What is troubling you, Morna?' Jane looked at her anxiously. 'I thought you particularly wanted to read that new play?'

'I did – I do,' Morna said, giving her a rueful smile. 'To be honest, I don't know what's wrong with me tonight. I just have a feeling that something catastrophic is about to happen.'

'Dear me, do you think the seamstress will ruin that beautiful material you chose for your bridal gown? I thought she was rather clever at her work, but one never knows about these things.'

Morna laughed, her brows shooting up in surprise. 'Jane! You are making fun of me.'

'Just a little, my love. At least it made you laugh. Something I've noticed you seldom do these days.'

'Oh, Jane,' Morna said, sinking on to the sofa beside her. 'I'm so unhappy. I should never have promised to be Sir Richard's wife. It was a foolish, foolish thing to do!'

'It was indeed,' Jane agreed immediately. 'So why go through with it? You wouldn't be the first young woman to change her mind.'

'You don't understand. Philip lost the estate to him at the card table. If I don't marry him now…'

'He'll turn us all out?' Jane patted her hand comfortingly. 'I dare say we should manage, my love. I would be quite happy in a little cottage with you, and if necessary we could take in some sewing.'

Morna shook her head, amused at the idea of her cousin becoming a seamstress. Jane's stitching was hardly of the finest!

'We should be far from destitute. I still have most of what father left me, and mother's jewels, but Philip would lose everything – and it would be a terrible scandal. Besides...' She had been going to add that it would not ease the ache in her heart, but held the words back. Not even to Jane could she confess the whole truth. The memory of Jared's bitter accusations had stayed with her constantly since the night of Lady Alexander's ball, haunting her dreams and robbing her of the innocent pleasure she had taken in her first visit to town. Of what use were fine clothes to her, now that her life was over?

She knew she would be unhappy as Richard's wife, but she was already miserable. So what did it matter whether she married him or not? At least the marriage would ensure Philip's future... Sighing, Morna picked up her book again and attempted to read it. Her thoughts were so confused; and no matter how often she tried, she could find no worthwhile solution to her problems. All she had ever wanted was to be Jared's wife, but he had shown his contempt for her only too plainly. She had not heard from him since the night of the ball… She did not even know if he was still in London.

In the shadows of the trees, the masked highwayman waited, pistols at the ready. Hearing the rumble of carriage-wheels in the distance, his mouth firmed into a grim line. Now he would discover what his opponent was made of. If Stainton were not a fool, he would have armed both himself and his coachman, which was why Jared had chosen pistols. Somehow he must disarm them both while keeping both alive: the coachman because he was an innocent onlooker, and Stainton because it was not a part of his plan to kill him.

Urging his mount forward, Jared stationed himself in the oncoming vehicle's path. He levelled his pistols at the coachman, shouting a warning. The horses came to a shuddering halt, but their driver made no move towards a weapon of any kind.

'Do nothing foolish, man, and you'll come to no harm.'

Jared manoeuvred his horse so that he was on a level with the coach door. 'Give me your purse, sir,' he commanded.

The door opened and Sir Richard looked out. 'You've tried this once too often, sirrah,' he cried, his voice carrying loudly through the darkness. 'Take him, men!'

At his words, two burly-looking men

jumped out of the far door of the carriage, taking up positions just out of reach of Jared's guns. Seeing that they were both armed with double-barrelled shotguns, Jared realised he was at a disadvantage. It was clear that he had been led into a trap like any green youth, and he cursed himself for a fool. It had all been made too easy for him, he saw that now, but how could he have guessed that Stainton suspected him of being the highwayman who had previously held up his coach? Unless...

Suspicion, half-truths and thoughts of evasive action were jumbled in his mind as he sought for a means of escape. Firing one of his pistols just above the head of one of the men sheltering behind the side of the coach, Jared wheeled his horse about, kicking his heels in hard as he made for the safety of the trees.

Common sense told him that it was useless to stand and fight; his only chance was to make a run for it. His opponents were on foot and he could outdistance them, chancing a ball in his back.

Too late, he saw the party of horsemen ahead of him, spreading across the road to cut off his retreat. He tried to turn his horse to avoid them, but even as he did so a shot rang out. He was aware of a sharp, stinging pain as the ball creased his temple. His horse reared up in fright and he struggled to hold it, but then he was falling, and there was only the blackness enfolding him as he slumped forward and slipped over the animal's neck to the ground.

CHAPTER FOUR

'Have you forgotten you were to have the first fitting for your wedding gown this morning?' Jane asked as she found Morna sitting, still not dressed, when she knocked and entered the girl's bedchamber. 'If you don't hurry we shall be late.'

Morna had been staring at her reflection in the mahogany-framed mirror standing on her dressing chest. She picked up a silver-backed brush and began to stroke her long hair with sure, deft movements, curling the shining black tresses over one finger.

'Should I have my hair cut for the wedding, Jane?'

'Cut your beautiful hair!' Jane cried, dismayed. 'Why should you do that?'

'Curls across the forehead are fashionable...' Morna broke off and clutched her silk robe round her as her brother burst into the room unannounced.

'Philip, I'm not dressed yet! You might have knocked.'

'Beg your pardon, Morna,' he apologised awkwardly. 'I didn't think... Lord, I can't believe it! You'll never guess what happened last night. It's the damnedest thing I ever heard of...'

A cold chill ran down the girl's spine as she saw the excited yet apprehensive look in his eyes. 'What is it, Phil? Why are you staring at me like that?'

He came to stand beside her, picking up a Bristol blue scent-flask and fiddling with it. 'This is pretty, Sis. Is it new?'

'No. Father gave it to me for my sixteenth birthday.' She took it away from him and frowned. 'Stop prevaricating, and tell me why you came here in a rush to tell me something you know I won't like.'

Robbed of the scent-bottle, Philip began to tug uncomfortably at his cravat, casting an agonised glance in Jane's direction. Morna saw his expression and shook her head.

'There's nothing you can say that Jane can't hear.' She threw a look of command at her cousin. 'No, don't go. I have no secrets from you. Go on, Philip, tell us what has happened?'

He shrugged his shoulders, his face sulky. 'Very well, have it your own way. Jared Trenwith was arrested for highway robbery last night...'

Morna dropped her brush with a little

clatter, her face turning pale. 'Oh no! He can't have been so foolish. I tried to warn him...' She caught her brother's arm. 'Where did it happen? Tell me more, Philip. Where have they taken him?'

'To Newgate, I think.' Philip stared at her stricken face. 'He attempted to hold up a coach on the Heath, but they were waiting for him. He was wounded as he tried to escape.'

'Wounded?' Morna's eyes darkened with anguish. 'He's not dead? Oh, please tell me, he's not dead!'

'No, it was merely a flesh wound. He was alive when they carried him off to prison.'

'I must see him.' Morna looked at her brother pleadingly. 'Will you arrange it for me, Phil – please?'

'You'll only make a spectacle of yourself, chasing after him when he's shown plainly he has no time for either of us. Forget him, Morna, he's not worth your trouble.'

Her face reflected her reaction of mutiny. 'If you won't help me, I shall go alone.'

'I'll come with you if Philip refuses.' Brother and sister looked at Jane in varying degrees of surprise. She clasped her hands in front of her determinedly. 'If visiting this highwayman means so much to you, Morna, then it is clearly my duty to accompany you. I could not allow you to go to such a terrible place alone.'

Philip's gaze travelled from one stubborn female face to the other, a wry smile twisting the corners of his mouth. 'It seems I have no choice. I'll arrange this visit since you are set on it, but I see little point in it. I doubt if he'll want to see you – and if he does, there is nothing you can do to help him. He was taken in the act of committing armed robbery, Morna. He'll be tried, sentenced and hanged.'

'No...' Morna whispered, her hand flying to her trembling lips. 'There must be something we can do – there must!'

Jane moved towards her, her usually gentle face angry. 'Philip, don't stand there like a fool, upsetting your sister. These things are not always as bad as they first appear. My dear late mother's brother is a magistrate. I shall write to him at once and ask what can be done.'

Morna turned to her, gripping her hands gratefully. 'Please do, Jane. I cannot believe there is no hope for him. I will not believe it. Jared is not a wicked man – he was driven to what he did by the evil of – of others.'

Jane bent to kiss her cheek; then she hurried away, shooing Philip before her and closing the door firmly behind them. For a moment Morna stared unseeingly into the mirror in front of her, a single tear sliding down her cheek.

Suddenly it did not matter that Jared had

rejected her love. She remembered only that he had once been her friend, and that she loved him. 'You must not die on the gallows,' she whispered fiercely, brushing the tear from her face and lifting her chin with new determination. 'You shall not! Oh, please God, you shall not!'

The sharp clanging of the grim-looking gate behind her made Morna jump. It had such a final, hopeless sound. She glanced uneasily at the gaoler's uncompromising features and then at her brother for reassurance. He attempted a grin but failed, and she guessed that he was thinking he could find himself a prisoner here for debt if he continued to gamble so recklessly. It was a sobering thought for any man, and she hoped it would make him stop and think next time he was invited to play cards for large stakes.

'The prisoner has a cell of his own,' the gaoler informed them gruffly as they began to walk down a long, dark passage. 'I likes to see my guests has all the comforts of home – so long as they can pay for them.'

His suggestive leer made Morna bite her lip as the idea came to her. 'I shall pay for anything he needs. It would be worth your while to give him special attention, sir.'

'Seems this particular gentleman o' the road has a few friends left. I won't take your money, miss. I've bin paid already and I'm

118

an honest man. I asks only what's due to me, see. Don't take no bribes – so it's no use your asking.'

'I wouldn't dream of it,' Morna lied, her hopes of securing Jared's freedom in that way fading as swiftly as they had flared to life. 'I only meant that he should have decent food and – and a warm blanket at night. It is so cold in here!' She shivered, hugging her velvet cloak round her.

'They soon gets used to it. Most of them are here for years – unless they're gallows-meat or transported to the colonies.'

'Doesn't anyone ever leave here as a free man?'

'Not often.' He grinned at her again. 'Stands to reason, don't it? The debtors can't pay or they wouldn't be in here in the first place. The rest of them – well, they're guilty, see, and they pays for their crimes one way or the other.'

Morna held a scented kerchief to her nose, inhaling the perfume she had sprinkled liberally on it. As they went deeper into the prison, the air was becoming more and more fetid. It caught in her throat, choking her and making her long to be outside in the fresh air once more. And to think that Jared was a prisoner in this terrible place! She pictured him riding the fine black stallion he was so proud of on the moors, and tears stung her eyes. He was such a proud man:

he must be hating every second he was forced to remain here!

'Here we are, then.' The gaoler stopped, jingling a bunch of keys importantly. 'I'll have to lock you in with him, miss, but you just give a shout if he bothers you. I'll be in my room just a little further on, and I'll be back in a second if he bothers you.' He glanced at Philip. 'You going in with the lady?'

'No. I – I'll wait with you in your room, if I may?'

'Suit yourself, then. Are you sure you want to go in, miss?'

'Quite sure.' Morna looked at him, her eyes sparkling. 'Your prisoner is a friend of mine, sir. He won't harm me.'

Shrugging his shoulders as if to say it was her responsibility, the man unlocked the wooden door, squinting through the little grille at the top. 'He's awake now, anyways. I'll be back in ten minutes, then.'

'Thank you.' Morna gave him a tremulous smile, then stepped inside the gloomy little room. She waited until the key was turned and she heard the sound of retreating footsteps, her eyes accustoming themselves to what light there was from a tiny barred window high above on the wall. 'Jared – are you awake?'

There was silence for a moment, then a muffled groan. Her eyes focused on the bed, and she saw the shape of a man's body lying beneath a thin grey blanket. Thinking he must be ill, she moved instinctively towards him.

'Don't come near me!' Jared swung his legs over the side of his bunk. 'I'm not dead yet, Miss Hamilton, so you can save your gloating for another day! Maybe they'll give you a ringside seat when they hang me, so that you can watch me twitch...'

'Oh, please don't!' Morna caught her breath on a sob as his cruel words lashed her. 'I haven't come to gloat over you. How could you say such a terrible thing? Why should you believe me capable of being as cruel as that?'

He stood up, towering above her as he took a few steps towards where she was standing. 'Why have you come, then? Not to weep over me, I hope? I can't stand wailing women!'

Morna's head went up, her eyes sparkling with pride. He would get no tears from her. 'Why should I cry for you?'

'Why, indeed?' His brows met in a frown. 'Well?'

She could see the blood-stained bandage round his head, and was thankful that here at least was something practical she could do for him. Gazing up at him, she took a packet of clean linen from her purse.

'Will you let me wash your wound for

you?' she asked, her manner outwardly calm despite the beating of her heart. 'That filthy rag can cause an infection if it is not removed.'

Jared put his hand to his brow, his eyes narrowing. 'Since it pleases you to play the ministering angel, I'll not deny you. There's water in the jug. I still have at least one friend, you see.'

He sat down on the solitary stool, watching impassively as Morna poured water into a pewter bowl. Flinching only once when she removed the bandage which had stuck to his open wound, he stared at the wall straight ahead, ignoring her as she worked.

'There, that is much better,' Morna said as she tied the bandage neatly. 'You were lucky, Captain Trenwith; the wound is not deep.'

Jared caught her wrist as she would have turned away, his fingers enclosing it in a grip that held without hurting her. 'Why did you come?' he asked, his voice grating harshly. 'Did Stainton send you? Is that why you are here, to tell him I was suitably humbled by your magnanimity?'

'Richard does not know I am here. He went out of town some days ago. Besides, why should I tell him?' She gasped as she saw the sudden blaze of fury in his eyes. 'Did – did Richard have something to do with your being arrested and brought here?'

'Do you mean me to believe you did not know he set a trap for me?' Jared's mouth curled with scorn. 'You surprise me, Miss Hamilton. I have been passing the time by imagining you planning it together...'

'You thought that of me?' She stared at him, her eyes wide with distress. 'I knew nothing of any trap. I swear it, Jared. I knew nothing!'

Jared rose to his feet, his fingers still holding her wrist, looking fiercely at her from his superior height. 'You expect me to believe you are totally innocent in all this? Yet only you knew my secret, Morna. Until the night I stopped his coach, I had never met Stainton face to face, though I had watched him from a distance many times. He could not have guessed my identity that night. It was too dark for him to have seen enough to enable him to recognise me again when we did meet. Indeed, I know he did not guess my identity. Only you could have told him, Morna.'

'No...' she whispered, shocked and hurt that he could think her so vindictive. 'No, you're wrong – terribly wrong. I would never have betrayed you, Jared. You know I could not!'

He was breathing heavily, a strange, tormented look in his face as he stared at her. She protested her innocence, but how could he believe her when all the evidence was to the contrary? Yet even now, when he knew she had betrayed him, her eyes were accusing him, tearing him apart. He clenched his hands at his sides, hardly knowing what he was saying, clutching at a slim thread of hope.

'Why should I believe you? You are engaged to that swine. Why should I believe anything you say?'

'Because...' Morna's throat caught with emotion. She wanted to confess her love, to throw her arms round his neck and cling to him as she begged him to listen, but pride held her back. She could not bear it if he rejected her again. 'Because you know I care for you. I have always cared for you as – as a friend.'

'You care for me?' Jared's crack of laughter was like the lash of a whip. 'You care for me – but you will marry Stainton, knowing what he is, because he can buy you anything you want. Isn't that the extent of your devotion? You're like the rest of your kind, Morna, greedy and selfish – using a man to take what you want from him and giving nothing.'

Morna was silent. His bitter rejection of her friendship left her feeling numb and at a loss. What could she say to him when he would not listen? She had come here to help him, but it was clear he blamed her for what had happened. Sadly, she turned towards the door, intending to leave. Before she could pass him, he caught her arm, swinging her to face him.

'Where are you going?'

'I thought you wanted me to go.'

She lifted her eyes, looking at him unhappily. He took her chin in his hand, his mouth twisting in an ugly sneer as the bitterness rose in him.

'Does it really matter to you what I want, Morna?'

'Yes,' she whispered. 'You know it does...'

A despairing moan broke from him. 'Then you'll have no objection if I take what I want?'

His hand slid round her throat, and she felt his fingers tighten as though he would squeeze her very life from her. Then his mouth was covering hers with a fierce, blind passion that sought only to take. He was hurting her, punishing her for being a woman as his hands tightened on her slender neck, threatening her existence. She thought that he meant to kill her, and she stood submissively, wanting only that it should be over quickly. If Jared hated her that much, she did not care to live.

It was her submissiveness that saved her. Since he had been thrown into the stinking cell, Jared's thoughts had dwelt continuously on the revenge he would exact if he were free. The knowledge of Morna's betrayal had festered in his mind like a canker, eating at his sanity until he thought he would go mad. For a moment as his hands encircled her throat, he felt an insane desire to kill her, to see her lying at his feet like a puppet. Then he looked into her eyes and saw the calm acceptance there. She was gazing up at him with the eyes of a frightened doe.

He felt a sudden sickness inside, realising what he was doing. Disgust at his own behaviour surged through him and he thrust her away from him with a groan. God, was he going out of his mind? Had he really come so close to murder? She was still staring at him with those misty eyes, and he knew that look would haunt him long after she had gone. He watched her put her hand to her throat, and he wanted her to scream or shout at him for what he had done, but she said nothing. She just looked at him.

'Go away,' he said at last. 'Go back to Richard, and leave me in peace! If I hurt you it was your own fault – you'll drive me to madness yet, Morna. I don't want you to come here again, do you understand me?'

'You didn't hurt me,' she whispered, blinking hard as she heard the key turning in the lock and knew it was time to go. 'I understand you, Jared, but I don't care what you do or say to me any more. Your words can't hurt me, because I pity you. You're so eaten up with bitterness that you've forgotten how to trust. You've forgotten there is goodness and trust!'

'I've never found a woman worthy of trust.' His eyes looked through her.

'Then I'm sorry for you,' Morna said quietly. 'Goodbye, Jared. I pray you will find peace of mind before it's too late.'

She lifted her clear eyes to his for a moment and saw a flicker of something that might have been regret; then she turned and went out without a backward glance.

Jared closed his eyes as the door clanged behind her. For a moment he stared into the pit of Hell and the blood pounded in his temples, then his shoulders straightened and he opened his eyes, facing the inevitable. It was over. He had sent her away, and she would forget him. But could he forget her?

The small courtroom was packed to capacity as Morna took her place in the public gallery. She glanced round as she took her seat between her cousin and Philip, thinking that, from their laughter and fancy clothes, the audience might have been gathered to watch a play, not a trial. Because of the severe overcrowding of the prisons, Jared's hearing was taking place much sooner than she had expected, and the courtroom was packed. His trial had attracted a great deal of attention on account of both his standing as a former army officer in India and his firm refusal to speak one word in his own defence.

He was not without friends, the most prominent of whom was possibly Edward Marston. Besides engaging a well-known barrister to defend Jared, Lord Marston had taken the stand to tell the court of the occasion when Captain Trenwith had risked his own life to save his friend.

'We were on patrol in the hills, my lord,' Teddy Marston said, as the ladies in the gallery held their breath and craned forward to listen more carefully. 'Suddenly a party of fierce, warlike natives swept down on us without warning. I was dragged to the ground by one of these damned fellows and a couple of them had started to beat me when Captain Trenwith rode up firing into the midst of the devils. He then leapt from his horse, threw me across the saddle and rode off with me. I can tell you, sir, I should not be here today if it were not for his swift action.'

Lord Marston's testimony brought cheers from the crowd and even the judge seemed impressed, though he frowned and said it was a pity that such a man should be in the dock before him. Several more officers of Jared's old regiment had also testified to his former good character, but when the judge asked him if he had anything to say that might throw some light on the case, he remained steadfastly silent.

He had not spoken during the whole of the first two days of his trial, except to give his name and rank when asked for it by the clerk of the court. His behaviour had angered the judge, who had warned that he would pass a severe sentence unless Jared could show good cause for attacking Sir Richard Stainton's carriage.

'They are coming,' Philip whispered to his sister as a buzz of excitement issued from the benches. 'Jared's a stubborn fool, but you have to admire him. He looks as if he hasn't a care in the world.'

'Why doesn't he explain his reasons for attacking that coach?' Jane wondered aloud, her hand closing protectively around Morna's. 'Uncle William says he might get away with a short prison sentence if he pleaded his case. Judge Moreton is said to be a fair-minded man.'

Morna's eyes were fixed on the prisoner's face as he stood proudly in the dock. He was staring straight ahead, apparently unconcerned that his life hung in the balance. It seemed to Morna that he was almost daring the judge to do his worst.

'I think Jared would rather die than spend his life in prison,' she said, pressing her cousin's hand as Jane opened her mouth to reply. 'Hush, the judge is coming now.'

A strange hush fell over the courtroom as

Judge Moreton took his seat. In his wig and robes of red velvet, Moreton was an impressive figure, his face hard and inscrutable. His dark eyes swept over the assembled company, coming to rest at last on the prisoner.

'You have been found guilty of the charge brought against you, Captain Trenwith,' he said. 'Have you anything to say before I pass sentence upon you?'

Jared raised his head, a look of contempt on his face as he met Moreton's angry stare. For a moment it seemed as if he would not speak even now, and a woman leaned over the balcony to toss a pink silk rosette and a kiss in his direction.

'Speak, you foolish man,' she cried. 'Beg his lordship's pardon and save your neck. You're too handsome to die so young!'

An outburst of laughter greeted her interruption and there was some clapping. It was quickly squashed by a look from the outraged judge, and the atmosphere was charged with tension once more.

'Well, sir, have you nothing to say?' Moreton's thick brows met in a frown.

'I have nothing to say that would alter your decision, sir,' Jared broke his silence at last. 'I am guilty in the eyes of the world. I did hold up Sir Richard Stainton's carriage, and my reasons for doing so are my own.'

'Then you must accept your punishment,

sir.' Moreton's eyes were cold as they met the prisoner's. 'Highway robbery is a serious crime, punishable by death…'

He paused as a ripple of horror went round the courtroom, and a woman screamed.

'Silence! I will have order in court.'

Silence descended once more and the piercing eyes came back to Jared's impassive face. 'I have been asked to show mercy, and because of the testimony in your favour given by men of good character, I am tempted to do so. I am a moderate man, Captain Trenwith, and despite your apparent lack of regret for this heinous crime, I believe you might yet be brought to repent of your wickedness. Therefore, I shall show compassion in your case.'

Moreton paused again, waiting for absolute silence as he looked at the prisoner. 'You will be sentenced to a period of seven years' hard labour in the colonies. Transportation will take place within one month on the first suitable vessel leaving for New South Wales.'

Watching intently from the gallery, Morna thought she saw a flicker of something like shock register in Jared's eyes. The emotion was quickly mastered, and perhaps only she had noticed it. She knew instinctively that he had expected death. Hanging would have been a cruel but swift end, and in his present mood of bitterness he might even have welcomed it. To be transported to the colonies as a convict was perhaps the worst fate imaginable for a man like Jared Trenwith. For seven years he would be little better than a slave, forced to work for the master of a chain-gang.

There was a moment before Jared was led away, a moment in which his eyes were drawn to the public gallery as if searching for someone in particular. A sharp pain went through Morna as he seemed to look straight at her, and she felt as if his soul was silently reaching out to her in his moment of absolute despair.

'I love you...' Morna's lips formed the words, though no sound came out. 'I shall always love you. Goodbye, my darling. God protect and keep you...'

Just for an instant Jared smiled, almost as though he had read what was in her heart and mind. Then two warders came to take him down, and his expression became distant again as he walked proudly between them.

'The man must be made of stone,' someone whispered just behind Morna. 'Everyone knows transportation is a living hell!'

'Come along, my love.' Jane was on her feet, smoothing the fingers of her York tan gloves. 'We can do no more here.'

Morna allowed her cousin to lead her away. She felt numb with grief, unable to think clearly. Jared had been condemned to seven years of misery. He was going away from her, to a land he had never seen; a savage, hostile environment where he would be treated worse than a beast of burden. Forced to work under the burning sun, he might be beaten, half starved or simply driven until he dropped of exhaustion.

'No, I won't let it happen. He can't die like that!'

Morna had cried her thoughts aloud. Hearing murmurs of agreement, and one or two cries of 'Shame', she blushed as Jane hurried her through the curious crowd. People were staring at her, whispering behind their hands.

Outside the courtroom, Philip looked at her awkwardly. 'I'm sorry, Morna. I know it's a shock for you, but – but it's probably for the best.'

'For the best?' Morna's eyes glinted with anger. 'How can a savage, inhuman sentence like that be for the best? But I won't let Jared die. I'll find a way to save him yet!'

'Perhaps a pardon?' Jane said. 'If we went to see the judge and told him the true circumstances...'

'He would refuse to listen,' Morna said bitterly. 'A man who calls transportation showing compassion is a man with no heart.'

She looked at her brother thoughtfully. 'Do you know Harry Robson, Philip? He's a cousin of Jack Robson. Apparently, he thinks New South Wales is a land of opportunity for those who can afford to buy land and settle it.'

'Can't say I've heard of either of them,' Philip replied. 'Look, do you need me any more? I thought I'd just take a walk down to my club.'

Morna looked at him angrily. 'If Richard has returned, you may tell him I wish to speak with him at his earliest convenience.'

'Richard has been back in town for ... several days,' Philip faltered as he saw the look on her face. 'I rather think he's been avoiding you. Wants to give you a chance to get over this business...'

'Philip! You knew I wanted to see him as soon as he returned. The wedding is scheduled for next week.'

Her brother's gaze dropped beneath the accusation in her glittering eyes. 'Won't you think about it for a while, Morna? It is going to be a bit difficult for me if...'

'Do you really believe I would marry him now? After what he has done to Jared?'

The scorn in her voice made Philip flinch. 'He had the right to defend himself, Morna. Trenwith was breaking the law, after all.'

'I told you why Jared was playing that masquerade.'

'Oh, that nonsense about Richard being a cheat. You can't expect me to believe all that!'

'Why should I expect anything from you? Go to your club, Philip.' Morna's look of disdain made him shudder. 'Come, Jane dearest, I think we'll pay a call on Lady Alexander before we go home.' She walked past her brother to the waiting carriage, ignoring his half-hearted apologies.

Philip stared after her, his face flushed with a kind of shamed annoyance. Sometimes his sister was impossible to understand! Then he shrugged, turned and walked swiftly in the opposite direction, trying not to let his thoughts dwell on that gloomy prison he had visited with her a few weeks ago. If Morna carried out her threat to break off her engagement, he was ruined. He had debts she knew nothing about, and he might find himself an inmate of Newgate before the month was out!

Morna looked up expectantly as her cousin came into the room. Jane nodded, and a little shiver went down the girl's spine. She got to her feet, nervously smoothing the froth of lace at her throat. It was time to face Sir Richard at last, and despite her resolve, she could feel butterflies in her stomach. Her wedding day was less than a week away, and she knew the scandal would anger her fiancé. She would be branded a heartless jilt, and he would be embarrassed by all the gossip this last-minute cancellation would cause.

Jane reached out and pressed her hands comfortingly. 'You must not be afraid of him, my love. This marriage was never right for you. No matter what else you decide to do, you must break it off now.'

Morna straightened her back, a determined gleam in her eyes. 'I am not afraid of Richard! I should never have agreed to marry him, I realise that now. Even if he had not harmed Captain Trenwith, I should have learned to regret my foolish decision in time.'

'For my part, I am glad you have come to your senses at last. I never did like Sir Richard!'

Morna smiled at the vehemence in her cousin's normally gentle voice. 'Well, I must not keep him waiting.'

'If you need me you have only to call, Morna. I shall not be far away.'

'I do not believe Richard will offer me violence in my own house,' Morna said, smiling as she touched her cousin's hand.

She was not as confident as she pretended, however, and her heart was hammering wildly as she walked down to the salon where Sir Richard was awaiting her. Pausing on the threshold of the pretty little room, she saw him standing by the fireplace, his back turned to her. He swung round as she entered, a cool smile on his thin lips.

'Philip told me you wished to see me urgently, Morna. I hope nothing is wrong –

you are not ill?'

Her eyes met his steadily as she studied his face, noting the hard line of his mouth and the barely-concealed arrogance of his manner. She was seeing him clearly now, knowing how ruthless he could be, and she realised that Jared had been right to condemn her for her willingness to marry such a man. Even if she and Philip had been left penniless, she ought never to have considered it – not for one second!

'No, I am not ill,' she said calmly. 'In fact I am feeling better than I have for weeks.'

'I am glad to hear that, my dear.' He reached out for her, obviously intending to embrace her.

Morna moved away. 'I have something important to say to you, Richard.'

His eyes narrowed in suspicion. 'I hope you are not about to do something foolish – something that you would most certainly regret?'

The warning note in his voice made her head go up, and her eyes glinted with pride. 'I shall not regret what I am about to do, sir, though I am sorry for the embarrassment it may cause you.' She slipped the ring he had given her from her finger and held it out to him. 'I cannot marry you, Richard. I have never loved you, as I am sure you knew, and now I do not even like you. In fact, I despise you.'

'This is plain speaking indeed!' His lips curled with scorn. 'So, you would throw away a fortune for a whim? You disappoint me, Morna. I thought you had more sense. You will never marry your highwayman lover. Have you any idea what seven years in the colonies can do to a man? If he lives – and I doubt that! – he'll be broken in body and spirit. He's as good as dead.'

'Do you think I don't know that?' she cried shrilly. 'I would have kept my promise to marry you if you had not set that trap for Jared. Oh, I know you must have seen us together at Lady Alexander's ball; it was the only way you could have learned the truth about him. You thought he was my lover, but he sent me away. He told me you cheated his father out of a fortune. I would have married you even then – God forgive me! – but now I hate you. I would rather beg in the streets than be your wife!'

'It may come to that, Morna. Your precious brother owes me more than he can hope to pay. He'll end in the debtors' prison if you make me a laughing-stock before the whole of London.' His face was white with anger. 'You are of good family – there is old blood in you, and that still counts for something. With you as my wife, the gossip would be at an end. Already doors have opened to me that were closed before...'

'I knew there must be some reason you

wanted to marry me!' She lifted her head proudly. 'What kind of gossip, Richard? Is it because you spend so much time with young men of a certain type...' Her eyes widened in horror. 'Have you corrupted my brother as well as ruining him? I know you cheated him out of his estate. You stole it from him – as you stole Jared's father's...'

'Be careful what you say, viper! You can prove none of this.' Sir Richard moved closer to her, his voice softly menacing. 'I have not corrupted your brother, though it would have been easy enough. Ask yourself why he was so unhappy when he came back from university, Morna. And you cannot prove that I cheated at the card table. I have witnesses who will swear that Philip went on gambling against my advice. Everyone who knows him will say that he is a young fool who drinks too much and gambles recklessly. There are also other, less pleasant, rumours that might somehow begin to circulate if you cross me. I warn you, Morna, I'll ruin you both. You won't make a fool of me and escape unscathed!'

'One day someone will expose you for the wicked liar you are...'

Morna gasped as he raised his hand to strike her. Even as she shrank away from him, there was a sudden noise behind her and a small table clattered to the floor. Glancing over her shoulder, she saw Philip hurtling towards them. He threw himself at Sir Richard, taking him by surprise and knocking him to the ground.

'Don't you dare to hit my sister, you swine!' he yelled furiously. 'I've taken many an insult from you because you found out about that incident at university. It wasn't true, but I knew everyone would believe you if you circulated the stories. The dons believed it even though I tried to tell them I wasn't involved. You've used it to torture me for months but you won't harm Morna.'

'You insolent puppy! I'll teach you a few manners before I've done with you.'

Sir Richard scrambled to his feet, launching himself at Philip. Morna screamed as they fell over a sofa, crashing into a delicate table and sending a tray of crystal glasses flying. They rolled to and fro on the floor, struggling violently and punching whenever they got the chance.

'Stop it,' Morna cried. 'Oh, please stop fighting! You are behaving like unruly children.'

Neither of them listened to her pleas. It was a messy, vicious struggle and one neither man seemed likely to win. They were both too angry to judge what they were doing, hitting out wildly and causing as much damage to the furniture as to each other.

Finally, Philip managed to land a telling blow on Sir Richard's chin. It stunned him and he went limp, not moving as the younger man struggled to the sofa and collapsed, gasping for breath. He wiped the blood from his mouth, watching with satisfaction as Sir Richard pulled himself up off the floor.

'You'll pay for this – both of you!' he muttered, touching his chin anxiously.

'We've heard your threats before, sir,' Morna said contemptuously. 'As you see, they do not frighten either of us. Please leave now, or my servants will throw you out!'

'I'll make you sorry you scorned me, you proud bitch!' Sir Richard snarled. 'Your brother will rot in prison – and not one hostess in London will receive you. You will be a social outcast.'

Morna laughed in his face, her eyes bright and unafraid. 'I care nothing for you or the society you live in, sir. It is a shallow, despicable world, for it allows parasites like you to live on the blood of others.'

Sir Richard's lips were white with temper, but her defiance left him with nothing to say. He was sure that she meant every word and he was powerless to destroy her. He threw one last look of malevolence at Philip, then turned and strode from the room, slamming the door behind him.

Morna rushed to her brother's side, giving him her kerchief to wipe away the blood trickling from the cut on his lip.

'Are you badly hurt, Phil?' she asked anxiously. 'You were very brave to defend me like that – but you shouldn't have done it.'

'I couldn't let him hit you.' Philip attempted a grin and winced. 'I may be a fool, but I still have a sense of honour despite what some people may think. You didn't believe those filthy lies he was telling you when I came in?'

'No, of course I didn't.' Morna smiled at him. 'And you are not a fool. That man is very clever. I wasn't sure what hold he had over you, but I knew there was something. He makes people do what he wants them to. He cheated you as he's cheated others.'

'He's an expert in the art of blackmail.' Philip's face crumpled. 'He never actually puts the threat of exposure into words, but it's always there. I got mixed up with something at Oxford, Morna, and I was accused of... Well, I expect you can guess. It wasn't true, and the dons gave me the benefit of the doubt, so I wasn't expelled, but the rumour leaked out and Richard got hold of it somehow. I've been such a fool! I've signed the estate over to him – and he still has my notes for thousands more. I can't even remember signing half of them.'

'You probably didn't,' Morna said. 'We can't do anything about the estate, but don't pay him a penny more.'

'I couldn't if I wanted to.' Philip

shuddered. 'I don't know what to do, Morna. I don't think I could stand being locked up for years – I'd rather kill myself.'

'You mustn't say such things!' Morna gave his arm a little shake. 'I still have most of mother's jewels and the money father left me. We can go away together, Phil. We'll start a new life where he'll never find us.'

'You don't know Richard if you think that. He would follow us to Hell itself to get his revenge.'

'He won't follow us to the colonies.'

Philip stared at her, his first reaction one of astonishment. 'You can't mean it? Have you any idea of how hard the journey would be? Morna, you're not really considering it, are you?' He frowned as he saw she was serious. 'But you don't know the first thing about New South Wales.'

'That's where you are wrong!' Brother and sister looked up as Jane came towards them, setting a small table to rights and shaking her head at the state of the room. 'Your sister has not been idle these past few hours. Tell him your news, my love.'

'I went to see Harry Robson after the trial. He told me that *Sea-Sprite* would be leaving for New South Wales in ten days' time. She has been used for carrying convicts before, and Jared is sure to be one of them on this trip. The ship also accommodates a few passengers. Mr Robson is returning on board her himself. He has offered to help us get started, Philip. He knows of some land outside Sydney Cove, with a small flock of merino sheep, that might suit us. It belongs to a friend of his who wants to move to the west...'

Morna paused, looking hopefully at her brother, but she saw by his face that he was not convinced.

'It would be a new start for us all, Phil,' she said, looking at him pleadingly.

'I'm not a sheep-farmer,' Philip protested, frowning. 'I don't know the first thing about it.'

'We can learn.' Morna laid her hand on his arm, gazing earnestly into his face. 'I know it isn't what you wanted, but it might be better for you to get away. You haven't been truly happy since you came back from Oxford, have you?'

'You want to go because you think you can help Jared, that's it, isn't it?'

'Yes, I can't deny that was my reason for enquiring about the possibility of settling in New South Wales – but it would be good for us all, Phil.'

'Better for you, perhaps.' Philip stared at her sullenly. 'He'll still be a convict, you know. You can't change that.'

'I can buy his bond.' Morna's eyes sparkled defiantly. 'I can't set him free – only a pardon from the Governor could do that – but he can live and work with us as part of our family. Oh, Phil, he was your friend once, can't you forget your quarrel with him?'

Philip got up and went to stand by the fireplace, staring moodily into the flames. 'If you would pay my debts we might manage to find a small estate here…'

'Morna and I are going away,' Jane interrupted him. 'If you were not such a selfish young man, you would see how much this means to your sister. You can come with us or you can stay here and find yourself employment; but if you are sensible you will look on this as a great adventure. New South Wales has made Harry Robson a rich man, and it could do the same for you if you are willing to work.'

Morna laughed and went to stand by her brother, taking his arm and looking at him. 'Cousin Jane is becoming quite a tigress in my defence, isn't she? Surely you can see how exciting it could be, Phil? A new country – a new beginning…' She gave his arm a little squeeze, a teasing smile in her eyes. 'Say you'll come with us, please?'

His mouth twisted in a rueful grin, unable to resist such an appeal. 'Since you're both so set on it, I haven't much choice, have I?'

She gave a little scream, grabbing his waist to whirl him round the room in a dance of delight.

'You won't regret it,' she cried, her face

alight with a new hope. 'Everything will turn out right for us. I know it will.'

Then the light died from her eyes as she remembered that Jared was still in prison. Nothing was certain yet. The problems and difficulties of the voyage lay before them, and the conditions on board for the convicts would be even harder to bear than those for the passengers. Neither she nor Philip knew anything about farming – all that had been left to their tenants and all she really knew of the colony was what she had gained from a brief conversation with an enthusiastic young man. It was a daunting task she had taken on, and for a moment her courage almost failed her. How could she possibly hope to succeed? Then her chin went up and her face settled into determined lines. She would do whatever she had to because the alternative was to abandon the man she loved to his fate.

And that was something she would never do! No matter how often he denied her love, she would fight to save him from himself – and from the bitterness which had so nearly destroyed him. Then, perhaps, one day, he would turn to her with love in his eyes.

She walked away from Philip, to stand looking out of the window at the setting sun. Somewhere across the city of London with its church spires and gracious buildings there was a dark, ugly prison which smelt of fear and was always cold. At this moment Jared was alone in his cell, facing the prospect of a terrible future. Her heart called out to him, and she wished she could tell him not to despair. There was still hope for the future and one day, much sooner than he thought, he would be free again.

Sighing, she fought down the longing to see him. Her plans and hopes for the future were no more than that. Jared was a convict, and must travel to the colonies as such. She could do nothing to ease his suffering, and only if she succeeded in buying his bond would she tell him what was in her mind. To arouse his hopes now could only make things harder for him if something should go wrong!

'Oh, please, God, let me succeed,' she whispered, tears stinging her eyes. 'Help him to face what he must until I can set him free. I don't ask you to make him love me. Even if he hates me for the rest of his life, I want him to live. I want him to live...'

CHAPTER FIVE

The docks were crowded with people: sailors loading cargo among a hubbub of noise and seeming confusion; well-wishers come to wave goodbye to their friends; carriages forcing a passage through the mêlée, and a string of filthy, wretched-looking convicts chained to one another by the ankles as they shuffled towards the vessel which was to carry them to their destination.

As Morna watched anxiously from the ship's rails, a group of small boys gathered about the prisoners, pelting them with refuse from the gutters and jeering. Most of them ignored the taunts, apparently too apathetic to care; others scowled or muttered beneath their breath. One or two caught a missile and hurled it back at their young tormentors.

Morna's eyes searched the faces of the convicts, her heart torn with pity as she saw the blank hopelessness in their eyes. Anger stirred in her at the barbaric way these men were being treated. It was time that this savage custom was done away with, she thought. It was not justice to herd men like animals in the hulks, no matter what crime

148

they were guilty of; and some of them had done nothing more than steal a pheasant from the woods of a country squire. It was wicked and inhuman to punish men this way!

'There he is,' she whispered to Jane as she suddenly saw Jared at the end of the line.

Somehow he had managed to retain the appearance of a gentleman. Although his clothes were creased and stained, he had shaved recently and his hair had been cut very short. He held himself proudly, his eyes contemptuous as he stared straight ahead. It was almost as if he refused to believe what was going on around him, as if he had forced his mind to reject what was happening to him.

'Oh, thank God,' Morna whispered as she saw his spirit was unbroken. 'Jared, my love. My love...'

The sailors were urging the convicts across the gangplank. Morna saw that they carried long, thin sticks which they used to prod the men, occasionally striking anyone who moved too slowly. She caught her breath as she saw one of these bullies turn his attention on Jared.

'Oh no!' she breathed, flinching as if it were she who would receive the blow. 'Please don't...'

The sailor drew his arm back as if to strike, but something in his victim's face must have stopped him, for he contented himself with a muffled oath.

'Get a move on, you!'

Morna breathed again, glancing at her cousin as the convicts began to shuffle on board and climb down the ladders to the lower holds, where they would be kept for most of the journey.

'Come, we must not let Jared see us,' she said in a low voice. 'He would hate it if he knew I had seen him chained like this. He is so very proud.'

She turned away, almost bumping into a young ship's officer. He caught her arm as she swayed, smiling and shaking his head as she tried to apologise.

'It was my fault, Miss Hamilton,' he said. 'I should have taken more care.'

'No, it was my fault,' she insisted. 'But you have the advantage of me, sir. I do not know your name.'

'Ah, it is my duty to know the names of the passengers. I am John Blackwell, first officer of this ship and at your service, Miss Hamilton.'

Morna smiled as she saw the gleam of appreciation in his eyes when he looked at her. He was only a few years her senior, fair-haired and with an engaging manner. She liked the warmth in his eyes and the gentle way he had steadied her without being in the least familiar.

'Well, Mr Blackwell, I am pleased to meet you. If you will excuse me, I shall go to my cabin now. I – I do not care to watch those poor wretches being herded like animals into a pen.'

'No, I agree it's a bad business,' he said with a frown. 'When I have my own ship – and I hope that will be on our return to England next time – I shall refuse to carry convicts. Now that more settlers are going out, I think the practice of sending forced labour there will gradually die out – but unfortunately, until it does, someone must transport them.'

'Yes, I suppose so – but could they not be treated a little more kindly?' Morna saw that the last of the prisoners were coming on board. 'I must go now.'

She turned her face away quickly as Jared glanced in her direction, praying that he had not recognised her. It would be time enough to let him know she was on board when they reached New South Wales. Until then, it could only increase his suffering if he knew she had seen him chained like a dog.

Taking Jane's arm, she nodded to the young officer and walked swiftly in the direction of the passenger cabins at the other end of the ship. She did not dare to glance back, and so missed seeing the sudden flash of pain in the eyes of the very last convict to descend into the darkness of the holds.

There was a grating noise as the hold was opened and a chink of light appeared above them. Jared tensed himself, preparing for the mad scramble and the fierce fighting over the scraps of food that would shortly be lowered down to them in baskets. Food! He laughed mirthlessly at the thought. Until a few weeks ago – or was it months? – he wouldn't have fed such swill to the pigs. Yet now he would fight as desperately as any of the others to make sure he got his fair share – more, if he could manage it! All he thought about was survival, though why he or any of the others even wanted to survive was beyond imagination.

His thoughts were suspended as the baskets came down, Plunging into the thick of it, he used his feet, and elbows to claw his way through and seize two chunks of the coarse brown bread, a cup of water and a hunk of dried meat. Succeeding, he retreated to a quiet corner and sat down on the ground to eat. He bit into the meat, tearing at its leather-like strands as he forced himself to chew slowly. The taste was rancid, almost choking him, but he made himself swallow it all. He had to eat or he would die.

Hearing a faint moan, Jared turned his head slightly. Lying on the floor close by was an old man, his matted hair and beard almost entirely grey. His eyes were closed and his emaciated body twitched as if he were in pain.

Jared hesitated, knowing from experience that some of the men would use any trick to steal food. Then pity stirred in him and he bent over the old man. Slipping an arm beneath his head, he held the cup of water to his lips.

'Here, drink a little of this,' he said.

The old man opened his eyes, his lips moving greedily at the side of the cup. He swallowed a few drops of water and sighed, but when Jared showed him the bread he shook his head.

'Save it for yourself,' he croaked. 'I'm dying – I've no reason to live. Even if I reached Australia, I couldn't hope to survive for seven years. No, its better if I die now.'

'It might be better for us all,' Jared said bitterly, but in his heart he knew he would fight to live. After seven years he would be free – free to seek the revenge he thirsted for.

Chewing the dry bread, he closed his eyes, shutting out the stink and foulness of his surroundings. One day he would kill the man who had done this to him. He had sought a more subtle revenge for his father's suffering, thinking to play Robin Hood and win back the money Stainton had stolen from his victims, not only for himself but for young fools like General Millington's boy.

He would have been content to see Stainton beaten at the card table and exposed for the cheat he was – now only his enemy's death would satisfy this gnawing hunger for revenge inside him.

And when Stainton was dead, he would think of a suitable punishment for his enemy's widow – the woman who had betrayed him. Jared's teeth tore at the bread with a savage fury, frustration grinding at his belly as he remembered their last meeting. Why had she come to visit him in that foul prison? After she had left, her presence had lingered like the sweet smell of her perfume, haunting him by day and night so that he woke from tormented dreams, crying her name and covered in a fine, cold sweat. He knew that she must hate him now. He had driven her away deliberately, choosing his words with an icy calculation that was meant to hurt. He had seen himself as a surgeon lancing the wound that would finally cut the ties between them, but he had been wrong if he believed it would end once she was gone. Instead, the memory of her stricken face stayed with him constantly, a nagging ache that would not be denied. He cursed himself over and over again for being a fool. She was only a woman, not even wildly beautiful, and he had ample proof of her betrayal. Yet he could not put that sweet, sad look she had given him out of his mind.

'I pity you,' she had said. 'You have forgotten how to trust. I pray you will find peace of mind before it's too late.'

'Damn you,' he whispered hoarsely. 'Why won't you give me peace? Why must you torment me even now – even here?'

He had expected to hang when he sent her away. He had defied the court, inviting the maximum punishment, even wanting it. It would have been a swift end and he did not fear physical pain. Yet he had never once considered the alternative. The shock of his sentence had stunned him for a moment, so that he was hardly aware of what it meant. Then, as realisation came, he had felt a wave of such despair sweep over him, bringing him close to breaking-point. It was then that he had let his eyes travel round the packed courtroom for the first time, searching for her, though he knew she would not be there. When he saw her he could scarcely believe it. She had smiled at him, and her lips moved as if in benediction.

For a moment he had felt so close to her that he could almost smell the fresh scent of her skin and feel the warmth of her lips beneath his. Afterwards, he had thought he must have imagined it. It could not have been Morna he had seen, but the image of her that haunted his dreams. She had not been in the courtroom any more than she was on board this ship, though he had deluded himself into thinking he had caught sight of her moments before he descended into the bowels of this stinking hell.

'God, do they mean to keep us for ever like rats in a trap?'

Jared did not realise he had spoken aloud until he heard a cackle of laughter somewhere to his right. Turning his head, he saw a grinning face only inches away.

'Ain't no God down here, mate!'

The creature who crawled towards him through the half light seemed at first sight more animal than human, with its snub nose, twisted lip and shock of thick black hair covering all but nose and eyes. Seeing the instinctive revulsion in Jared's eyes, the man, for it was after all a man, snickered and squatted cross-legged on the floor beside him, eyeing the second piece of bread hungrily.

'Pyke's me name, sir,' he said. 'Had another one once, but I've forgotten it. You couldn't spare a bit o' that bread, I suppose?'

'Why didn't you get your own?'

'None left, sir.' Pyke dragged his left foot forward so that Jared could see his club foot. 'It takes me time to get there, see?'

Knowing he was probably a fool, Jared broke the bread in half and gave one piece to the little man. He watched as Pyke stuffed it into his mouth, almost choking himself in his hurry to swallow it.

'How long is it since you've eaten?' he asked when the other had digested the food.

'Three – four days.' Pyke shrugged. 'It don't take much to keep me alive. I'm used to being hungry.'

Sighing, Jared gave him the other half of the crust. 'In future, stay near me when the baskets come down and I'll get food for you, too.'

To his surprise, tears welled up in Pyke's eyes and he began to blubber noisily like a child.

'In Heaven's name, what's the matter, man?'

Pyke sniffed, wiping his face with the sleeve of his filthy shirt and making pale smears across his dirt-streaked cheeks. 'That's the first time in me life anyone ever did me a good turn,' he choked. 'Folks don't like me 'cause I'm ugly, see? I shan't forget this, sir.'

Jared smiled wryly. 'Why do you call me, sir? I'm a convict like you.'

'I knows quality when I sees it, even here.' Pyke shifted so that he could see Jared's face. 'You're Captain Trenwith, ain't yer? I heard you was took for highway robbery.' He grinned as he saw faint surprise in the other's eyes, and tapped his foot. 'I might be a bit slow on account o' this, but I'm sharp in other ways. I listens and I hears things. You'll find me useful when we get to the colonies, sir.'

'If we ever get there,' Jared muttered. 'We must have been stuck in this hold for months already.'

'Three weeks to the day, sir.' Pyke grinned as Jared looked at him in disbelief and took a piece of wood from inside his shirt. He had made twenty-one distinct cuts on it. 'I keep count, see?'

Jared took the piece of wood from him, examining it carefully. 'How did you do this?'

'Don't ask no questions – too many ears about.' He tapped the side of his nose significantly. 'I told you I could be useful to you, sir.'

Suddenly, Jared threw back his head and laughed. Obviously he had made a friend of this ugly little creature, and strangely it had eased the deep bitterness inside him. He was no longer alone in this terrible place. There was someone he could talk to, someone to share the endless hours of inactivity in semi-darkness.

'Tell me,' he said. 'What terrible deed have you done to deserve this pleasure trip?'

'Ah now, that's a long story,' Pyke replied with a grin. 'I wouldn't want to make a nuisance of meself, sir.'

Jared yawned and stretched out on the floor with his arms beneath the back of his head. 'Well, as it happens, I have an hour or two to spare just now...'

'But surely the captain must allow them to come up on deck sometimes?' Morna looked at the first officer, her eyes angry. 'We've been at sea for a month, and they haven't had a breath of fresh air. It's inhuman – and unhealthy. Those prisoners were sentenced to seven years of penal servitude, not to die in a filthy hold!'

'I know it must appear cruel, Miss Hamilton,' John Blackwell replied uncomfortably. 'But some of them are difficult to control; they try to jump overboard and they attack the crew. Captain Smithson feels that several weeks below deck subdues them, but he will bring them up soon, I assure you.'

'When?' Morna insisted, knowing that she was blaming the wrong man but unable to control her impatience. 'Would it help if I were to speak to the captain?'

'I could not advise that.' He shook his head, frowning. 'Captain Smithson is fair, but a man of uncertain temper. He might resent your interference, and that would only make things worse for the prisoners.'

Morna turned away, gazing out at the endless sea and sky. Tears stung her eyes as she imagined Jared's suffering shut away in the holds with another thirty or forty men. The air in there must be fetid by now, and she had seen the meagre portions of food that were sent down in the baskets twice a day.

If only there were something she could do to help him, Morna thought desperately, some way she could ease the misery he must be enduring, but she knew she was powerless. She could not even buy his bond until they reached New South Wales. A tentative enquiry had brought a sharp reply from Captain Smithson.

'The prisoners' bonds will be auctioned in accordance with the law when we get to the colony, Miss Hamilton. It is not my custom to show favouritism to a particular convict.'

She had not dared to argue. Captain Smithson was a harshly-spoken man with stern features. Though not unattractive, he had a forbidding manner and she suspected him of being rather contemptuous of passengers like herself and her family. He was above all else a seaman, and he considered the settlers slightly mad, although he was happy enough to take the fares they paid for the privilege of sailing on his ship.

Morna and her cousin were the only women on board, and there were two other men besides Philip and Harry Robson, both of them young officers who had been appointed to the Governor's staff. She had spent several hours talking with Mr Robson, who had told her a great deal about the climate, vegetation and conditions she could expect to find in her adopted country. He was becoming a good friend, and it was comforting to know that he and his family would be their neighbours.

'Emily will enjoy having you near,' he informed her on one of their frequent walks about the deck. 'With the children such a tie, she doesn't get into Sydney Town much these days, so you can expect an invitation to dine every week.'

He had already described his wife in great detail, and Morna had a clear picture of a fair skinned, sweet-faced woman only five or six years older than herself. Emily had been carrying her third child when Harry left on his business trip to England, where he had bought more stock and vital supplies for his property. He was naturally anxious to get home and make sure that she and the child were well.

'I know Rupert will have taken care of her,' he confided to Morna. 'He promised not to sell out until I got back, and to keep an eye on Emily and the stock. So I'm glad I can bring him good news. As soon as you've inspected the homestead and made up your mind, he'll be on his way over the mountains.'

Morna nodded, remembering what he had told her about his friend's restless nature. Ever since the way had been found through the Blue Mountains in 1813, more and more settlers were moving further westward now that the country was opening up and so many exciting discoveries had been made. There was the great river called the Murray, which had been first seen by Europeans in 1824, only five years ago, but Morna knew that her brother would want to settle close to Sydney itself; which was growing into a sizeable town. He had already made friends with the two young officers on board, and was talking of parties at the Governor's residence almost as if he had never left London.

Philip was drinking more than she liked, but the voyage was tedious for them all, with the long hours of enforced idleness, and she could only pray that his mood would improve once they reached their new country. Surely, when they were settled on the land, he would see the possibilities open to them all?

Morna had begun to keep a journal, in which she recorded every scrap of information she could gather about sheep-farming. She even had a list of sheep diseases and the symptoms to look for. Philip scoffed at her industry, refusing to take an interest and dismissing her efforts as unnecessary.

'We shall hire an overseer,' he said carelessly. 'There'll be no need for you to concern yourself with all this nonsense.'

Taking no notice of his attempts to dissuade her, Morna continued to learn all she could. It helped to pass the time, and to turn her mind from fretting over Jared. She could get no news of him, except that John Blackwell had told her none of the convicts had so far died. That meant that Jared must still be alive, though there was no doubt he was suffering like the other prisoners. She could only hope that he was at least managing to get his share of the food...

'He must have died in the night,' Jared said, touching the old man's face. 'He's stone cold, poor devil.'

'Maybe it's a blessing for us,' Pyke said. 'He couldn't have lasted much longer anyways.'

'At least he's not suffering now.' Jared frowned. 'What did you mean by "a blessing for us"? He was no trouble.'

'It will get us up on deck, if we're lucky. Someone's got to put the body over the side – and they'll not get a sailor to fetch it. Especially if we tell them he died of a fever.'

Jared looked at him, his eyes narrowed thoughtfully. 'You're right, Pyke. If we spread the word on this, it might get us all on deck for some fresh air. A few moans when they open the hatch, and the sight of a dead body, should throw a scare into them. They won't want us all dead when we finally arrive.'

'Just make sure we're the ones to tell about

the body – at least we'll get a breather.'

'Don't worry, I'll manage that,' Jared replied with a grin. 'That was a good idea of yours, my friend.'

Pyke winked and tapped his nose. 'Didn't I say I'd be useful to you? I'll pass on the word to some of the others.'

Morna's hand tightened on her cousin's arm as they approached the hatch leading to the hold where the convicts were held. It was wide open, and something unusual appeared to be happening.

'I wonder what's going on?' She looked at Jane, a flicker of excitement in her face. 'Do you think they can have decided to let those poor men come up at last?'

'Here's Mr Blackwell,' Jane said. 'He'll tell us what the fuss is all about.'

The young officer came hurrying towards them, holding out a hand in warning. 'I shouldn't come any nearer, ladies. Two of the prisoners are bringing up a dead man. Apparently he died of a fever, and we're afraid some of the others might have contracted it.'

Morna's heart caught with fear. 'Do you know who the dead man is?'

'Not by name, but he was an old man. I very much doubt he could have stood up to the conditions in New South Wales, Miss Hamilton.'

'Will you be letting the prisoners up for some exercise now, sir?' Jane asked. 'This fever is surely the result of their being kept below decks for more than six weeks.'

'You may be right, ma'am. At least, the captain has decided they should come up a few at a time. We are going to douse them with sea water. If I were you, I should go to your cabin for a while.'

'Is that an order, Mr Blackwell?' Morna looked at him defiantly.

'No. I was merely thinking of your comfort, Miss Hamilton. It will not be a pretty spectacle, I assure you.'

'We are neither of us squeamish. We shall stay here for a while. I am tired of my cabin and I need a little air.' She smiled at him. 'I shall be sure to stay well clear of your prisoners, sir.'

'It would not be wise to approach them. They are rough creatures – and most of them have not seen a woman in months. Especially a young and pretty woman.'

'They are coming up now.' Jane touched her cousin's arm urgently. 'Surely that is him, Morna?'

Morna glanced towards the open hatch. Two men had climbed out on deck. One of them was a small, ugly creature with a misshapen foot, but the other was unmistakable Jared. His hair had grown and he had a beard, but she recognised him at once.

She saw him blink in the bright light, stumbling a little as he struggled to accustom himself to the daylight after the gloom of the holds. Then he bent to pick up the old man's body, carrying the weight of it while his companion made a show of helping by holding the feet.

They walked to the rails and paused. Jared seemed to be asking the sailor something, and his reply was clearly audible to the two women.

'Say a prayer yourself then – if you know any.'

Morna watched as Jared made the sign of the cross over the old man's body and murmured a few words she could not catch. She shuddered as the corpse splashed into the ocean.

'God rest his soul,' she whispered. 'The poor man...'

'Amen,' Jane added softly.

Now the sailor was gesturing towards two buckets, obviously telling the prisoners to draw water from the sea. When they had done so, he ordered them to douse each other, giving them short, stiff brushes to scrub themselves with. He pointed to the hatch as two more prisoners came up, clearly directing Jared and his companion to stay where they were. It soon became plain that he intended them to undertake the task of drawing water from the sea and sluicing the other prisoners while he stayed at a safe distance. The convicts continued to emerge two at a time, each man being sent for a short walk after he had scrubbed himself before being ordered below once more.

'Jared will be up on deck for some time,' Morna said, looking at Jane excitedly. 'Go and fetch some food from our stores: ham, cheese, bread – anything you can find. I shall see if I can persuade Mr Blackwell to give it to him.'

'Is that wise? John Blackwell would be in trouble with the captain if he were seen.'

'He need not be seen if he is careful. Besides, I think he will risk it if I ask him!' Morna smiled naughtily. 'Bring the food, Jane, while I flirt with our charming first officer.'

Jane shook her head in mock reproof, knowing that the young man was half in love with Morna and would likely do as she asked. She hurried away to get the food, smiling a little as she saw her cousin approach the first officer.

Morna lifted her eyes to the young man's, fluttering her lashes and smiling at him. She was prepared to flirt shamelessly with John Blackwell if it would help Jared. Her laughter rang out as she responded to his gallantry, completely unaware that she had attracted the attention of the taller of the two convicts.

Jared stiffened as he caught sight of the girl talking to the handsome young officer. She was wearing a gown of blue silk with a fashionable pelisse in a darker shade. As she tipped her head to look teasingly at her companion, a lock of shining black hair slipped from beneath her straw bonnet.

It couldn't be her! A muscle throbbed in Jared's neck as he heard the sound of her gay laughter. Was he going crazy? Had the weeks below decks turned his brain soft? It couldn't be her. She would be married to Stainton by now and living in London – unless her husband was also here on this stinking tub!

A red mist formed in his brain as a terrible anger swept over him, robbing him of his self-control. If Stainton were here now, he would kill him! In his sudden rage, he let go of the bucket as he tipped its load of salt water over a convict. The wooden missile struck the unfortunate man a glancing blow on the head, stunning him for a moment.

Even as Jared realised what he had done, the convict gave a snarl of rage and lurched at him, his crooked hands going for Jared's throat. Bracing himself instinctively, he repelled the attack, throwing off the man's dangerous embrace.

'It was an accident,' he said. 'In Heaven's name, don't be a fool!'

'I ain't taking that from no one,' the other man growled.

He launched himself at Jared again, and this time succeeded in knocking him off-balance. They went down on the deck together, rolling over and over in a fierce struggle. Suddenly something snapped in Jared's brain. All his pent-up frustration boiled over, and the convict became Stainton in his mind. His one desire was to slaughter the enemy who had subjected him to so many endless days and nights of misery. He made a sound in his throat that was inhuman as his hands closed on the other man's throat. He wanted to kill, kill, kill...

When the sailors dragged him off his victim, he fought like a wild man, felling three of them before they finally managed to pin him to the deck, where he lay panting and gasping for breath. He felt himself dragged to his feet, his hair almost pulled from its roots as they held him to bind his hands behind his back. As the insane rage cleared from his brain, he became aware of a large, hard-featured man observing him from a few yards away.

'Is the brute secured?' Captain Smithson asked, his lips tight with anger. 'Who started the fight?'

'It was this one.' A sailor pushed Jared forward. 'He threw a bucket at the other.'

'Is that true?' The captain's mouth curled

in a sneer as Jared remained silent. 'Answer me, you scurvy dog!'

'It was an accident, sir.' Pyke hobbled forward. 'The bucket slipped from Captain Trenwith's hand and this man here went for him. The captain were only defending himself.'

Smithson's eyes narrowed dangerously. 'Speak when you're spoken to, cripple. There's only one captain on board this ship, and that's me.' His eyes narrowed in thought as he looked at Jared more closely. 'You're no seaman, that's for sure. Were you in the military, Trenwith?'

Jared met his eyes with a cold stare. 'Yes, I held the rank of captain in the Indian cavalry regiment.'

'Yes, sir!' Smithson bellowed. 'You will address me as sir, Trenwith. Well, was it an accident?'

'The bucket slipped from my hand, but I was equally to blame for the fight ... sir!'

The note of sarcasm in Jared's voice as he added the last word was not lost on Smithson. His heavy brows met in a frown as he studied the prisoner's face, noting the pride which was still evident despite the weeks of hardship below decks. In the captain's experience, it was often necessary to make an example of one man as a lesson to the others. Discipline had to be tight on board ship, where the crew were outnumbered by the prisoners. Slackness led to rebellion, and, in extreme cases, mutiny.

'This man will receive twenty lashes,' he barked to the boson. 'The other dog, five. Bring six of the prisoners up to witness the punishments.'

'Curse you!' The convict Jared had fought with spat on the deck, struggling madly as he was dragged away.

His punishment was swift, and executed as soon as the six witnesses were on deck. Jared was taken to the front of the line so that he could see the other man's agony as the cruel whip bit into his flesh, and though he screamed twice, he was still conscious when they cut him down. He lay on the deck moaning until two sailors pulled him to his feet and took him to the hatch, forcing him to go below.

Then it was Jared's turn. He walked proudly between the two members of the crew who escorted him to the mast, his face stony as they bound his wrists and ankles spreadeagled against it. One of them tore his shirt away, exposing his naked back. He braced himself, waiting for the first blow, promising himself that he would not cry out no matter how painful it was. The first blow surprised him, bringing a gasp from between his clenched teeth. He took a grip on his nerve; he would be better prepared next time.

Exercising rigid control, he absorbed the next several lashes without crying out, though his body writhed, and the muscles bulged in his shoulders and neck. The tenth stroke broke his skin and he felt a trickle of blood run down his spine. After that there was only pain; unimaginable, soul-destroying pain. He heard a scream as from a distance. Dear God, had he made that sound? No, surely it was a woman's cry... A woman was sobbing and screaming for the punishment to stop. The thought trailed through his mind, blotting out the agony for a precious moment... Was it her?

Then a last, savage blow more terrible than all the others cut through the mist in his brain. He cried out once and slumped against the mast, no longer conscious.

'Stop it!' Morna cried. 'Stop it this instant! Can't you see you've nearly killed him?'

Captain Smithson looked down into her face and saw the passion there. Until this moment he had thought her almost plain, an insignificant scrap of a girl. Now he saw that she was magnificent, her dark blue eyes full of fire, and she was beautiful. A woman after all, not a girl.

'The punishment was necessary,' he said, feeling a sudden need to defend himself. 'However, it is finished. I shall have him cut down.'

'And what then?' Morna's eyes seemed to

fill her face as she looked at him. 'If you send the prisoner back with the others, he'll die. Is that what you want? Do you want his death on your conscience?'

Smithson stared at her, feeling confused and uncertain, knowing he should assert his authority. Yet there was something about her at that moment that made him want to see her smile at him. His own weakness angered him. It was ridiculous to be swayed by a woman's tears. But what a woman! In her anger she was a goddess, a she-wolf defending her young.

'On your own head be it,' he snarled, wondering why he did not send her to her cabin. 'Nurse the dog back to health if you've a mind to it. But he goes back with the others as soon as he can walk, do you hear me?'

'Yes. Thank you. Oh, thank you, Captain Smithson.' Morna's smile was blinding as she gazed up at him, causing him to blink. 'Will you have your men carry him to my brother's cabin, please? Philip can move up to the top bunk so that I can nurse him.'

'Do as you please,' Smithson growled, but his tone was softer, though he glared at her as he jerked his head at one of the crew. 'Trenwith's bond will fetch a decent price. It would be a pity to lose him, after all.'

His words were meant to be overheard by the sailors. He needed to justify this unusual softness for the sake of discipline. Turning away, he strode towards a seaman who had ceased his task of coiling a rope to watch the little scene.

'Get on with your work, Harris, or you'll taste the lash yourself!'

'Ay, ay, sir!'

The sailor swung into action and Smithson smiled to himself, feeling better. He had not gone soft in the head; it was bad business to lose too many convicts. If the woman wanted the trouble of looking after the prisoner, it made good, financial sense to let her do it. Trenwith was strong, and his bond would fetch a good price at the auction.

Unaware of the conflicting emotions she had raised in the captain's breast, Morna bent over Jared's unconscious body, restraining her tears as she saw his torn and bloodied back. Such terrible injuries! How had he borne them so bravely? She wanted to beg the crew to be careful as they lifted him, but she knew she had been incredibly lucky in persuading their captain to let her care for the prisoner at all, and she dared not complain as they half carried, half dragged the unconscious man to her brother's cabin.

Thankfully, Philip was not there when they arrived. She knew he would protest at the intrusion, but it was the only arrangement possible. She directed the sailors to lift Jared on to the lower bunk, thanking them with a tight smile before they left. She had begun to sponge away the blood on his back when Jane came in.

'I saw what was happening as I returned with the food. I – I could not bear to watch, Morna. You were braver than I.'

Morna shook her head, her eyes misty with tears. 'He was so brave, Jane. I was screaming and crying, but he cried out only once at the end. No matter what they do to him, they cannot break his spirit.'

'I'll empty this,' Jane said, taking the bowl of bloody water from her. 'It might be better for him sometimes if he were a little less stubborn.'

'That he could never be.' Morna smiled sadly. 'He would die before he gave in.'

'That's what I meant.' Jane showed the girl a jar of salve and some clean linen bandages. 'I went to our cabin to fetch these. Shall I help you to bind them?'

'Yes, for I cannot lift him alone.'

The two women worked side by side, applying salve to the torn flesh and binding the soft linen firmly. He groaned once as they lifted him, but he did not regain his senses. Morna was anxious, wondering whether they should try to bring him round, but Jane shook her head.

'It's nature's way of helping him to cope with the pain,' she reasoned. 'We'll leave

175

him to rest now, my love. Later, when he wakes, we'll bring water and a nourishing broth. There's no more we can do for him at present.'

Morna looked at the face of the man she loved, half buried as it was in the pillows beneath his head. 'No,' she said. 'I shall watch over him for a while in case he wakes and harms himself. You go and rest, Jane.'

Jane frowned. 'I thought you didn't want him to know you were on board until we reached Australia?'

'I was wrong,' Morna said. 'I should have told him of my plans before we left England. It would have given him something to hope for.'

Jane hesitated, her eyes anxious as she looked at the girl. 'Have you considered his wishes in the matter, Morna?'

'What do you mean?'

'He may not want to be your bond-servant. He might feel humiliated at the very idea. Don't forget you were once his friend and neighbour. He might prefer to be bought by a stranger.'

'That's ridiculous!' Morna cried. 'I have no intention of treating him like a servant. He will be free to live as one of the family.'

'I know that, my love.' Jane sighed as she saw the look on the girl's face. 'But the fact remains that in law he will be a servant for seven years. I do not think Captain Trenwith's pride will let him accept the situation easily. You must not expect him to be grateful to you.'

'I do not want gratitude,' Morna said indignantly. 'How could you think it?'

'I know what you want.' Jane smiled a little sadly. 'But you cannot buy love, my dearest one. If it is not in his heart to love you, you cannot change that – nor should you try. You will only end by hurting yourself.'

'Oh, Jane…' Morna caught her breath on a sob. 'I love him so very much. I did not know just how much he meant to me until I saw him tied to that mast today. But you are right, he is too proud to accept the situation easily. Perhaps it will be better if I do not tell him until it is certain. Once he understands the alternative, he will come to terms with what I have done.'

'You must do as you think best. I wanted only to warn you, my dear. I do not like to see you so unhappy. What you have done is commendable, but you must not try to hold him against his will.'

'I know. I have always known that I could not do so.'

Morna sighed as her cousin went out, settling down to watch over her patient. Jane was right, she knew. If Jared suspected what she had done for his sake, he would feel his obligation keenly. She must not humiliate him more than was necessary. When he asked why she was on board, as he would surely do as soon as he saw her, she would invent a story to satisfy him. It was better that he should resent her presence than be humbled by the knowledge of what she had risked to follow him half across the world. Her own pride forbade that he should be grateful to her. No, she would rather see anger in his eyes than shame.

Leaning over to touch her lips gently to his cheek, she smiled. 'One day you will know the truth, my love, but until then – hate me if you must.'

'You should rest now, Morna,' Jane said, seeing the tiredness in the girl's face. 'Since Philip has refused to be concerned in this, I shall sit with Captain Trenwith tonight.'

Morna nodded and got up, easing the stiffness in her back. It was a week since she had witnessed the brutal beating that had resulted in Jared being almost out of his mind with fever. He had lain in a semi-conscious state for most of that time, muttering wildly and thrashing restlessly on his bunk. Philip had moved his things to the cabin of his new friends, preferring to sleep on the floor than to stay with the sick man.

'If you insist on nursing him, Morna, you must do so without my help,' he said. 'Though, I warn you, he won't thank you for your trouble when he comes to his senses.'

Ignoring both his warning and his sulky expression, Morna continued to watch over Jared day and night. Together she and Jane had bathed his feverish body with cool, refreshing water, shaved his beard and tended the lacerations on his back. The torn flesh had begun to heal with their careful nursing, but the fever raged on and on, and his strength was impaired by weeks of deprivation.

Morna had hardly dared to leave his side, relinquishing her place only when her cousin insisted she must rest or be ill herself. Looking at Jared now, the girl was reluctant to go, lingering even as her cousin gave her a gentle push towards the door.

'You will call me if there is any change?'

'Of course, my dear. But you must get some sleep. You look exhausted.'

Giving a little sigh, Morna allowed herself to be shooed from the cabin. She went up on deck, breathing deeply of the fresh air. The sun seemed to be sinking into the sea, setting it on fire. She could hear the whisper of the wind in the sails, and the rhythmic swish of the waves against the ship. It was peaceful, and it relaxed the tension from her body as she arched her back, letting the breeze catch her long hair, cooling the back of her neck.

'And how is your patient tonight, Miss Hamilton?'

Morna was startled as she heard the captain's voice behind her. She forced herself to smile at him, knowing that without his co-operation she would not have had the chance to nurse Jared.

'He still has a fever, Captain Smithson.'

'I regret that it should be so. It would be a shame if he were to die after you have nursed him so devotedly.'

'Yes.' Morna held back the angry torrent of words that sprang to her lips. Now was not the time to tell Smithson she thought him a heartless monster. 'If you will excuse me, sir, I am tired. I think I shall go to my cabin.'

Captain Smithson caught her arm as she would have turned away. 'The punishment was necessary, you know. If I allowed the convicts to fight, they would go beserk. I do not like this trade, Miss Hamilton, but it has to be done.'

She heard the note of pleading in his voice and relented a little. 'I know you have to keep discipline tight on board ship, Captain, but was it necessary to inflict such a cruel punishment? Would it not have been enough to give both men five lashes?'

'Perhaps.' He let go of her arm. 'Good-night, Miss Hamilton.'

She saw his cold expression and feared that she had annoyed him. 'I am sorry if I have offended you, sir. It was not my intention. I am tired...'

'Yes, you are tired.' He smiled oddly. 'I almost wish I could change places with Trenwith. Do not be anxious, Miss Hamilton. I have given you my word, and I shall not break it. You may have your convict – until he is well enough to join the others.'

He resumed his walk round the deck, leaving Morna to stare after him in surprise. Perhaps Captain Smithson was not quite the monster she had thought him, after all.

She was smiling as she went to her cabin, her thoughts happier than they had been for some time as she began to brush her long hair, enjoying the soothing sensation. She might yet persuade the captain to let her buy Jared's bond before they reached Australia. Then he need not go back to those foul holds with the others...

Morna was sleeping peacefully when her cousin came to wake her. Jane smiled as she sat up in alarm, and nodded reassuringly.

'The fever has broken at last, Morna. Captain Trenwith is awake and asking for food. I thought you would like to take it to him?'

'Oh, Jane, that's wonderful!' Morna cried, jumping out of bed. 'If you prepare a tray, I will be ready in five minutes.'

'The soup is already hot. I warmed it myself before waking you.'

Jane sat down as the girl disappeared behind a curtain to strip off her high-necked night chemise, reappearing in a hurriedly donned gown of pale grey wool. Her hair was clustering about her face in wayward tendrils, but she shook her head as Jane's brows went up.

'My hair can wait!' Morna laughed excitedly. 'Oh, Jane, you know how I have longed for this moment – to be able to speak to him at last! To see him almost well again...' She caught her breath on a sob of joy. 'What did he say to you when he woke up?'

Jane turned away to tidy the bed. 'He was still a little light-headed. He seemed to think I was someone else.'

'I expect he thought he was at home, and that you were Naomi, his housekeeper, come to wake him.'

Naomi was not the name Jared had called on waking, but Jane did not feel it necessary to tell Morna what he had muttered so desperately seconds before he opened his eyes.

'I expect you are right,' she agreed. 'Now don't let Captain Trenwith eat too fast. A little at a time is best. He's still very weak.'

Morna nodded, her heart singing as she picked up the tray and made her way along the narrow passage to what had been Philip's cabin. She paused outside the door and knocked, mostly to give herself a moment before entering. Jared's voice inviting her to enter sent a shiver down her spine. What would he say when he saw who had brought his food?

Jared was sitting propped up against a pile of pillows when she went in. He looked towards the door in anticipation, obviously expecting Jane, and the smile of welcome froze on his lips.

'You!' he muttered. 'I thought I'd been dreaming – but it was you. You were with that officer...' He scowled as he saw she was carrying a tray. 'I thought the other woman was bringing my food.'

Morna set the tray down, keeping her face averted while she fought to control her disappointment. She had thought he might be aware of her caring for his every need while he was racked by the fever, but it seemed he remembered nothing. Perhaps it was best that way, she thought, her emotions under tight control as she turned to him.

'Jane came to wake me,' she said in a calm, light voice that betrayed none of the turmoil inside her. 'We have been looking after you between us since – since you became ill. She sat up with you all night and she is tired. It is my turn now.'

'You mean since I was beaten?' Jared's eyes narrowed in suspicion as he looked at her. 'Why am I not with the other convicts? How did you manage to persuade the captain to let you nurse me – and why?'

'Such a lot of questions.' Morna smiled and dipped the spoon in the soup. 'Why don't you eat instead of bothering about unimportant things?'

'Leave the tray, I shall feed myself,' Jared said harshly, but as he reached for the spoon his hand shook, spilling the hot liquid on to his naked chest. 'Damn it!'

The fever had left him too weak even to feed himself. He scowled at her as she calmly wiped the mess and refilled the spoon, his eyes resentful. Why was she here? Why was she bothering with him after all the things he had said to her? He was too weary to think clearly and his confusion made him angry. He would have liked to send her away, but he was too weak to attempt it. Morna felt the smouldering anger in him as she patiently fed him the nourishing broth, crumbling the bread so that he could swallow it more easily. When the food was finished at last, he lay back, obviously exhausted.

'What does your husband think about your nursing me?'

It was a stupid question to ask, but there was a devil in him that needed to be appeased. Somewhere in a tiny corner of his mind he knew that he was being too hard on

184

her, but he could not help himself.

'Nothing. I do as I please.' Morna turned away to tidy her tray. She was unable to tell him she was not married to Richard. If she did, he would demand to know the reason for her change of heart.

'You were always wilful,' Jared said, sounding almost amused now. 'You never listened to your father or those unfortunate governesses! I should have thought Stainton capable of taming you, though.'

He sounded suspicious, and Morna's chin went up as she looked at him. 'No man will ever tell me what to do, Captain Trenwith. I am not accountable to Richard, to my brother – or to you!'

'Especially not to me.' Now there was a definite glint of humour in his eyes. Just talking to her was making him feel better, he thought. Or maybe it was the food. He felt a sudden sting of remorse for taunting her, as he realised it was probably due to her that he was alive at all. 'I think I must owe my life to you. I am not sure whether to thank you or curse you.'

Morna turned her head away as she heard the mockery in his voice. 'The respite is only temporary, I'm afraid. When you are well, you will have to return to the holds. I'm sorry.'

A muscle flicked in his cheek as he saw what he thought was sympathy in her eyes, and a strong surge of resentment went through him. 'I don't want your pity, Morna. I'm grateful for what you've done, but I don't need your help any more.' He attempted to rise, cursing as he fell back against the pillows. 'God damn you and your husband! I swear I'll kill him if I get the chance! Your charity in nursing me won't save him if I survive the voyage.'

'You should conserve your strength,' Morna said, realising that she had made a mistake in offering him sympathy. Naturally, it was the last thing he would want from her. 'The sooner you are well, the sooner Philip can have his cabin back.'

She picked up her tray, preparing to leave. He made a violent lunge at her in a vain attempt to grab her arm, his face creasing with agony as he felt the pain from his back. Morna paused, hiding her hurt at his weakness behind a mask of indifference.

'What do you want? I have things to do.'

'Why did Philip come with you?' he muttered, his eyes narrowing in suspicion. It had been worrying him why she was on the ship at all. Stainton wasn't the type to leave town during the season – and definitely not for a trip to the colonies. No, there had to be something else – but what? 'Has Philip's gambling ruined you, too? Is that why you decided to leave England?' He glanced at her hand and saw that it was ringless. 'Did

Stainton jilt you? Is that why you're not wearing his ring?'

Morna hesitated. Her cousin's warning had made her reluctant to tell him the truth just yet. If he was sent back to the holds, he would have too much time to sit and think. He had already made it clear he resented her help, so how much more would he hate the idea of being her bond-servant then? No, she must wait until it was done and he saw for himself that it was the only solution.

'The answer to all your questions is yes,' she said at last, 'but do not concern yourself on my account. It was not a love affair, as you know. I have already received one proposal of marriage on board this ship, but I shall not make up my mind until after we land. It was a shock when Richard changed his mind, of course; but they tell me women are in scarce supply in the colonies. I am sure to find a wealthy husband if I take my time. After all, one man is very like another, don't you agree?'

Jared had been lying there imagining all kinds of impossible things, and her statement hit him like a douche of cold water. Like a fool, he had begun to believe he had misjudged her, but now he saw that he had been right all the time.

'Are you really such a cold-hearted bitch?' His lips curled with scorn. 'No wonder Stainton changed his mind. I suppose even he needed a show of affection from his wife!'

'And you are insolent sir.' Morna was angered by his scorn, even though she knew she had provoked it. She was less in his eyes than the man he had sworn to kill! 'I do not know why I wasted my time nursing you. In future, my cousin will bring your food.'

'That will please me just as much as it does you!'

Jared hurled the words after her as she went out. Morna closed the door behind her, blinking back her tears. She must not let his bitterness hurt her. It was better that he should think her a cold-hearted bitch than that he should guess the truth. If he was obliged to feel grateful to her, he might try to pretend some affection for her out of a sense of duty – and that she could not bear!

CHAPTER SIX

'I thought he was sleeping at first,' Jane said, her expression concerned as she looked at Morna in the flickering candlelight. 'I am sorry to disturb you, but I fear the fever may have returned.'

'You were right to wake me.' Morna reached for her thick bedwrap, thrusting her feet into a pair of soft slippers. 'He seemed so well the other morning that I thought the danger was past.' She looked at her cousin's pale face as Jane sank down on the edge of the bunk. 'You look tired, Jane. Please stay here and rest for a while. I shall do all that is necessary to quiet him.'

'Well...' Jane hesitated, giving in with a sigh. 'I do have a headache – and you are better with him when the fever is on him. He seems to respond to your voice somehow.'

Morna laughed mirthlessly. 'You would not have thought so when I took him his soup – but it is my turn now. It was selfish of me to leave so much to you these past few days. It was just that – that he seemed to prefer your company to mine.'

Jane shook her head, looking close to exhaustion. 'You know I have been glad to help. I shall come in a little while.'

'I shall stay with him tonight. Sleep now, dearest,' Morna shut the door softly as she went out, carrying her lantern. Its soft light cast little shadows on the wooden panelling as she hurried to the next cabin. Opening the door, she heard an agonised cry from the bed and went quickly to Jared's side. Placing the lantern on a hook in the low ceiling, she bent over the tossing figure in the bed, placing her palm against his forehead. It was surprisingly cool.

'Danielle... No!' Jared muttered. 'You

cannot leave me…'

Morna stiffened as she heard his cry. She thought he was merely having a bad dream, but she could not go without making sure he was not ill again. She put her hand on his naked shoulder, shaking him gently.

'Wake up,' she said. 'You're having a nightmare. Wake up, Jared.'

She bent over him again, smoothing the dark hair from his forehead. As she did so, his arms suddenly closed round her and she was pulled down across his chest. She struggled, trying to fend him off without causing him pain, sure that he was still in the grip of his dream.

'Let me go, Jared,' she said. 'I am not Danielle. You are dreaming.'

With a muffled groan, he rolled her over him so that she was trapped between him and the wooden side of the ship. His mouth was suddenly on hers, joined in a passionate kiss that took her by surprise, shocking her into an instinctive response. His kisses covered her face and throat hungrily. She tried to protest, but his mouth stopped the words. Then his fingers were tearing at the ribbons at her throat, his hands pushing back the flimsy silk of her chemise so that her breasts were exposed to the yellow glow of the lantern. Its light seemed to turn her flesh to gold silk, and he drew a shuddering breath.

'So beautiful... So beautiful,' he murmured, sounding feverish. 'Why do you haunt me so? Your face is always with me...'

Did he mean her or someone else? Morna could not be sure. Was he still half asleep, imagining that she was a woman he had once loved?

His mouth covered one rosy nipple, sending little tremors running through her. She gasped, her head swimming, knowing she should stop him. He was still dreaming, in the grip of a fever, believing she was a woman called Danielle. It was not her he wanted. Yet her body was responding to every move he made, and she could not find the strength of will to prevent his hands caressing her breasts.

His touch was arousing such strong emotions in her that she cried out, arching towards him as desire spiralled through her. She tried to look at his face, wanting to know if his eyes were open, but he had buried himself in the dark tresses of hair as they spread out across the pillow. Whispering his name in wonder, she felt his hands moving beneath her nightgown, parting her legs, probing the silken flesh which throbbed and pulsated to the searching of his fingers. Then a shiver of something like fear went through her as his hands gripped her hips, pulling her body firmly beneath him. She moaned a feeble protest, knowing she was a fool to let this happen, realising that even if he was by now aware of who she was, she was only a substitute for Danielle. He was fulfilling a basic need long denied him. He was using her to relieve the frustrations of the months he had spent in such wretched misery.

Yet even as she acknowledged all this, her body responded to his urgency. She could hardly breathe for the wild beating of her heart and the weight of his body on hers. Then his mouth possessed hers, his tongue forcing entry even as the pulsing heat of his manhood pierced her.

Morna's muted cry was lost beneath his exquisitely tender kiss that seemed to compensate for the brief pain he had caused her. She felt him deep inside her, his hips grinding against hers as he thrust into her accommodating softness. It was over swiftly, as though in his urgency he had lost control, spilling himself inside her too soon. He gave a groan as he sank on to her, his face pillowed in her breasts, his strength spent. She lay still, shocked and bewildered by what had happened. There was a vague sense of disappointment, too. This was not as she had always imagined it would be. Something was missing, though what, she was not sure.

It was several minutes before she dared to speak, whispering his name softly.

'Jared, let me go now. Please.'

He neither moved nor answered. The sound of his regular, gentle breathing suggested that he was asleep. She shook his shoulder but there was no response. Determined to be gone before he woke again, she began to ease herself from beneath his weight. Once, she had the feeling that he was deliberately making escape difficult for her, but repeated requests to wake up met with no reply. At last she managed to shift his body sufficiently to allow her to wriggle free.

Standing by the bed, she looked at Jared as he lay where she had rolled him, his eyes closed. Was he feigning sleep? She could not make up her mind. Yet why should he pretend? Unless he had kept an image of Danielle in his mind and did not want to destroy it. Perhaps it was best for them both this way, she thought, her emotions too confused to know what she wanted.

Morna straightened her nightclothes, glancing once more before she left at the man in the bed. He had not moved, and she was fairly convinced that his sleep was genuine now. She sighed, slipping quietly out to the passage and feeling thankful that no one was about as she went quickly to her own cabin.

Jared lay still for some time after she had gone, hardly daring to breathe for fear of betraying himself. After a period in which he felt himself floating in a dreamlike state, he rolled over on his back, opening his eyes as he stared blankly into the darkness, tortured by the confusion of his thoughts. He was unsure why he had feigned sleep, except that it had seemed to be the only means of escape – escape from a situation that was too difficult to face just yet.

He had woken from his nightmare only moments before Morna came into the cabin. At first he thought she was a part of his dream. He had called for her so many times in his haunted slumber, and then she was suddenly there. And he wanted her – he wanted her in his arms so desperately. Without really knowing why he did it, he had spoken Danielle's name, and once the deception had begun he could not stop it. Any more than he could stop himself making love to Morna once he felt the softness of her yielding body beneath him and sensed the urgent response in her as she opened to him.

He had been swept away on the tide of his need for her, long denied by both his body and his mind. He had taken her with feverish haste, fearing that any moment she would begin to fight him. Then it had been all over too swiftly, and he realised what he had done. The sharp pleasure he had felt at the moment of possession was quickly replaced by shock and remorse. Exhausted by the sheer physical act of making love, he had felt drained of energy, unable to cope with the outrage he was sure she would feel. So he had pretended not to hear her as she tried to wake him. A surge of disgust at his own behaviour swept through him. Even if she had betrayed him, he had no right to use her in that way – and if she hadn't... He would not let himself examine the alternative. It was better that he continue to fuel his anger against her, otherwise he would go mad!

Moving quietly so as not to wake her cousin, Morna poured water into a bowl and washed the trickle of blood from between her thighs. Then she sponged a stain from her night-gown before slipping into bed. Lying on her back with her eyes closed, she was aware of the burning sensation between her legs, the reminder of her shame.

Now that she was alone, she could not understand why she had let it happen. The act of love had left her feeling vaguely unsatisfied, used and guilty. Why? Why did she feel like that, when at the beginning her heart and body had responded so willingly to Jared's touch? She had felt as if she were about to experience something wonderful, and now she just felt strangely empty. Why?

The answer came to her with blinding clarity. It had not been an act of love on Jared's part, only the satisfaction of his lust.

He had used her like a whore, as a substitute for the woman he really wanted. That was why the early promise of their brief union had not come to true fulfilment.

She had surrendered her maidenhead to him, offering it with her heart and love. Jared had taken her sacrifice carelessly, squandering it for a moment's pleasure. It had meant no more to him than that. She could not even be sure he knew it was her he had made love to. It might have been any woman.

The pain struck her through like the blade of a knife, bringing hot, stinging tears to her eyes. How could he use her so carelessly when she loved him with her entire being? Then anger surged deep within her, anger and resentment at the way he had destroyed her innocence.

'I hate you, Jared Trenwith,' she whispered fiercely in the darkness.

Yet, even as she said it, she knew it was a lie. She loved him still, despite what he had done to her – but she would never tell him so now. She meant nothing to him: no more than any woman of the streets.

In future she would not give him a chance to hurt her. She would treat him with the coldness he deserved. And she would put the memory of this night out of her mind. It had never happened...

In the morning, Morna had something more important to occupy her mind. Jane was burning with a fever. She complained of aching limbs, and a faint rash had begun to spread across her skin.

It was some time before Morna could leave her cousin; but as soon as she had seen her settled comfortably, she prepared a tray of food for her other patient, knowing that she was the one who had to take it to him now. Her pulses raced as she paused outside his door, trying to achieve a calm but distant manner. How could she face him again after what had happened between them? And yet she must. Entering the cabin, she saw the bunk was empty, and frowned. Why had he risen from his sick-bed? He was still far from well. Putting down her tray, she glanced round the small space as if expecting Jared to suddenly appear from nowhere.

'Jared – are you here?' she whispered, her voice catching.

'He has gone.'

Philip's voice behind her made Morna jump.

'Gone – where?' She stared at him in dawning suspicion. 'But he was too weak. The captain promised me he would not send Jared back with the others until he was completely recovered. He promised me!'

Her brother shrugged, unconcerned. 'I

only know what John Blackwell told me. Ask him what happened if you don't believe me.'

'I shall speak to Captain Smithson. He gave me his word.'

'He must have changed his mind.' Philip looked at the tray of food. 'I may as well eat this, since Trenwith won't be needing it.'

Morna flashed him an angry glance, but made no answer. She was too concerned about Jared's fate to argue with her brother. Going up on deck, she made her way directly to the bridge, where the captain was standing alone. He turned as she approached, his thick brows meeting in a frown.

'Good morning, Miss Hamilton.'

'Is it true you sent Captain Trenwith back to the holds?' she demanded, her eyes cold.

'Yes, he has returned to the other prisoners.'

'But you promised you would not do so until he was completely recovered.'

'Trenwith assured me he was perfectly fit. Apparently he was concerned for a friend of his...'

'What do you mean?' Morna stared at him in disbelief.

'He came to me himself and asked to go back.'

'He asked to go back down there – to that terrible place?' she whispered, shocked. 'Why?'

'He was afraid the cripple – a man called

Pyke – would die without his help.' Captain Smithson frowned. 'Trenwith is a strong man. I am confident he will survive the voyage. You will be pleased to learn that I have given instructions for the convicts to be allowed on deck for a short time each day. Two of my crew have gone down with a fever. If it should affect the prisoners, it could lead to an epidemic down there. I hope to avoid a tragedy by improving their conditions.'

He was looking at her intently, and Morna knew he expected her to express approval of his actions. Forcing herself to smile, she said the words he wanted to hear. Then added,

'I am sure you will do everything you can to combat the threat of an epidemic, sir. Unfortunately, it may already be too late. My cousin is ill – and if two of your crew have the same sickness, it may already have begun.'

'I am sorry to hear Miss Jane has come down with fever. You must take care not to contract it yourself, Miss Hamilton. I have some pastilles which, if burnt day and night, may help to keep the air free of infection. If you wish, I shall have some sent to your cabin later.'

'Thank you, you are very kind,' Morna's smile was unforced this time. 'Now, if you will excuse me, I must return to my cousin.'

'Of course.' He inclined his head. 'You

must let me know if I can be of further assistance.'

'I shall,' Morna promised, holding her fine wool shawl closer about her shoulders as she hurried below, glad to be out of the wind. Dark clouds had gathered overhead while she talked with Captain Smithson, and the sky was black with the promise of a storm.

Jane was lying quietly when she entered the cabin. Having first made certain that her cousin wanted nothing, Morna lay down on her bunk and closed her eyes. She was tired, and she would need all her strength to nurse Jane over the next few days. It would be as well to sleep now if she could.

Closing her eyes, she shut out the last picture she had of Jared, forcing it from her mind. He had asked to go back to the holds. That could only mean he was more concerned about the fate of his convict friend than about her feelings. In future he must fend for himself; she would not try to help him again.

The storm that hit them that night was only the start of the misfortunes which were to beset *Sea-Sprite* and her crew. It raged furiously all through one night and the morning after, tossing the ship to and fro like a straw in the wind.

Morna was too busy trying to keep her

cousin from throwing off the bedclothes to be afraid for her own life. Indeed, she was scarcely aware of the huge waves crashing over the deck as she bathed her cousin's heated brow. Jane's fever had suddenly become much worse, and she tossed end-lessly in the little bunk, crying out in her delirium.

There was no sleep for Morna that night, or for many nights to come. Philip visited the cabin, standing on the threshold to tell his sister about the damage caused by the storm. The ship had taken on water during the night and one of the masts was down.

'Captain Smithson has decided to heave to while the necessary repairs are done,' he said. 'We can't afford the delay, because some of the water-casks were lost, but it seems we've no alternative.'

Morna sighed wearily. 'I expect the cap-tain knows what he's doing. He's a capable man.'

Hearing the sigh, Philip looked at her in concern. 'I hope you're not coming down with this fever, Morna. At least six of the crew have it – and a score of the convicts. You should rest for a while. Shall I sit with Jane?'

She smiled at him, feeling a temporary return of their old closeness. 'Thank you for the offer, but I know how you hate to be in a sick-room, Phil. I am not ill – just tired. I shall try to sleep when you leave. Jane seems to be resting at the moment.'

Then she slept from sheer exhaustion, waking to find Jane trying to get out of bed. She coaxed the fretful woman back between the sheets, helping her to swallow a little water and gently reassuring her that she was not too much trouble.

Jane's illness lasted for ten days, and then she began to recover. Although they had not realised it, she had been lucky, having had only what proved to be a mild attack of a virulent disease. Three of the crew were dead and seven of the convicts by the time the epidemic began to wane. One of the victims was John Blackwell, the young first officer who had been so kind to Morna when she first came on board.

She found it hard to believe that such a strong man could die so quickly. He had seemed so full of life the last time she had seen him, and it was strange that he should succumb to the disease when others had recovered. She shed a few tears for him, thanking God again for the recovery of her cousin.

Morna herself had escaped the sickness completely, as did Philip and Captain Smithson. Jared, too, had come through unscathed, as Morna discovered when she went up on deck for a breath of fresh air one morning.

Jane was sleeping peacefully when she left the cabin, feeling the need for some exercise after being cooped up or so long. Taking a stroll around the deck, she saw Harry Robson standing at the rails and called to him, happy to see that he, too, had survived. He came to her at once, catching both her hands in his and kissing her cheek.

'Miss Hamilton, how glad I am to see you!' he cried. 'I was very much afraid you would take the fever from your cousin.'

'As you see, I am quite well.' Morna smiled at him warmly. 'It was good of you to send that bottle of brandy for Jane. I am sure it helped her to recoup her strength once the fever was over. You have not been ill yourself?'

'No, I was one of the lucky ones.' He offered her his arm. 'I have missed your company. Please, will you not walk with me for a while?'

Morna had a strange feeling of being observed. She glanced up at the rigging, smothering a gasp as she saw a man working on the halyards attached to the mainmast. Her eyes met Jared's, and her cheeks begin to flame as she saw the clear accusation in his icy gaze. What right had he to look at her like that?

Harry Robson followed the direction of her gaze, and frowned. 'The captain has decided to allow one or two of the convicts to help with the repairs, since several of his crew are still weak after their illness. You need not be alarmed, Miss Hamilton. No harm will come to you while I am with you.'

The memory of her seduction was uppermost in her mind. Determined that Jared should not guess how much his callous behaviour had hurt her, Morna smiled brightly at her companion. Taking his arm, she deliberately turned her back on Jared, her head high as she allowed herself to be led in the opposite direction.

The shock of seeing Jared unexpectedly had unnerved her. She listened to Harry's conversation, answering in what she hoped were the right places, but her thoughts were in total confusion. From the way Jared had looked at her, anyone would have thought that she had betrayed him! He could at least have had the grace to look ashamed of himself, she thought bitterly.

Her one consolation was that her foolishness in allowing him to take advantage of her would have no disastrous results. That morning, she had begun to bleed as usual. It was only when she knew for certain that she would not bear Jared's child, that she had realised the possibility had always been there. Because of Jane's illness, she had not had time to worry about the dangers inherent in her situation, and now the time for anxiety was past.

It was over. She could put the incident behind her and forget that it had happened. Except that she knew it would always be there, at the back of her mind.

Morna stood at the rails with the other passengers, watching the shoreline become land, trees, and buildings you could see were houses rather than just a hazy blur on the horizon. They were approaching Sydney Harbour at last, the long months of the voyage behind them. Overhead, the sky was a cloudless blue, reflected in the gentle ripple of the sea. Here and there the surface was broken by a crest of white spray, which hung like diamonds in the brilliant sunshine before vanishing forever.

To the weary passengers, worn out with the vicissitudes of a long and difficult journey, the sight was a touch of Heaven. Morna smiled at her cousin, knowing that Jane shared her excitement in this moment of triumph. They had done it! They had crossed thousands of miles of ocean, surviving storms, shortages of food and water, and sickness. And they were not hardened sailors, but two women who had hitherto led sheltered lives in the safe environment of their country homes. There was a special pride in this moment that only they could share.

The sails were being hauled down now, and the deck was a hive of activity as the crew scurried about, making ready to drop anchor. *Sea-Sprite* would stand a little way off, and her boats were being lowered to ferry the passengers and most of the sailors ashore. The convicts were to stay on board until arrangements had been made to house them securely. This meant that a skeleton crew must also remain, and the glum faces of those chosen were proof of the resentment felt by the unlucky few.

'You must stay with us, Miss Hamilton,' Harry said as they watched the passengers' possessions being loaded into one of the boats. 'Emily will be pleased to have your company until you have settled your business with Rupert. We can stop by and see him on the way out to our homestead if you wish?'

'That is very kind of you, Mr Robson,' Morna said, frowning slightly. 'But I must stay in Sydney until the convicts' bonds have been auctioned. Shall I be able to find accommodation in town?'

'There is a boarding-house of sorts.' Harry pulled a wry face. 'I would not recommend it for ladies like yourself and Miss Jane. You would be far more comfortable with us – and the auction will not take place for several days. I can bring you into town whenever you wish.'

'Then we shall be delighted to accept your invitation.' Morna smiled at him. 'Excuse me, I must speak to Captain Smithson before we leave.'

Smithson came to meet her as she approached, his hard features softening into a look of welcome. Over the past months a mutual respect had developed between them; if they were not quite friends, they were no longer enemies.

'So what do you think of your first sight of New South Wales, Miss Hamilton?'

'The harbour itself is breathtaking.' She fanned herself with her hand. 'Tell me, is it always so hot?'

He gave a harsh laugh. 'We're lucky to have this breeze on board, Miss Hamilton. You will find it a little overpowering at first. The heat and the flies drive some English ladies to tears, but I'm sure you will manage.'

'Indeed, I haven't come all the way to complain of the heat,' she agreed. 'Mr Robson has invited us to stay with him and his family until we can buy land of our own. But I must know...'

'You want to make sure of Trenwith's bond. If you would like to come to my cabin now, I think we can agree a price.'

Morna looked at him in surprise. 'I thought... You said his bond would be auctioned with the others?'

A self-conscious smile hovered on his lips. 'I think I might make an exception in this case.'

'Oh, thank you!' Morna reached out impulsively to clasp his hand. 'You cannot know how much this means to me. To know that Jared will be spared the humiliation of being paraded for prospective buyers as if he were an animal!'

'It isn't quite like that,' Smithson said gruffly. 'Settlers watch the prisoners in the exercise yard and make their bids to me. The highest bid secures the settler the right to the convict's labour for seven years – they do not own the man, as they would a horse.'

'But they are still slaves,' Morna insisted. 'They cannot leave their master if he mistreats them?'

'No,' he agreed. 'There are some who abuse the system, of course, but many treat their bond-servants as one of their family. You will find life very different here, Miss Hamilton. In Sydney itself things are not too difficult, but on the farms, especially those in outlying districts, it is a question of survival. If a convict is trustworthy, he earns the right to be treated as a human being – if not...' Smithson frowned. 'The trouble-makers are sent to Van Diemen's Land: very few of them ever come back.'

Morna shivered as she heard the note of horror in his voice. If the prospect appalled a man as hardened to the brutal realities of life in the colonies as Captain Smithson, it must indeed be terrible. She knew that convicts were expected to work hard wherever they spent their years of servitude, but the settlers worked hard themselves. Australia was a virgin land, most of it still unexplored by the settlers; it required dedication, tears, sweat and blood to clear the unbroken ground and make it produce the food the colonists needed to survive without being constantly dependent on ships from home.

As if he had read her thoughts, Captain Smithson smiled encouragingly. 'The early years were very difficult, Miss Hamilton, but Sydney is a thriving town now. Many people have made fortunes from the land, and there are still real opportunities for those with the vision to see them.'

'What kinds of opportunities?'

'I have for some while been considering opening a superior general store.' His eyes narrowed as if in thought. 'There are stores there already, of course, selling the stuffs that are basic to the needs of most settlers – but it has occurred to me that more and more ladies are coming out now...'

'And you think there may be an opening for better commodities that are not yet available in the colony?'

He nodded, his face taking on a speculative look. 'With the right person as my partner, it could be a lucrative venture. The only trouble is, I don't know exactly what the ladies need, and I might bring in all the wrong goods.'

'Not if someone were to make it their business to discover what is wanted and give you a comprehensive shopping-list. How soon do you leave for England, Captain?'

Smithson chuckled. 'I thought the idea might appeal to you, Miss Hamilton. In two weeks I shall be sailing for Van Diemen's Land; I transport stores and men both ways. It will be two months before I set out for England.'

Morna laughed as she saw the question in his eyes. 'Yes, I should very much like to be your partner in this venture, Captain Smithson – and I can already tell you of several items that Mr Robson forgot to mention when he advised me on what we should need.'

He offered her his arm with an awkward gallantry. 'If you will be so kind as to write them down for me, Miss Hamilton. I shall make out the bill of sale you require. It would be best if you leave Trenwith with the others until a few days have passed – to avoid the charge of favouritism.'

'Yes, I understand,' Morna agreed instantly.

Within a few days she would have her own house. When Jared saw that she meant him to live as a part of the family, he would quickly lose his resentment. He would see that she had acted in his best interests. In the meantime, it might be advisable for him to have a chance of seeing what fate awaited his less fortunate comrades. It might make it easier for him to accept the situation. For, no matter how often she denied it, in law he would still be her bond-servant. She had the right to have him beaten if he disobeyed her, and she could sell his bond at any time.

It was a situation neither of them would find easy, Morna reflected as she watched Captain Smithson set his seal on the document that made her the legal owner of Jared's bond, but the alternative was unthinkable. With his reputation as a trouble-maker, any show of rebellion could result in another beating – or banishment to the dreaded penal settlement on Van Diemen's Land.

Even though she could not forgive the callous way he had treated her the night she had gone to wake him from his nightmare, she still intended to help him through the period of his servitude. If he had not come to terms with the situation at the end of seven years, he would be free to go wherever he wished. But seven years was a long time; surely by then he would have learned to be less bitter? She could only hope it would be so for his own sake.

'Well, we made it, Captain!' Pyke grinned as the hatch opened above them, revealing a patch of blue sky. 'Pretty soon now they'll be taking us ashore. I heard them talking when I was up on deck yesterday. Seems they've been preparing a nice little place for us! Course, I don't suppose it will have all the comforts of home like here.' He winked at Jared cheekily.

Jared grinned at his friend. The months of confinement had cemented the bond between them. Now at last they were to be freed from this hell-hole. After the first few weeks at sea, conditions for the prisoners had shown a vast improvement. Both he and Pyke had spent several days on deck, helping with repairs to the ship when half the crew were sick; and after the crisis was over, Jared had been made a trustie, which meant that he spent part of every day supervising the other convicts who were allowed twenty minutes each for exercise. He usually managed to find Pyke something to do, either drawing sea water or handing out food to each man as he came up on deck. It was a more civilised way of feeding the prisoners, ensuring a fair distribution, and Captain Smithson had readily agreed to the idea when it was put to him.

The new routine meant the convicts were in much better health than they might otherwise have been. There had been no more deaths after the fever waned. Smithson had been pleased with the results of his experiment, and he often stopped to watch

Jared and Pyke at their work.

'You've shown yourself worthy of trust,' he remarked to Jared one morning shortly before the ship's arrival in Sydney Harbour. 'I shall not forget it, Trenwith.'

Pyke winked at him as Smithson continued his walk round the deck. 'It's as well he don't know what you've been planning for weeks, Captain.'

'We'll have maybe two days before they split us up, Pyke. If we're going to make a break for it, that will be our opportunity,' Jared replied, his eyes cold as he watched the captain walk away. 'Once we're on shore, Smithson is bound to relax his guard. They will all think we're too exhausted to try and escape so soon after we land.'

Their whispered conversation that morning was one of many which had helped to pass the time during the weary nights. Perhaps neither of them really believed in the plans they made, knowing that the chances of getting away were very slim. And even if they succeeded in eluding their guards, they would have to cross the mountains to gain their freedom.

Jared knew it was an impossible dream, but the faint hope had kept him alive inside, preventing him from slipping into the apathy so many of his fellow convicts felt. Planning his escape with Pyke had saved his sanity, blocking out the gnawing frustration which made him want to lash out at his guards in a frenzy of hatred. It had also helped to stop him thinking about *her*, remembering things which were best forgotten. The feel of her silken skin, the taste of her lips as she responded to his kiss.

Yet as the prisoners were called up on deck for the last time, Jared found himself wondering if she would be there. Had she gone ashore already? Would he ever see her again, now that the voyage was over? Did she think of him at all, or was she already making plans to marry that settler he had seen her kiss on deck? God damn her for flaunting herself in front of him with her new lover so soon after the death of the young officer she had been flirting with only a week or so earlier! She was a heartless wanton and he would think of her no more! He shut the picture of her out of his mind, trapping it with other, forbidden, memories. He could not afford the luxury of dreams which could never come true. His only aim now was to escape if he could..

He became aware of the slowness of the convicts' exodus from the holds. What could be causing the delay?

'What's going on, Pyke?' he asked as the little man came back after squeezing his way through to the ladder. 'Why is it taking so long?'

Pyke's face was unusually grim as he

looked at him. 'They're putting the chains on, Captain. It seems they're frightened some of us might try to escape once we leave the ship.'

'Damn them all to Hell!' Jared muttered, the blood pounding at his temples as he clenched his hands, 'May their souls burn for ever!'

There was to be no escape for him or any of his fellow prisoners. They were to be chained like dangerous beasts, held at the mercy of their guards until they were sold into slavery. Anger burned deep inside him, a bitter bile forming in his throat. All at once his control was broken as he started to force his way through to the front, a desire for murder burning in his heart. Pyke lunged at him, hanging on to his sleeve like a little terrier dog.

'It won't do no good, Captain,' he said. 'Even if you killed a couple of them, they'd get you in the end. Then they'd hang you as an example to the rest of us. It ain't worth it. Believe me, it ain't worth it.'

Jared glared at him, frustration making him want to strike out at someone – anyone! Then the molten rage began to cool, settling into a solid knot of bitterness in his chest.

'You're right, Pyke. It's not worth it. I have to wait – wait for the right moment, that's all.'

His face hardened into a granite mask. He

would wait, for seven years if need be. Then he would take his revenge on all those who had tried to destroy him!

It was a long, dusty drive out to the Robsons' farm, despite the occasional shade from trees whose branches spread across the road. Once or twice Morna caught sight of brightly-coloured birds chattering loudly among the gumtrees, and a small, fluffy creature asleep in the fork of two branches. Seeing her curiosity, Harry Robson told her it was a koala beer, and just one of the many exotic animals she could expect to encounter.

Morna was wearing the thinnest of her cotton gowns and a broad-brimmed straw hat, but her underbodice was sticking to her and she could feel the sweat trickling between her breasts when they finally arrived. Even though she had seen a few gracious houses in Sydney amongst the smaller, wooden buildings, nothing had prepared her for the large house Harry Robson had built for his wife. It was painted white, and a long, shaded veranda overlooked a carefully-tended flower garden.

The surprise was even greater after the heat, flies and sheer discomfort they had endured in Harry's wagon. It was laden with supplies and bumped uncomfortably over every rut in the road. Used to the ease of well-sprung carriages, Morna had endured the ride without complaining, conscious of Harry's kindness in bringing all her supplies as well as his own.

'Well, here we are then,' he said, helping Jane and then Morna down from the driving box. 'What do you think of it?'

'It's lovely,' Morna said, looking up at the bright curtains billowing at open windows. 'Somehow I hadn't expected to find anything like this out here.'

Harry laughed. 'Well, it wasn't like this when I first bought the land. We lived in a very primitive shack for five years – but I promised Emily a decent home and I finished this just before I left...' He broke off as a woman came out on to the veranda, excusing himself hastily as he ran to greet her, sweeping her up off her feet and embracing her passionately.

Witnessing their joyful reunion, Morna found herself envying the other woman just a little. How wonderful it must be to be loved like that, she thought. To know that you were the centre of one man's world, the reason for all he strived to achieve. Would she ever experience such happiness? She turned away from the happy couple, feeling the sting of tears.

When Emily came forward to greet them, welcoming three perfect strangers into her home with a warm, sweet smile, Morna knew why Harry was so much in love with his wife. The pleasure she showed in receiving her unexpected guests was genuine, and soon she was drawing them into the cool of the house out of the fierce sun.

'You must be exhausted,' she said as Morna sank gratefully into one of the tall, spindle-backed chairs that Harry had made himself. 'You must have a glass of my special fruit punch and rest for a while, then I shall take you to your rooms.'

A small girl of perhaps two or three came into the room, followed by a slightly taller boy. They looked shyly at the strangers, clinging to their mother's skirts as they sucked at freshly-baked gingerbread and watched with wide, wondering eyes. The children, like the house, were spotlessly clean; as was the two-month-old baby boy Emily proudly fetched from his cot and placed in her husband's arms.

Although Emily had two convict women to help her in the house, it was hardly surprising that she looked a little tired, Morna thought, noticing the strain in her hostess's face, though she had successfully hidden it until her husband left them to go on a tour of the property. With three children to care for, this big house and all the washing and cooking to see to, besides tending her beloved flower garden, Emily must be busy from dawn to dusk.

'You must let me help with the chores while we are here,' Morna said as she was shown into a simply furnished room, made gay by a pretty patterned bedspread and matching curtains at the windows. The whole room smelt of the perfume emanating from a vase of flowers on the wash-stand.

'Certainly not,' Emily said. 'You are my guests, and I cannot allow you to tire yourselves. You must rest after that awful voyage. I know just what it is like. I was a child when my parents came out nearly fifteen years ago, and I can tell you it was pretty rough out here then. I think it must have been terrible when the first settlers arrived in Botany Bay. But, of course, they were convicts and the site was unsuitable, so they founded a new colony at Sydney.'

'Captain Arthur Phillip was the first Governor of New South Wales, wasn't he?' Morna asked with a little frown. 'I've heard some of the history from your husband, but I still know so little.'

'Oh, Harry knows everything,' Emily said, smiling proudly. 'But I can tell you anything you want to know. Governor Phillip founded his settlement at Sydney in 1788. He was confident of the colony's success despite all the setbacks. He helped to get the first settlers established before he retired.'

Emily laughed and pressed a hand to the middle of her back. 'I was working in the

219

garden early this morning and I'm feeling the strain of it. Please forgive me, but I think I must sit down for a few minutes.'

Morna pulled out a chair for her, looking anxious. 'You have so recently risen from childbed, and you must have so much to do. I insist on helping you. Besides, I hope we shall become real friends, and I would like to do what I can.'

'Oh, we shall be friends,' Emily said, her hazel eyes glowing with enthusiasm. 'You cannot know how often I have longed to have a woman living near by. Rupert is a good friend to us, but he has never married and he talks of nothing but moving out to near Lake George – and it is comforting to have a woman to gossip with sometimes.' She looked at Morna admiringly. 'Your gown is so elegant! Is it the latest fashion in London?'

'Well, it was when I left,' Morna laughed. 'It may not be now.'

Emily pulled a wry face. 'Men never think about such things, do they? Harry brings me beautiful materials, but no patterns or pictures of the latest fashions – and oh, how I would love a stylish hat and some pretty shoes.' She looked down at her serviceable black boots. 'In the evening it would be nice to wear a pair of satin slippers sometimes.'

'Well, I have a pretty hat which might suit you. I shall give it to you as a present. And if you tell me your shoe size I shall have some brought out next time *Sea-Sprite* returns with a cargo. Captain Smithson and I are to be partners in a business venture – a shop that will cater for just the kinds of pretty trifles you long for, Emily.'

Emily clapped her hands in delight. 'And I shall be your first customer. Harry is so generous to me, but I have nothing to spend the money on. Some of our neighbours have grown wealthy of late; I am sure they would be glad of such a shop.'

'Captain Smithson will have a long shopping-list,' Morna chuckled. 'Every day I keep adding to it. The poor man will begin to wish he had never suggested the idea.'

Emily shook her head. 'When are you going to view Rupert's place? I do hope you will not be disappointed in it. The house is not like this one, I'm afraid – but Harry will be pleased to make alterations to it.'

'Your husband has already been more than kind, but he will want to attend to his own affairs now.'

'Harry is never too busy to help a neighbour – and if he says he is, I shall want to know the reason why.' Emily's eyes sparkled with a militant light. 'I want you to be happy here, Morna. Then you'll stay and we can be friends.'

'Oh, I am determined to stay,' Morna assured her. 'Harry told me that there would have to be a good many changes, so I am prepared for the worst...'

'Oh, it really isn't too bad.' Emily got to her feet. 'There, I am better now. Please, you won't tell Harry that I felt a little tired?'

'No, of course not,' Morna smiled at her. 'As soon as I unpack, I'll look out that hat I was telling you about – but it won't be until we are settled.'

'Then you're determined to stay. I'm so pleased.'

'Oh yes,' Morna said. 'Whatever the house is like, I am determined to settle here.'

That there would have to be a good many changes was made clear to Morna the next morning when she saw Rupert Prowther's homestead for the first time. It was built in a similar style to the Robsons' with a veranda, a large kitchen, a sitting-room, three bedrooms, besides outhouses for washing and storage, but it was smaller and the wood was painted an ugly green. No pretty curtains softened the windows, nor was there a lovingly tended flower garden to brighten the outlook. However, the roof was sound, as were the barns and the shearing shed. The vegetable plot behind the house had been recently dug, but there was little sign of planting.

'I haven't bothered much lately,' Rupert explained, seeming slightly ashamed as he shooed a hen from the veranda. 'I've only been waiting for Harry to get back before I sell out.'

The small flock of merino sheep looked healthy enough to Morna's inexperienced eyes, but it was clear a lot of work would have to be done to make the farm a viable prospect. Much of the land was still covered with scrub bushes and stones. It would need clearing and putting down to grass if the flocks were to be built up to a worth-while size.

'You can't consider this place,' Philip said, drawing her aside as the host took his guests inside for a cool drink. 'Let's go back to Sydney Town, Morna. You can open your shop and I'll find something to do.'

'What?' Morna looked at him, frowning. 'You haven't any training, Phil. The farm will provide us with a home, and we can grow most of our own food. The shop may turn into a profitable venture in time, but that's for the future. We should gradually build up our flocks and buy more land.'

'We'll be rich when we're too old to appreciate it'. Philip scowled. 'Well, if you're set on this godforsaken dump, don't expect me to stay here all the time.'

'I have learnt to expect very little from you, Philip.' Morna's eyes sparkled with anger as she looked at his sulky face. 'You must do as you please, but Jane and I will try to make the farm a home. If you want to live here, you'll have to do your share of the chores.'

He laughed grimly. 'Since you hold the purse-strings, I've no choice, have I? I'll do what I must – but don't expect me to be happy about it.'

Morna sighed, feeling hurt at the unfairness of his accusations. She had never dwelt on the fact that it was her money that had brought them to New South Wales, nor had she reproached him for wasting his own inheritance. She had hoped that Philip would see the possibilities of making the shabby house into a real home for them all, as she did. Of course it was not Hamilton Towers, but the past was gone and it was no use in sighing for what could never be.

For a brief moment her courage failed her. It was all so useless. Philip hated the farm, the house and the whole idea of living here. And tomorrow... Tomorrow she must face the problem that had haunted her for months.

What would Jared say when he knew she had purchased his bond? Everything she had strived for suddenly seemed meaningless. Perhaps it would have been better for everyone concerned if she had simply stayed in England and left Jared to his fate. He would only hate her when he knew what she had done...

'Morna, my love,' Jane's voice broke the

tangled spiral of her thoughts. 'Come and see what I've found.'

There was a note of excitement in her cousin's voice, and Morna hurried to see what she was pointing at.

'Look! Look there, Morna, is it not perfect?'

Following her cousin's pointing finger, Morna saw a tiny pure white flower thrusting its way through a mass of rocks and strangling scrub. Its petals were so delicate that it should never have survived in such a place.

Morna slipped her arm through her cousin's, suddenly full of new hope. 'Let's go in now, Jane,' she said. 'I want to ask Rupert how soon we can take over.'

CHAPTER SEVEN

Morna dismounted from one of the horses she had bought as part of the farm stock, brushing a thick layer of dust from her skirts. She looked enquiringly at Philip, but he shook his head.

'I'll stable the horses for you, Morna but this was your idea. You will find me having a drink with Laurence Starr at the officer's club if you need me.'

Morna watched him walk away, leading the three horses loosely by the reins and felt a surge of frustration. They had been in New South Wales for four days, and Philip had spent most of them with the young officers he'd met on board *Sea-Sprite*. He'd shown no interest in the move to their own farm, though he had helped to unload the wagon before riding back to Sydney Town to meet his friends.

Rupert Prowther had three male convicts already working for him. He had recommended Morna to buy the remainder of their bonds, assuring her they were all to be trusted.

'Dickon has only nine months before he's a free man, Miss Hamilton. Sam and Benjamin both have two years left, but they know I've treated them well and they won't give you any trouble. I haven't bothered to lock them in their cabins at night for years; they've all enough sense to realise there's no point in running away. Most runaways end up dying of starvation, or they're captured and brought back to be punished.'

Having spoken to the three convicts, and assured them they would be treated as trusted servants, not slaves, Morna agreed to purchase their bonds. She particularly liked Dickon, who was a thickset man of perhaps fifty, and who seemed quite capable of controlling the other two. He told her that he hoped to find work as an overseer when his sentence was finished, and eventually buy his own land.

'Then you'll be pleased to know I intend to pay each of you a small wage,' Morna said. 'It won't be much – at least until the farm begins to support itself.'

'You're not obliged to pay us anything, Miss Hamilton. We work for our food and clothing.'

'I know.' She raised her eyes to meet his, seeing the faint distrust there. 'But I meant what I said, Dickon. In law you are all my bond-servants, but I do not regard you as such. I have always paid the people who work for me, and I see no reason to change my habits.'

'Then we'd best keep it to ourselves, miss, or you will be unpopular with a lot of people hereabouts.' He grinned at her. 'I reckon we'll be grateful for whatever you give us.'

The memory of that conversation lingered in Morna's mind as she stared at the wooden shack just behind a securely fenced yard in Sydney Town. Several prisoners were still sitting or walking about in a desultory manner, and she felt her heart miss a beat as she saw the man she had come to fetch. He was standing with his back to her, staring towards the great range of mountains that divided the costal plains from the interior. Then she noticed he was shackled by the thick chains around his ankles, and indignation surged through her. How dared they treat him like that?

She had been unconsciously delaying that moment when Jared would realise who had purchased his bond, but now she was concerned only that he should be released from those chains.

The officer inside the stuffy, dingy hut took his time in examining Morna's papers. She tapped her foot impatiently when he last got to his feet and shouted for a subordinate.

'Bring Trenwith in,' he said. 'This lady has come to collect him.'

'Alone?'

Morna heard the whisper, and glared at them. 'Yes, I am alone,' she snapped. 'And you can take those disgusting chains off the man before you bring him in here.'

They both looked at her in amazement. 'I couldn't advise that, ma'am,' the officer said. 'He's fresh off the ship and he'll likely try to make a break for it.'

'You may leave the responsibility for Captain Trenwith's behaviour to me,' she said, her eyes glinting dangerously. 'He is a man, not an animal.'

The officer shrugged, obviously thinking her a fool. His subordinate went out and there was an uncomfortable silence. Morna turned to look out of the window at a row of wooden houses on the opposite side of the street. They were on the edge of town, well away from the larger houses and the Governor's residence, but she had seen a general store a little further along the road and she meant to investigate its stock before she went home.

Hearing a door open behind her, Morna stiffened. Her heart was pounding so wildly that she could not bear to turn round immediately.

'Here he is, Miss Hamilton.'

Morna turned her body slowly to face him, her eyes flying to Jared's. She saw the surprised anger in him and dug her nails into the palms of her hands. She must appear perfectly calm; he must not guess how nervous she was.

'Hello, Jared,' she said, her voice devoid of all emotion. 'Are you ready to leave?'

'You?' he ejaculated, and she saw the dawning realisation in his face. 'No, be damned. I'll not be owned by a woman! Take me back...' He turned on the guard, his eyes blazing with a fury that made the soldier step away. 'Take me back – do you hear?'

'Hold him, Chambers.' The officer was on his feet, a loaded pistol cocked and ready. 'Make one move, and you're dead, convict. I told you he was dangerous, Miss Hamilton. Shall I have the chains put back?'

'No, you will not – and you can put that pistol away.' Morna crossed the floor, looking up at Jared with a little, teasing smile on her lips. 'Do you imagine I am foolish enough to believe anyone could really own you, Jared? I have purchased the bond which entitles me to your labour for seven years, that's all.'

'Why?' he glared at her, his face tight with anger. 'Why will you not leave me in peace?'

'Do you know what they do with trouble-makers?' Morna asked coolly, her smile vanishing. 'They send them to settlements in Van Diemen's Land. You may ask this officer what your chances of surviving seven years in such a prison would be, if you wish.'

'He'd be dead within the year. They know how to handle his sort there, miss.'

Morna saw a muscle tighten in Jared's jaw as he heard the officer's scornful words. 'Don't you want to live?' she asked softly. 'I know you hate me now – but one day you will see that I did what was right.'

'Shall I indeed?' Jared's brow arched in mockery. 'Perhaps, if one man is as good as another, a mistress is as good as a master.'

'Watch your mouth, convict!' The officer crashed his fist down on the table-top. 'Do you want me to send a soldier with you, miss?'

'I don't think that will be necessary.' Morna's eyes held a challenge as she gazed

230

up at Jared, ignoring the words that had been meant to sting and wound her. 'I have some shopping to do before we go back to the farm – are you coming with me? Or perhaps you prefer the company here?'

She thought there was just the flicker of a smile before he shut it out, his mouth thinning. 'Since I have no choice, pray lead on, Miss Hamilton. Do you wish me to walk two steps behind like a puppy-dog – or in front so that you can make sure I don't run away?'

'Why not at my side, like a man?'

Morna nodded to the astonished soldiers and walked out, not bothering to glance back to see if Jared were following. It was all or nothing now. If he refused to accept the chance she was offering him, his future would be out of her hands. In a moment she heard the sound of his footsteps, and then he was beside her, matching his stride to hers. She stifled an urge to smile and walked on in silence, not looking at him. When they reached the general store, she stopped and turned to him.

'I want to buy a few things, Jared. I'm sure you would be bored – so would you fetch our horses from the stables? They are just up there.' She pointed to a building at the end of the street. 'Philip left them there half an hour ago. Mine is a black mare; you will be riding the chestnut hunter. It's not a thoroughbred, I'm afraid, but I think it will be up to your weight. Here, you will need this to pay the ostler.' She pushed some silver coins into his hand.

Jared hesitated, his eyes narrowing as he looked at her, searching for a clue to the workings of her mind. His initial reaction had been one of shock and anger, believing in that first instant that her motives for buying his bond must have been some kind of revenge. Then, when she had looked up into his eyes and he had seen the gleam of mischief there, he had felt a strange sensation, almost of light-headedness as he struggled to come to terms with this new situation. Why was she doing this? Why was she giving him money and a horse?

'Is this some kind of test?' he asked at last. 'To see if I shall try to escape?'

Morna saw the doubts in his face, and sighed. Somehow she had to reach him, to make him see that she was not his enemy. 'If you wish to run away, you will have an ample opportunity once we reach the farm. I'm sure you know by now that you wouldn't stand much chance of getting clear. Unless you could find your way across the mountains, of course. Dickon tells me most escapees come back half-starved; the others die in the bush or live to regret their foolishness ... in Van Dan Diemen's land.'

'Dickon?' Jared's eyes pierced her, feeling

a dart of jealousy as he heard the warmth in her voice. 'Another of your suitors, I suppose.'

Morna laughed, her eyes sparkling with mischief. She had not missed the jealous note in his voice, and it pleased her. Jared could not be completely indifferent to her if it made him angry to think of her with other men.

'He would be most amused to hear you say that. Dickon is my servant – at home I should probably have called him my bailiff. He has been of immense help to me since I took over the property.'

'A tame lap-dog to dance to your tune,' Jared scoffed. 'Does he thank you when you lock him up at night?'

Morna heard the resentment in his tone, and thought that this was exactly the reaction she had feared. Jared was coming to realise what the position was, and fighting against it.

'Dickon has only nine months to serve, but he has already said he hopes I will keep him on when his time is over. There is nothing so very terrible in working for a living, Jared. Nor in serving a mistress.'

Jared stared at her in silence, watching the way her eyes darkened with emotion. Despite the bitterness twisting inside him, he was sensible enough to understand what she was offering him, and he knew that he could have fared far worse. He had seen the other convicts leave one by one, witnessing the fear in their eyes as they went to an uncertain future. Some of them might be lucky enough to find a fair master, but many more would be treated little better than slaves. Jared knew that he ought to be on his knees thanking Fate for giving him an opportunity to survive the next seven years, but there was a perverse devil inside him that made him want to strike out at the woman who had saved him. She had to be plotting some kind of devious revenge – and yet, if she wasn't... The realisation that he had wronged her made him angry again.

'Perhaps not for some.' His face darkened as he felt a twist of pain inside. 'Do you expect me to thank you?'

'No, I don't want either your gratitude or your forgiveness,' Morna said coldly. 'I knew you would resent any bonds – even those as tenuous as I hold over you. But what difference does it make? You despise me, and I – I feel only indifference towards you. I have tried to put right a little of the wrong that was done you, that's all.' Her eyes glinted with sudden temper. 'And now I'm going into that shop. You may do exactly as you please!'

She turned and climbed the two wooden steps that led into the rather dark interior of the store, refusing to glance back even though every nerve in her body was tingling with apprehension. If Jared was foolish enough to try and escape, nothing she could do would save him from the consequences. He would be hunted down by the military and brought back to face a beating – or worse! Since she had no intention of locking him into his cabin every night, he must learn the realities of the situation. If he stayed with her, it must be by his own choice.

Morna deliberately took her time in the store, examining the rather limited selection of materials on display in the haberdashery corner. She thought the cloth mostly of poor quality, and the colours were dull. There was nothing here to delight the feminine eye. There was, however, a good stock of spices, flour, dried fruit and beans. Also tools of every description for farmers, carpenters, metalworkers and blacksmiths. It was clear that it would not be good business to compete in these areas.

Making several small purchases, Morna left the store at last. Her heart missed a beat when she realised there was no one waiting for her outside; then she saw that Jared had tethered the horses under the shade of a tree a little further down. He was sitting on the side of the road, rubbing at his ankles, which had no doubt been chafed by the chains he had been forced to wear; but when he saw her leave the shop, he untied the reins and led the horses towards her.

He made no comment as she handed him her packages, stowing them in the saddle-bags and then turning to help her to mount. Mounting himself, he looked at Morna questioningly.

'There was a third horse – is your brother not coming with us?'

'He is with some friends,' Morna replied shortly. 'We shall not bother him. Don't be anxious, Jared, I am quite capable of finding the way home.'

A reluctant smile entered his eyes. 'Yes, I am sure are,' he said. 'You came to collect your property alone, and now you are preparing to leave town alone with a convict. Hasn't it even occurred to you that I could murder you and leave your body hidden where no one would find it for months?'

'It would hardly matter to me whether they found me or not if I were dead, would it?' Morna laughed wickedly. 'Don't be a fool, Jared. I know you won't kill me. Why should you? I'll give you the horse if you want it, and money. Besides, you wouldn't kill a defenceless woman – you've too much pride.'

'Defenceless? You?' His eyes glittered with angry amusement. 'Don't be too sure, Morna. You might just drive me to it one day.'

'Indeed?' Morna flicked back her long

hair, looking up at him provocatively. 'I'm going home. Come with me if you want a decent meal. It's roast lamb and baked potatoes tonight, with fruit pie to follow.'

It was a cruel thrust and she knew it, laughing as she saw real agony in his eyes. Urging her horse on, she was aware of a feeling of intense happiness inside her. It did not matter at this moment that Jared was resentful and suspicious. He was free at last – free to ride by her side and breathe the fresh air. He was no longer a prisoner at the mercy of uncaring strangers. He was with her again, and for now nothing else mattered.

A pleasant breeze had sprung up, easing the fierce heat. She felt it on her flushed cheeks, refreshing her as she rode. She did not need to look at Jared to know that he, too, was enjoying the sensation of freedom. His horse was racing side by side with hers, matching her pace and her mood. She laughed aloud, unable to keep her feelings inside another moment. And she heard him echo her laughter as if he had suddenly realised the chains were gone for ever.

It was a two-hour ride to the farm. By the time they arrived, they were both covered in dust, and the horses were sweating. Morna dismounted without waiting for anyone to help her, though Dickon had come out of the barns to meet them.

She smiled up at Jared as he paused a

moment before slipping from the saddle. 'Dickon will show you your cabin. You'll find clothes, soap and a razor waiting for you. Dinner will be ready in an hour. I expect to see a vast difference in your appearance by then. Don't keep me waiting, Captain Trenwith.'

He swept her an elegant, mocking bow and she was suddenly aware of the muscled strength of him. 'I shall try not to disappoint you, Miss Hamilton.'

Morna licked her lips nervously, trying to hide the surge of excitement she felt. 'My cousin Jane is an excellent cook, sir, but she likes everyone to be on time. If you are late, you may find your dinner has been given to someone else. Neither Sam nor Benjamin are averse to a second helping of Jane's roast lamb.' Morna's eyes were glowing as she turned and ran into the house. It was all going to work out as she had planned all those months ago. Jared was resentful now, but once he had settled down, he would be happy enough. It was hard, back-breaking labour, cutting down the scrub, clearing timber and prising boulders from the land, but it was work a man could take pride in at the end of the day.

As time passed, Jared would feel less bitter. The scars on his back and ankles would begin to fade, and perhaps the deepest ones inside him would heal, too. Here he could live and work as he pleased, and when the land prospered, he also would prosper. She was willing to share it with him as a friend – or as her husband.

Suddenly the smile died from her eyes as a memory she had tried to banish rose unbidden to her mind. In her excitement she had forgotten the way he had used her to satisfy his lust that night... She had forgotten how cruelly he had rejected her at his house all those months ago. She had forgotten the bitter, taunting words he had used to drive her from his prison cell.

'What kind of a fool are you, Morna Hamilton?' she whispered, her eyes dark with pain. 'How many times will you let him hurt you before you stop loving him?'

The answer came swiftly. Never! She would never stop loving him. Only death could break the invisible bonds that bound her to him. She would die rather than give up the hope that one day he would take her in his arms to kiss her tenderly, and this time it would be her name he whispered in the darkness. It would be her, Morna Hamilton, he called to in his dreams!

Morna's back was straight and her head was high as she went upstairs to wash and change her gown. She would not let Jared guess how much she loved him, but one day he would turn to her. He would come to her because he could not live without her love.

He might not know it yet, but he was *her* man. He had always been hers. She had known it instinctively for years, and nothing he could do would ever change that.

Her love had brought her half-way across the world. It was strong enough to survive anything that life or Jared Trenwith could do to her!

Morna watched as Jared finished eating and touched the napkin to his lips. He had eaten slowly, carefully, almost as if it were an effort for him to swallow. She saw how loosely the clothes she had provided hung on his body, and she felt a stab of pain in her heart.

'Good night, Miss Hamilton.'

Morna nodded as Sam, Dickon and Benjamin got to their feet and left. Jared sat where he was, looking at her with an odd expression she could not read.

'You have no overseer,' he said as the door closed behind the others. 'Aren't you afraid we shall all run away?'

'Where would you go, Jared? If you could manage to cross the mountains you might avoid capture – but you would live in fear of being recognised. You could never return to England, and you would be obliged to work for a living. Here, you will be your own master...'

'My own master?' Jared's face tightened

with anger. 'Am I free to live where and how I choose? Can I walk the streets of Sydney without being questioned as to who my master is and why I am there?'

'I cannot change the law, Jared – but here on my land, you will certainly be free.'

'On your land?' Jared smiled ruefully. 'It is a little unusual for an unmarried lady to be granted land here, isn't it? But, then, you were never bothered by conventions, were you?'

Morna's eyes snapped with temper. 'If you are saying that I don't know how to behave like a lady...'

'Then I should not be a gentleman.' His eyes clouded. 'But of course, I am a convict now – and you are my mistress. I was not insulting you, Morna, merely thinking aloud. So it is your intention that I should come and go as I please?'

'Yes.'

'And you will not try to stop me if I leave?'

'No. If you stay, it must be from choice.'

'If I take my chance and cross the mountains, will you return to England?'

'There is nothing for me there now.'

'So we are both in exile?' He gave a harsh laugh and stood up. 'It seems then that neither of us has much choice. Good night, Morna. I shall leave you now – with your permission.'

'You do not need my permission, Jared.'

241

His brows went up, but he said no more. After he had gone, Morna carried the dishes into the outhouse where Jane had been heating water to wash them.

Jane looked at her face and frowned, seeing the hurt she was trying to hide. 'You look tired, Morna. Why don't you go to bed? I can do these.'

Morna shook her head. 'No, I'll help you. You've been busy all day. The house looks much better already.'

'There's a lot to do yet, but we'll make it into a home, Morna.'

'Yes, I expect so.' Morna sighed, drying her hands as she finished washing the last of the pots. 'I think I shall go to bed now.'

In her bedroom, she undressed and pulled on a high-necked chemise, sitting down by the window to look out at the night. The moon was sailing high in the sky, giving her a clear view of the barns and stables. It was such a different outlook from the one of rolling lawns and roses that she had enjoyed at Hamilton Towers; the land itself, the trees and wildlife were all so strange to her, but she was not frightened at the prospect of making her life here. If only Jared could accept the situation, it would be a great adventure to be shared and lived to the full.

Suddenly she heard the sound of hoof-beats, and she saw a horse and rider canter across the yard towards the wide sweep of open country. Her heart stopped for one moment as she saw the horseman was Jared. She thought that he was leaving her, and she half rose from her seat as if she would somehow reach out and stop him. Then she sat down again, knowing she must do nothing at all. If Jared had decided to leave her, she must let him go. She could not hold him against his will, even if her heart was breaking. If Jared chose to risk punishment or even death, that was his right. She had done all she could to help him, and he must decide his own future now.

Unable to sleep, she sat by her window, keeping a long, lonely vigil. She was cold and frightened, her face white with strain as she sat there, hardly daring to breathe because it hurt so much. The pain inside her was crushing her, making her want to weep, but no tears fell. If Jared did not return, it had all been for nothing, and she would want to die.

Just before dawn, she heard the sound of hoofbeats once more. Her heart was pounding wildly, like the surf against the shore, as she watched anxiously. Then she saw Jared dismount and lead his horse into the stables. A few minutes later he came out again, to stand briefly looking up at the house. Morna drew back, not wanting him to see her. For a moment more he stood there, then he turned and went into his own cabin.

Morna stopped walking, pausing to watch the men at work. They had been clearing this area for the last few days and it was beginning to show a great improvement. Jared and Dickon were prising a large boulder from the earth. Both men had taken off their shirts, and the sweat was glistening on their skins. Knowing from past experience that they would put their shirts on as soon as she approached, Morna let her eyes dwell on Jared's back, happy to see that the hard welts where he had been beaten were beginning to fade into thin stripes.

When he had first arrived he had been painfully thin, but now he was putting on a healthy amount of flesh. She watched the muscles rippling beneath his tanned skin as he strained to free the stubborn rock, feeling a surge of love for him. How strong he was – and how much she wanted to feel those powerful arms holding her crushed against him!

Blushing at her wanton thoughts, Morna shifted her heavy basket to the other arm and began to sing, warning the men that she was coming. She smiled to herself as they made themselves respectable for her eyes. There was not a part of Jared's body she had not seen when she bathed him after that cruel beating, and while he was in the grip of the fever. Yet the men's modesty was a sign of respect, and it pleased her.

She wondered if Jared ever thought about the night she had woken him from his nightmare. Had he even known it was her he held in his arms and kissed so passionately – or had it all been part of the dream to him? Of late she had found herself thinking about the fierce emotions his kisses had aroused in her at the start of his lovemaking, and wondering if she had misunderstood what happened later. She was so inexperienced in these matters – could the vague disappointment she had felt afterwards have been caused by Jared's weakness, and not simply because he had used her body to satisfy his own needs? He had after all been ill, and his refusal to speak to her could have come from sheer exhaustion. Such thoughts led to speculation as to what it would be like if he made love to her now that he was so much stronger. Those thoughts intensified when she saw him doing hard, manual labour as he was now. There was something almost beautiful in the way he moved, the sheer power of those muscular shoulders, which sent tremors of tingling sensation through her entire body.

Banishing her immodest fancies, Morna smiled at the men. 'I've brought you food and some cold ale. At least, it was cold when I started out.'

Dickon came to take the heavy basket

from her. 'You shouldn't have walked all this way,' he scolded, sounding more like a revered uncle than her servant. 'Sam could have brought the food.'

'I wanted to see how you were getting on.' said Morna, her eyes straying to Jared, who was leaning on his pick-axe and watching her from narrowed eyes. 'Harry Robson has promised me some of his ewes as soon as we have the pasture ready, and that won't be long by the look of things. You've worked wonders between you.'

'Ay, it looks well,' Dickon said, glowing at her praise.

'Besides, I wanted to make sure you had a good meal. Tonight you'll have to fend for yourselves, I'm afraid. Jane and I are going to Emily's dinner.'

'You're not thinking of riding all that way alone?' Dickon looked shocked. 'Is Mr Hamilton not going with you?'

'Philip was invited – but he prefers to meet his own friends.'

'Then I shall accompany you, Miss Hamilton. I wouldn't feel right, knowing you two ladies were out there alone.'

Morna smiled as she heard the protective note in his voice. Dickon had told her he had been sentenced to seven years' penal servitude for killing a man who had attacked his young sister, and she rather thought he had adopted her in place of the family he had lost. She looked at him, a faint flush of shame in her cheeks as she said, 'I am not taking any of you with me. You would have to wait in the kitchen, Dickon. Emily is a sweet person and I love her, but she – she doesn't…'

'She doesn't dine with convicts – is that what you're trying to say?'

Morna met Jared's cold stare uncertainly. He was still so bitter, though most of the time he appeared outwardly content with his life. It was usually only when she tried to bridge the gap between them that he let his resentment show.

'The kitchen will suit me just fine,' Dickon said, ignoring Jared's outburst. 'I can spend the whole evening with my Mary.'

'Your Mary?' Morna laughed as she saw him blush bright red. 'And how long has this been going on? No, don't tell me – it's perhaps better that I don't know.'

'I used to ride over with messages from Mr Rupert,' Dickon said a little bashfully. 'Mary has eighteen months left to serve – but she's promised to wed me when we're both free. You'll be doing me a favour by letting me ride with you, Miss Hamilton.'

'Then of course you shall come,' said Morna. 'I'll be glad of your company. Now eat the food I've brought. I'm sure you must both be hungry.'

'Will you share it with us?' Dickon asked.

'I'm not hungry, but I'll have a mug of ale. It was hot and dusty on the road, and my throat is dry.'

Dickon poured her out a cupful from a stone jug, handing it to her. She perched on a pile of rocks they had been levelling into a wall to keep out marauding animals, sipping the strong home brew and smiling as the men devoured the savoury pasties, fresh bread and cheese she had brought. Almost all the food they ate now was produced on the farm and she was proud of their achievement. They had all worked hard these past months.

At times like these it seemed to Morna that there was a true companionship between them all. Sometimes, when Jared looked at her, she felt that he was happy just to see her near by – as she was to be close to him. He seldom said much, unless she asked him a direct question about his work, but she was conscious of him watching her when he thought himself unobserved, and sometimes she would see an odd, challenging look in his eyes, as if he could read her thoughts.

'I need some flour and bacon. Oh, there's quite a list of small things,' she said, forcing him to pay attention to her now. 'When we leave later this afternoon, will you take the wagon into town and fetch them for me, Jared?'

'If you wish,' he said, and for a moment

anger burnt in the grey eyes. 'I had thought of asking Sam to help me finish here. If you want the pasture ready for the spring lambing, there's no time to be wasted. Couldn't Philip bring what you need? He's in town often enough these days.'

Morna heard the note of condemnation in his voice and bit her lip. The past six months had brought no easing of the situation between these two men. Jared was coldly polite whenever they met, managing to conceal his feelings behind a frozen mask, but Philip made no such attempt to hide his dislike of the man who had once been his idol. He was growing ever more sullen as each week passed, refusing to do any of the work and losing no opportunity to taunt his sister.

Finding her scrubbing pots at the kitchen sink, he would turn away in disgust. 'Can you not find a convict woman to do that? You are my sister, Morna. You used to have a lady's hands – look at them now!'

'I'm not ashamed of them,' she had retorted. 'The house has to be kept clean; and the reason I don't buy more convict labour is because you spend everything we earn on drinking and gambling with your officer friends.'

It was not quite true. Philip had so far kept within the allowance she had agreed to give him when he promised to come out to

Australia. In fact she knew he had curbed his gambling, but he was drinking more than ever. She had tried to apologise for her flash of temper, but he had ridden off to Sydney Town in a sullen fit, staying there for ten days before he finally returned. Since then, an uneasy peace had existed between them.

'I thought it would give you a break to go into town, Jared,' Morna said now, avoiding the challenge in his eyes. 'But you are right, this work is more important. I'll drive in myself tomorrow.'

If she had expected him to relent and say he would go instead, Morna was disappointed. She saw by his stubborn face that he would go only if she made it a direct order. For some reason known best to himself, he hated to visit Sydney, preferring to stay and work even though the task of driving into town was a much easier one. She could only think that he disliked being reminded of the manner of his arrival in New South Wales. At least on the farm he could forget that he was a bond-servant in law.

Since she had never yet given him a direct order, except to be on time for dinner on the night of his arrival, Morna said no more on the subject. If he was hoping to provoke her, he too would be disappointed. Although she could not give him his freedom, he would never be a servant to her. He worked long hours, turning his hand to the cultivation of the vegetable garden after dinner; but he worked because he chose to do it, and he stayed because there was nowhere else for him to go. Yet she knew he often took one of the horses out after dusk, returning it to the stables just before dawn. He would leave her if he could, she knew, but so far he had stayed and she was careful to do nothing which might break the tenuous bonds that held him here.

Sighing, she gathered up the soiled napkins in which she had wrapped the food, returning them to her basket with the empty jug. Sometimes she thought that Jared would never cease to resent her, that he would carry his bitterness inside him for ever.

'I'll be ready to leave in two hours, Dickon,' she said. 'Before we leave, remind me to give you something. A gentleman should take his betrothed a gift sometimes, and I have a pretty scarf your Mary might like. It is new. I bought it for – for a special reason, and I have never worn it.'

Dickon thanked her, obviously pleased by her thoughtfulness, but she saw a flash of scorn in Jared's eyes and felt a sudden surge of anger. Why must he always misjudge her every action?

Smiling at Dickon, she gave Jared no more than a cool nod, walking away with her head held high.

'You look tired, Emily,' Morna said, kissing her friend's cheek. 'I had a favour to ask you, but I'm not sure if I should. You already work so hard.'

Emily shook her head, slipping her arm round the girl's waist. 'If I look tired, it's because I was up with Timmy last night: he has a tooth coming through and he was fretful. Besides...' She looked a little contrite. 'I'm not sure, but I think I may be with child again.'

'So soon?' Morna looked at her, surprise and faint alarm in her eyes. 'But you told me the doctor said it would not be wise for you to start another baby for at least eighteen months!'

'Harry doesn't know that. I haven't told him – and you mustn't, either. Promise me you won't worry him, Morna? He's had several of the sheep die of a mysterious illness, and he's worried enough as it is.'

'You know I wouldn't tell him anything you asked me not to, my dearest Emily, but if he had known, he would have taken more care. He loves you so very much.'

'It is because he loves me that I couldn't tell him,' Emily said, her cheeks pink. 'You will understand better when you are married, Morna. If Harry thought he might endanger my life, he wouldn't... I don't want to lose that side of our marriage; it means too much to us both. Besides, a man needs the comfort of his wife's body sometimes. Passion doesn't always matter so very much when you've been married as long as we have – though Harry can be very demanding – but it's the warmth of another body close to yours, and the sharing...' She laughed and looked shyly at Morna. 'Now, I have shocked you!'

'No, not in the least,' Morna said, pressing her hand. 'I envy you and Harry. It must be wonderful to have a relationship like yours.'

'I know I'm lucky,' Emily said, her eyes clouding slightly. 'There are moments when I wonder if I've been too fortunate; then I'm frightened I'll wake up and find it has been a dream.'

'You are not dreaming, Emily, but you should rest more.'

'Oh, I've practically nothing to do now. Harry bought the bonds of two young women from the last ship that came in. One of them was a ladies' maid, the other is a marvellous cook. I told him one would have been adequate – but you know Harry.'

'Yes.' Morna looked at her affectionately. 'If you really have too many servants, then perhaps I will ask that favour after all.'

'Of course you must,' Emily agreed instantly. 'If it is about the Governor's ball next month, I have already told Harry that you and Jane must come with us. You can stay here overnight.'

'It wasn't about the ball.' Morna frowned. 'I'm not sure I want to go, Emily.'

'Oh, but you must,' Emily insisted. 'Everyone wants to be there. Now, tell me what I can do for you?'

It was late in the evening when the two women and Dickon returned to the homestead. A full moon had made their journey easier, lighting the sky and washing the earth with a pale silver glow.

'You go in, Jane, I'll be with you in a moment. I have something to say to Dickon.'

Morna waited until her cousin had disappeared into the house before turning to her servant. Seeing his faintly apprehensive look, she smiled at him.

'There's no need to be anxious, Dickon. I have good news for you. Tomorrow morning you will take the small cart and ride over to the Robsons'. You will bring Mary and her possessions back here.'

'Bring Mary here? My Mary?' Dickon frowned. 'I don't understand you, miss.'

'I have bought Mary's bond.' Morna watched his face intently. 'You may start to build a new house for yourself on my land, Dickon. In a few months you will be a free man, and though I cannot set Mary free, on the day of your release I shall sell you her bond for one shilling.'

Dickon's eyes lit up with glow to rival the moon's. 'God bless you,' he choked, his voice caught with emotion. 'I don't know how to thank you, Miss Hamilton.'

Morna laughed; his pleasure in her announcement was reward enough, and she told him so. He stared at her for a moment and then impulsively caught her to him in a fierce embrace, hugging her and kissing her mouth in a surge of grateful affection.

'Forgive me,' he said gruffly, remembering too late his station as her servant. 'I should not have done that.'

'No, perhaps not,' she agreed, her eyes twinkling. 'But since it was a kiss honestly given, I shall accept it as it was intended. Good night, Dickon.' Morna waved as she turned to go into the house.

'You have ensured that my dreams will be sweet,' Dickon called as he gathered up the horses' reins and begun to lead them towards the stables.

The shadow came unexpectedly out of the darkness, and he was startled to find his path blocked. He looked into a pair of angry eyes, and frowned.

'What's wrong, Jared? Let me pass; I've the horses to see to, and it's late.'

'A pretty scene,' Jared's lips curved in a sneer. 'I ought to kill you for what you did just now. Her brother may not have the guts to do it, but I shall if you touch her again!'

Dickon stared at him, a look of incredulity spreading across his face. 'Damn your filthy mouth, Trenwith! What you saw just now was completely innocent – a token of gratitude – and if you weren't so eaten up with lust for Morna Hamilton yourself, you wouldn't thinking of others.'

Jared's hands clenched tightly, the veins cording in his neck. 'Get rid of those horses, and we'll settle this between us now!'

'I'll fight you, if that's what you want,' Dickon said coldly, 'but she'll demand to know the reason why. You can't go on treating a woman like that with contempt. She's taken a lot from you, but one day she'll see through you. You're a damned fool, Trenwith.'

'What do you mean by that?' Jared's eyes narrowed to murderous slits.

'Why don't you leave if you hate being here so much? I've seen you riding off at nights... Do you think I don't know what's on your mind?' Dickon glowered. 'I've a map of a pass through the mountains. Mr Rupert drew it in the earth one day and I memorised it. I'll give it to you if you want it.'

'Why don't you use it yourself?'

'Because of Mary.' Dickon shook his head. 'I could've gone years ago – but I stayed because of a woman. At least I'm honest enough to admit it.'

Jared glared at him, anger pounding in his

head as he felt the urge to plunge his first into the other man's face. Then he laughed harshly as the fury drained out of him. Dickon's words had forced him to admit the truth: there were no chains on him now, except those of his own forging. But perhaps they chafed all the more because he had not the strength to break them. If he was still haunted by his own desires, he could blame no one else.

'Perhaps I was wrong just now – and perhaps I am a fool. But if I ever see you touch Morna like that again, I'll kill you.'

Dickon watched as he strode away into the darkness, a puzzled frown creasing his brow.

'You're a strange one, Jared Trenwith,' he muttered. 'I'm dammed if I understand you. As for that poor lass, any man with eyes to see can tell she's breaking her heart for you...'

'Sam, will you hitch the wagon for me, please? I'm going into town...' Morna stopped abruptly as she walked into the stables and saw Jared grooming one of the horses. 'Oh, I thought Sam was in here.'

'He and Benjamin went to bring in that tree I felled yesterday. You said you wanted it for firewood.'

'Yes.' Morna nodded, feeling faintly disturbed as she saw the angry gleam in his eyes. 'Will you prepare the wagon for me, then? Dickon has gone to the Robsons'.'

She was wearing a sky-blue gown of some soft material that clung to her body, emphasising the slimness of her waist and hips. It was obvious that she was wearing very little beneath it, having left off her bodice and most of her stiff petticoats because of the heat. Suddenly he recalled the silken feel of her skin and the softness of her mouth as it opened for his invading tongue, and desire flared in him hotly, bringing with it a surge of acute jealousy.

'With another cry for help that will bring Harry Robson hurrying to your side, I suppose?' His lips twisted with scorn. 'How disappointed you must have been when you discovered your rich settler already had a wife! Especially after that charming officer died so inconsiderately of the fever.'

Morna was startled by the bitterness of his attack. 'I always knew Harry was married! Emily is my friend – and I don't understand what you mean about John Blackwell?'

Jared knew he was being unreasonable, but he could not stop. He had fought against his feelings of frustration and impotence for months, resentful of the situation but finding no solution that would let him keep his pride while reaching out for the greater prize.

'No?' He laid down the curry-comb he'd been using and turned to confront her. 'You told me you had received a proposal of marriage on board ship. Since Robson was already married, I supposed it must have come from Blackwell – but perhaps I was wrong?'

Morna bit her lip. She could not tell him she had lied simply to punish him for his cruel words to her, so she took refuge in anger.

'I do not see that any of this concerns you.'

'Why – because I am your bond-servant and not one of the wealthy settlers you hoped to meet?'

She flinched at the scorn in his voice, missing the agony beneath it. Why was he attacking her after all these months when he had deliberately kept his distance?'

As she remained silent, Jared moved towards her and she sensed the suppressed fury in him, and perhaps another, stronger emotion.

'You told me one man was as good as another,' he said, his voice quietly menacing. 'But it isn't quite as easy as that to find a rich husband, is it?'

She felt a tingle of apprehension run through her as she saw the way he was staring at her, his eyes full of a strange hunger. Part of her wanted to reassure him that he was the only man she would ever want, and yet she was afraid. Afraid that he would reject her offer of love again. She could not bear it if he still felt nothing for her after all this time.

Her head went up and her eyes glinted with pride. 'If I wanted a husband, I could find one easily enough! Emily told me there'll be plenty of men looking for a wife at the Governor's ball next month.'

When she looked at him like that he was torn between wanting to shake her and his desire to possess her. Sometimes he was so certain that she loved him and that only his own pride stood in the way of happiness such as he had never known. Yet there were other times when he found himself still doubting her, remembering that she had been engaged to a man he hated – that she had carried on with her plans to marry Stainton even after she knew what kind of a man he was. Only days after she had surrendered herself so willingly to his lovemaking, he had seen her walking and smiling up into the face of another man. And last night he had seen her kissing one of her own bond-servants! Anger flared in him again at the memory.

'But you can't wait until the ball, can you, Morna? You need the attention of a man now. Perhaps you were thinking of taking Sam as your lover – or maybe you prefer a more mature man? Dickon, perhaps?'

Morna gasped, suspicion in her eyes. He was jealous! 'You saw Dickon kiss me last night – that's what this is all about. Why?

You don't want me... Do you?' She held her breath.

'I had you once, remember?' The chill in his eyes made her shiver. 'Does Dickon know that? Has he lain in your bed yet? Is that why he runs after you like a lap d–?' Jared broke off as Morna slapped his face.

'How dare you!' she cried. 'That you should dare to say such things to me, when it was you...' She almost choked on the bile in her throat. 'You used me like a whore to satisfy your own lust.'

She saw a flicker of surprise in his face. 'You thought that?' he frowned, staring at her with an intentness that unnerved her.

'What else was I to think?' Morna's cheeks were flushed as she met the challenge of his eyes. 'You were dreaming of someone else. You believed I was Danielle...'

'No,' he corrected harshly. 'I may have spoken her name while I was asleep, but I knew who was in my bed. Believe me, Morna, I knew.'

She lowered her gaze swiftly, afraid to meet his piercing look. 'If you knew – but you wouldn't speak to me. I thought... I was so confused...'

'And disappointed, since you believed I had used you to satisfy my own needs.' Jared's look was amused now. 'What did you expect? I was still weak from the fever.'

Morna felt her face burning. 'I didn't

mean ... I didn't know.' She looked up at him suddenly, her eyes bright. 'I had no experience of men ... or of love...'

'And what do you think, now that you have?' The anger was back in his eyes. 'Are all men the same, Morna? Does Dickon satisfy you?'

'You devil!' she whispered, her throat tight: 'You know I haven't ... I couldn't...'

'Why? You were willing enough that night.' Jared moved closer to her, his hungry look seeming to burn into her. 'Would you let me make love to you now, Morna? I promise you won't be disappointed this time.'

Morna gasped, backing away from him. She felt her back pressing against the stable wall, and a shudder ran through her as he bent his head. His breath was warm on her face, and his body had a faint, tantalising scent of musk and horses. It was a very masculine smell and it sent little tremors of desire spiralling within her, sapping the strength from her limbs. She was trembling, her mouth tingling beneath his as he kissed her.

She moved her head aside, raising her hands as if to push him away. He caught them, twining his fingers in hers and holding her arms pinned against the wooden panels above her head as his mouth gently explored hers. His tongue traced the soft contours of her lips, teasing them apart with little dart-ing movements that brought a sigh from deep within her. He had never kissed her this way before, and it was driving her beyond the limits of control. She felt her head begin to spin as his mouth moved to the white arch of her throat, the tiny fluttering movements of his tongue making her moan softly. She knew she was close to surrender, and she had to stop him. She could not let it happen again like this.

'No...' she whispered. 'Please don't... Let me go, Jared... You must not...'

'Why?' he breathed, his teeth catching the lobe of her ear. 'You want me, Morna. I've seen it in your eyes when you look at me. I can feel it now.'

He slid her arms around his neck, his hands shaping the curve of her slim waist as they moved down to grasp her hips. Pulling her body close to his, he held pressed against him so that she could feel the pulsating urgency of his need for her.

'I want you, Morna,' he said, his voice harsh with desire. 'Forget who I am, forget who you are. Just for this little time remember only that we are a man and a woman who share a mutual need. You're a passionate woman, Morna, more so than you yet realise. You're the kind of woman who will always need a man...'

Suddenly she realised what he was saying to her, and she froze in his arms, shocked

263

and hurt.

'No!' she said, twisting her head away as he would have kissed her again. 'I am not a wanton – and I won't be used as one.'

'I wasn't calling you a wanton.' Jared's throaty chuckle made her flinch. 'Don't deny your nature, Morna; there's nothing to be ashamed of. You are a very desirable woman, don't you know that? You have a special quality that will always draw men to you – it is something that will grow more powerful as you grow older.'

She looked up at him uncertainly. This was a new Jared, a man she did not know. Was that look in his eyes meant to mock her, or was it the teasing, intimate smile of a lover?

'Why are you making fun of me? Is this your idea of revenge?

Jared saw the suspicion in her face and relaxed his grip, moving back so that she was free. 'Revenge – for what?' The laughter died out of his face, leaving his expression cold and distant. 'I am not a fool, Morna. Do you think I don't know I owe my life to you? Oh, I admit I blamed you at first, but I was out of my mind and furious at the whole world then. I realised long ago that you could have had nothing to do with Stainton's little plot. In fact, I blame only myself now. I was a careless fool...'

Morna drew a sharp breath. 'Then why

are you still so bitter? Sometimes I feel that you hate me!'

'Hate you?' He laughed harshly. 'Perhaps I do ... sometimes. What do you expect? I'm not Philip. I can't forget what I've lost by drinking myself into a stupor. I'll work for you, but I won't beg for favours.'

'I don't want that,' she breathed unsteadily. 'You must know I don't, Jared.'

'Then what do you want of me?'

'I want your love,' Morna's heart cried, but the words never reached her lips. There was a difference in Jared this morning; but even though he seemed less bitter, he was still as far away from her as ever. He had called her a desirable woman, and she had proof enough that he wanted to make love to her – but he was not in love with her.

She drew a deep breath and smiled, hiding the pain inside her. 'I should like us to be friends, Jared. Is that too much to ask? I don't want your gratitude. Anything I did to help you, you have repaid by working so hard for me. All I have ever wanted is – is that you should be happy here. It – it is your home.'

'My home?' Jared arched his brow. 'No, I don't think it could ever be that – not while I am your bond-servant.' He shook his head as she would have protested. 'No, it's not your fault. You have never made me feel like a slave, but in law I am your possession, just as much as these horses.'

'Can you not try to forget that?'

'Don't you think I have tried?'

She heard the mixture of frustration and pain in his cry and sighed. 'I'm sorry, Jared. What can I do?

'Nothing.' he smiled wryly. 'I'm lucky you bothered, after the way I behaved towards you. I have to learn to live with it. Just give me some time, Morna. Now, I'd better get that wagon ready and take you into town – as you asked me to yesterday.'

'I can drive myself if you're busy.'

'I can't let you go alone.' He grinned at her, and for a moment he was the handsome youth who had first captured her heart. 'But you knew that, didn't you? You always did know how to get your own way. Maybe I'm a fool to fight you.'

'What do you mean?' She gazed up at him, her heart racing madly. The barrier between them was beginning to crumble at last.

Jared shook his head, turning away to harness the horse he had been grooming earlier.

'I think you know what I mean,' he said and began to whistle cheerfully.

CHAPTER EIGHT

Morna watched as Jared drove on past the general store, halting the horses in the shade of a eucalyptus. It was autumn now, and the fierce heat of the summer had become a pleasant warmth that made her feel it was good to be alive. If a part of the quiet happiness inside her at this moment was due to what she hoped was a new understanding with Jared, she had tried not to let it show on the drive to town. It was too soon to hope for anything yet. She must be patient for a while longer. Even if he had begun to forget the bitterness of the past year or so, his pride still made it difficult for him to accept the situation. It would take time for him to come to terms with the inevitable, but now at least she had some hope for the future.

As she went into the gloom of the interior, Morna made up her mind that her shop would be light and airy, so that customers would feel encouraged to spend time there talking to their friends. She had already found a suitable building that could be altered to her specifications, and she was impatiently awaiting Captain Smithson's return with their first cargo, but it would be at least another three months before she could expect to see *Sea-Sprite* in port, even if the ship made good time.

'Good morning,' she said to the sharp-featured woman behind the counter. 'I have a list of supplies I need.'

'I'll do my best, Miss Hamilton,' the woman replied sourly. 'But we're short of several spices, and...' She broke off as a loud clatter came from the far corner and a pile of metal plates went flying. 'Pyke, you clumsy oaf! I've warned you to be careful.'

Morna was startled as the woman sprang from behind the counter and began to beat a small, ugly man with her broom. He did not cower away from her, but tried vainly to shield himself from her vicious attack. Seeing that he dragged his foot as he shuffled away from his irate mistress, something stirred in Morna's memory.

'The lazy, good-for-nothing creature,' the shopkeeper said angrily as she returned to her position behind the counter. 'Why I put up with him I don't know! A bargain, my husband said – I wish we'd never set eyes on him.'

'I'll buy his bond from you,' Morna said impulsively. 'How much do you want for it?'

The woman looked at her suspiciously. 'What do you want an ugly creature like that for?'

'I have my reasons.' Morna met her challenging look with a challenge of her own. 'Do you want to be rid of him?'

'My husband paid five pounds for the lazy creature.' She sniffed. 'No one else wanted a cripple – and my man calls it a bargain. I call it a waste of good food. He eats more than he's worth.'

'I'll give you ten pounds for Pyke's bond.'

'Ten pounds?' The woman's eyes gleamed with greed. 'Show me your money, then.'

Morna counted ten gold coins on to the counter, watching as the other woman bit each one. She expressed her satisfaction at last, taking down a battered tin box from a shelf and extracting a document from it.

'Please sign and date it,' Morna said. She waited until it was done and then turned to the little man, who had been following the procedure with interest. 'Pyke, you will find a wagon down the street. Please tell the driver – whom I believe you know – that I am almost ready. Oh – and tell him you are to be my driver in future.'

'Yes, Miss Hamilton, I'll do that.' Pyke grinned at her as he let the tin platters he had been restacking slide to the floor.

'You wretched creature! I'm glad to be rid of you. The shopkeeper shook her fist at him as he hastily made good his escape. 'You'll rue this morning's work, Miss Hamilton! Beats me why anyone should want such a vile creature.'

'Oh, I expect he'll look better when my men have finished trimming his hair and beard for him,' Morna said cheerfully. 'Now, can you fill my order or not?'

'Most of it, I suppose.' The woman moved about the shelves, grumbling to herself.

Morna smiled slightly, imagining the scene that must now be taking place further down the street. Jared would be pleased to be reunited with his friend, and she could easily find room for one more at the farm. Pyke might not be able to help with the hard labour, but he could tend her flower garden – and he could drive her into town. She would need to come more often once her own shop was opened, and it would save taking Jared from the land. Besides, even he could hardly accuse her of having an affair with Pyke!

Turning with her arms full of parcels, Morna found Jared in the doorway. She saw the smile on his lips as he went to pick up the sacks of flour and beans, and knew that this time her good intentions had not been misunderstood. He might not say so, but he was fully aware of what she had done, and of her reasons for buying Pyke's bond. She saw from the amused look he gave her when they went outside and discovered Pyke looking very important in the driving seat, that he had understood her message.

'That was good of you,' he said softly as he took her packages to load them in the wagon. 'And I am grateful to you for rescuing poor Pyke. You'll find him useful, though he is a cheeky, ugly devil!'

This last was said in a louder voice, and Pyke grinned at them. 'That's me, sir – but lazy I am not. I'll work fair and square for them as deserves it.'

'You certainly will, rogue,' Jared said with a mock scowl. 'Or I'll want to know the reason why.'

'Stop bullying my driver, Jared.' Morna gave him a provocative smile. 'Help me up and jump in the back. You'll have to give up your place to Pyke.'

His eyes flashed as he read the challenge in hers, but he made no comment, obeying her with a show of meekness that fooled no one.

Looking at Pyke, Morna lifted her eyebrows. 'I suppose you can drive a horse and wagon?'

'Ay, I can.' Pyke took a firm grasp of the reins. 'There ain't much I can't turn my hand to if I've a mind to it.'

'You should get Pyke to tell you his history one day,' Jared said, climbing into the back of the wagon and stretching out with a sigh of content. 'It would fill three volumes.'

Morna smiled, listening to the banter that passed between the two men as they rolled

271

forward. She had taken a definite stride towards a happier future for them all today. She did not expect a miracle. Jared would not suddenly change overnight, but there was definitely a new ease in his manner towards her, and she did not believe it was only because she had reunited him with his friend.

'You are turning the place into a sideshow,' Philip said, facing his sister angrily across the small parlour. 'Don't you know they're laughing at you in Sydney? You drive about with that – that cripple! – and you mock the law by selling a convict's bond for one shilling – and that's after turning down an invitation to the Governor's ball!'

Morna guessed that it was this last which had really angered him. 'Perhaps I shouldn't have done that,' she admitted, 'but I did have a nasty chill. As for the rest of it, I'm not sorry for anything I've done. Mary is happily married now. By making Dickon her legal owner, I gave them the right to that happiness, and I don't regret it. Dickon has just finished rebuilding my shop, and he and Mary will run it for me when *Sea-Sprite* arrives.'

Philip's mouth curved in a sneer. 'You must be out of your mind, Morna. You can't seriously mean to trust two convicts to run your business – they'll cheat you out of your profits.'

'No, I don't think so.' Morna laid a hand on his arm, looking up at him pleadingly. 'I don't want to quarrel with you, Phil. Everything is going so well now. We had more pasture for the lambs in spring, and the ewes are all healthy. With luck, we might be able to be granted more land next year.'

'We could build an elegant house in town,' Philip said, a spark of interest in his eyes. 'The Governor's wife has asked you to take tea with her one day next week. If you behave sensibly this time, we might begin to live decently again.'

Morna sighed. 'Can't you see that our life is here, Phil? I don't want to spend my time taking tea with the ladies of Sydney.'

'No, you want to waste it working like a drudge!'

'It won't always be like this. Besides, Pyke does most of the chores these days.' Morna looked at him. 'Maybe we shall build that house, Phil, and sooner than you think.'

'Do you mean it?' He frowned at her uncertainly.

'Yes. I kept some of mother's jewels in case we needed them for an emergency. I'll sell them and build that house, if you'll make an effort, Phil.'

'What do you mean by that?'

'I want you to stop drinking and take more interest in this place.' She saw him scowl and shook her head. 'I'm not nagging you,

Phil. I want you to be happy, truly happy – and you're not happy now, are you?'

'No...' He turned away, looking out at the flower garden, really seeing for the first time the changes Morna had made to the home-stead and the land. She had succeeded in making it a home, working long hours to sew the dainty cushions and matching curtains. It never could be Hamilton Towers, but it was comfortable. 'I'm not sure I know how to be happy, Morna,' he admitted at last. 'But that's not your fault. It's the way I am...'

'Maybe you would feel better if you stayed away from town for a while?'

'As you wish it, I'll try it for a time.' Philip swung round to face her. 'But I'll not take orders from Trenwith, do you hear me? He seems to imagine he's in charge these days.'

'Why do you hate him, Phil?'

Her brother glared at her. 'That's my business. If you want me to stay here – just make sure he keeps out of my way!'

'So the big day has arrived at last!' Jane smiled as she saw Morna come downstairs dressed in a pale green silk gown and a pretty straw hat that she had not worn since they left London. 'How long will you be gone?'

'Oh, about three days, I should think – a week at the most. Are you sure you won't change your mind and come with me, Jane?'

'Another time, perhaps. Someone must look after the men, especially now that they're so busy with the lambs.'

'I feel guilty about leaving you with so much to do, particularly as Mary and Dickon are moving into the rooms behind the shop.'

'Pyke will help me,' Jane said cheerfully. 'You've waited for this day a long time. Enjoy yourself and forget about the farm for once.'

Morna laughed and pressed her arm. 'I'm so excited, Jane! You saw a few of the goods Captain Smithson brought to show us. It will take me a day or two to sort everything out, even with Dickon and Mary to help me. I am sure we shall be busy once we open our doors. Emily has been telling everyone she knows that they must buy from us.'

'If the rest of the cargo is as good quality as that I saw, you will have no trouble in selling it,' Jane said. 'Here's Dickon now. You had better go.'

'Yes.' Morna kissed her cheek. 'Have you seen Philip?'

'He went out early to look at some of the ewes.' Jane frowned. 'He said he would be back in time to see you off.'

'Well, he's probably busy. I'm just pleased he's taking a genuine interest in the flocks at last. I must say goodbye to Jared. Do you know where he is?'

'I think he was with that young horse, earlier. Yesterday he and Sam were saying it was time she was broken in.'

'Then he'll be in the paddocks behind the stables.' Morna smiled at Dickon as she passed him on the veranda. 'There's only one small bag. I won't keep you waiting long, I promise.'

'I wanted a word with Miss Jane before we leave.' Dickon grinned at her. 'I'll know where to find you, Miss Hamilton.'

Morna's heart was beating rapidly as she walked towards the paddocks. Jared had refused to enter the house when Captain Smithson dined with them. She knew he still resented the cruel treatment that he and the other convicts had received on board *Sea-Sprite*, and he was angry with her for going into business with her captain. He had not put his objections into words, but his manner had become distinctly cooler these last few days. It hurt her that he should let something so unimportant damage the relationship that had begun to build between them, but she knew he would handle it in his own way. In the end he would see that what she was doing was for all of them.

Seeing him standing at the fence, watching the young horse prance nervously around the paddock she studied his face, or as much as she could see of it. The sun had turned Jared's skin to a deep bronze, making his features look even more carved than before. There was something in the proud line of his profile that made her heart catch. How much she loved him! It seemed that every passing day only intensified her feeling for him; and though he had not touched her since that morning in the stable, she believed he was beginning to love her too – at least, she had hoped it was so until the last few days.

'I came to say goodbye, Jared.'

He turned as she spoke, his eyes moving over her, noting the fancy silk gown and elegant hat. 'So you're going, then?'

'Yes. Won't you wish me luck?'

'I doubt you'll need it. Doesn't everything happen just as you want it to, Morna?' His face hardened. 'I hope Smithson appreciates your elegance.'

'I'm wearing this dress to impress the ladies of Sydney, Jared, not Captain Smithson.' Morna sighed, joining him at the rails. 'So you've decided it's time to break in Sunfire. You will be gentle with her, won't you? She's such a nervous creature.'

'In time she'll make a good riding horse for you, Morna.' Jared smiled suddenly. 'I'll treat her gently – for your sake as well as her own.'

Morna blushed as she saw the expression in his eyes. The ice had gone and there was a hungry gleam there now that made her tremble.

'How long will you be gone?'

'Three days ... perhaps a week.'

'Don't be too long. I shall miss you.'

'Will you?' she whispered, swaying towards him as the longing to be in his arms became too strong to be denied. 'Will you really miss me, Jared?'

Silently he reached out and drew her into his arms, his mouth caressing hers with the lightest of kisses that set her blood running hotly through her veins. She pressed herself against him, her fingers entwining in the thick hair that clustered at the nape of his neck. With a laugh, he put her from him.

'You little witch,' he murmured, his eyes ravenous as they absorbed every line of her face. 'You'll have me fast in your net yet. Go to Sydney, Morna. Go quickly before I lose control!'

'Will you think of me while I'm gone?'

She was living dangerously, but the look in his eyes was sending her heart on a dizzy dance of delight, and she sensed that he was closer to her at this moment that he had ever been.

'Yes, I'll think of you.' Jared laughed harshly. 'When do you ever give me a moment's peace?'

'What do you mean?' She swayed towards him enticingly, her mouth parting slightly as if inviting him to kiss her again.

'You minx!' Jared grated. 'Do you really

need to ask?'

'Oh, Jared,' she whispered. 'I...'

'Morna, I'm glad I've caught you before you leave.' Jared's teasing smile disappeared as he heard Philip's voice. He moved away from Morna, his features frozen as he turned his attention to the horse once more.

'Jared?' Morna said, disappointment sharp in her as she saw that the magical moment had passed.

'Say goodbye to your brother, Morna.'

She noted the grim line of his mouth, and sighed. For one moment she had thought the last barriers were set to tumble, but now he had them firmly in place once more.

'I shall have a special surprise for you when I return, Jared.'

He might not have heard her for all the notice he took of her words. Frowning, she went to join her brother. She took his arm as she walked with him to where Dickon was waiting with the wagon. After all, it was not Philip's fault that he had arrived at the wrong moment. He could not know that he had interrupted something special...

Philip pushed his plate away, leaving most of the food untouched. He leaned back in his chair, staring moodily in front of him, his mouth set in a sulky expression.

Jane looked at his plate with anger. She had cooked specially for him because he refused to eat with the other men, and it annoyed her when he wasted good food.

'Was something wrong with your meal, Philip?'

'I'm tired of mutton. Why can't we have beef for a change?'

'You know the answer to that. It's scarce at the moment, but I expect Morna will buy some when the next shipment of cattle arrives. She was talking of starting a small milking herd.'

'If it pleases my sister to grant a favour, I expect she will do so,' Philip sneered. 'We must all dance to her tune these days.'

'Philip! How can you say such a terrible thing? Morna goes out of her way to please everyone.'

'Oh, I know you worship the ground she walks on! She has you all bewitched, even Jared. I saw them kissing before she left.' Philip's eyes narrowed. 'If she marries him, I'll not stay here to see him lording it over us all.'

Jane save him a look of disgust. 'Where would you go? If it were not for Morna, you would have to work like everyone else.'

'Hold your tongue, cousin.' Philip glared at her. 'You've nothing to reproach me with! You live on my sainted sister's charity, too.'

'I am well aware of that, Philip, but at least I try to help her as much as I can.'

Scowling, Philip scraped his chair on the

floor and got to his feet. He went out of the house, his eyes thinned to angry slits as he walked, not really seeing his surroundings. In his mind was a picture of Morna and Jared embracing, a picture that filled him with jealousy and rage. He felt sick at the thought of them lying together; but even as he centred his anger on the two people he loved most in the world, he knew that the sickness was in his own mind. It was his own unnatural thoughts and desires which had ruined his life. He had fought against them for so long, feeling ashamed of his own nature, but neither the drinking nor the gambling eased the constant ache inside him.

Seeing the other men grouped about the paddock, Philip wandered over to join them. They greeted him with a polite deference, but he knew he was unwelcome. These men were all devoted to Morna, and he was aware that they despised him for his weakness.

'What are you doing?'

'We're breaking in the filly for Miss Hamilton, sir,' Sam answered as the others remained silent. 'She'll make a good riding horse for the mistress when she's ready.'

'Have you tried her with a saddle yet?'

Philip felt a stirring of interest as he watched Jared slip a simple rope harness over the horse's head. The filly shied a bit, tossing her mane before settling under his gentle but firm handling.

'Not yet, sir. Jared says we've to go carefully with her. She's a nervous creature. We're trying to get her used to a bridle in simple stages; then we'll put the saddle on and let her get used to the feel of it before Benjamin attempts to ride her.'

'Why Benjamin?'

'He's the lightest of us, sir. She's a ladies' mount – she wouldn't be up to either my or Jared's weight.'

'At this rate, you won't have her ready for weeks. Put a proper bridle on her, and I'll ride her myself.'

Sam looked at him awkwardly. 'Her mouth's too tender for a bit yet, sir. Besides, Benjamin has a way with nervous horses. You'd best leave it to him.'

Philip's eyes flashed with temper. 'Do as I tell you! All that horse needs is a firm hand. I'll have her broken before dinner-time.'

Sam hesitated, obviously unwilling to obey, but afraid of the consequences if he refused. After a moment he walked over to Jared and spoke to him in a low voice. Jared glanced towards the man who had given the order, his face registering his contempt.

'Leave this to me,' he said. 'Continue leading Sunfire round the field by the rope harness.'

Philip braced himself as he saw the anger in Jared's eyes. The tension had been mounting between them for weeks, both of them drawing back from the brink of confrontation time and again.

'Why did you give Sam an order you know he can't obey?' Jared demanded, his eyes scornful. 'You'll ruin that horse if you try to force her – highly-strung fillies have to be coaxed, not mastered.'

'Is that the way you've been playing it with Morna?' Philip asked, his lips curling in a sneer. 'You think you're pretty clever, don't you, Jared? But I know what you're about. I've seen you lusting after her...'

'Don't say any more, Philip, or you'll be sorry.' Jared's fists clenched at his sides as he struggled to control his anger. 'What is between Morna and me is private.'

'She won't marry you. Can't you see she's just leading you on so that she can laugh in your face when you finally ask her? She might be infatuated with you, but she'll marry a rich settler, not a convict she can twist around her little finger.' Philip laughed harshly. 'If you think you'll be master here one day, you're a fool!'

'God damn you for the unnatural wretch you are!' Jared cried, 'Morna is worth a dozen of you.'

Philip gave a cry of animal rage as something snapped in his brain. 'I'll kill you before I see you married to her,' he yelled. 'There'll be no peace for me until you're dead.'

As he spoke, he threw himself at Jared, his fists flailing wildly as he tried to smash them into the face of the man who had aroused his fury. Jerking and ducking to dodge the wild onslaught, Jared did his best to avoid a fight, but Philip would not be denied. He caught Jared a glancing blow on the chin, then punched him hard in the stomach.

Gasping in pain, Jared recoiled and stared at Philip with contempt. 'If that's the way you want it, you damned idiot, maybe it's best we get it over with.'

'Don't be a fool, man,' Sam warned. 'He wants you to attack him! Remember you're still a convict.'

Sam's warning came too late. Jared's fist shot out, connecting with Philip's jaw. He rocked on his feet, his head jerking back as another punch followed swiftly, sending him sprawling in the earth.

Standing over the prostrate figure of his opponent, Jared resisted the urge to teach Morna's brother a sharp lesson. He held out his hand, offering to help him to rise.

'I'm sorry,' he said as the younger man scowled and shook his head. 'I didn't want to hit you – but you asked for it.'

Philip got to his feet. He stood for a moment just staring at Jared in silence. A trickle of blood ran down his chin from the cut on his lip. He wiped it away, looking at the blood as if mesmerised; then his head came up and his eyes glittered with a deadly hatred.

'You struck your master, convict,' he hissed. 'Now you'll pay for it!' He swung round to face Sam and Benjamin, who were watching in horror. 'Tie him to that tree over there, and then fetch my whip. It's time this convict learned who is master here.'

Neither Sam nor Benjamin moved. They looked at each other uneasily, both of them realising the potential danger of the situation. Philip Hamilton was out of control. If he took it into his head to kill the lot of them, he need only invent a story of mutiny and his lies would be believed. The authorities in Sydney would not bother to question the deaths of three convicts, but if they attacked their master, all three of them could hang.

Sam looked at Jared, his face registering the sickness he felt inside. 'I – I can't do it.'

'Do you want to feel the lash, too?' Philip demanded. 'God help me, I'll shoot the lot of you scum if you cross me again!'

'Do as he tells you, Sam. He's quite capable of carrying out that threat,' Jared said calmly. 'He has a gun in the house.

Sam looked at him and then at Philip. Seeing the insane glitter in his master's eyes, he realised he had no choice. If he refused, Philip might fetch the gun and start shooting everyone. Nodding grimly at Benjamin, he took a coiled rope from the fence rails and followed Jared to the tree in the centre of the yard.

'Bind my wrists tight so that I can brace myself,' Jared said. 'It's not your fault, man. You're doing what you have to do.'

'God forgive me,' Sam muttered. 'I should kill him. I could do it, too, with my bare hands.'

'And hang the lot of us? Don't be a fool, Sam. I'd rather take a beating.'

Sam shook his head, binding Jared's wrists tightly with the rope and then pulling it firmly around the narrow tree-trunk. He stepped back, his face grim as Benjamin brought a long leather whip from inside the barn. It had belonged to Rupert Prowther, and Morna had ordered it to be destroyed. Unknown to her, Philip had rescued it from the fire, hiding it in the barn. All the men had known it was there and realised the significance of his action, but none of them had believed he would ever dare to use it.

'Give Sam the whip,' Philip muttered, his face white.

Benjamin avoided his fellow convicts' eyes as he obeyed. He retreated to a safe distance, obviously relieved he was not going to be forced to administer the beating.

'Get on with it,' Philip commanded.

Sam looked at the whip in his hand and then turned to face his master defiantly. 'No,' he said. 'I can't ... I won't do it. You can have me beaten, or shoot me if you must, but I won't do it.'

Rage flared in Philip's face. He darted forward and snatched the whip from Sam's hand, his fingers curling around the short, hard handle. His arm went back and then forward, the leather thong singing in the air as it snaked across Jared's back, cutting the coarse material of his shirt. Philip struck again and again, his high-pitched laughter ringing out as he saw his victim writhe and strain at the ropes.

'Now you'll learn some manners, convict!' Philip cried, his arm going back once more. 'I've only just begun to teach you how to behave.'

'Use that whip again and I'll shoot you, Philip.'

He froze as he heard his cousin's voice. He turned to look at her, his face incredulous as he saw her level his own pistol at him. She was pale and her hands were shaking as she grasped the gun tightly, holding it out at arm's length in front of her, but she had a determined gleam in her eyes. Philip realised that she was no longer the meek and mild drudge he had once thought her.

The whip fell from his hand. He stared at her, seeming stunned by her action for a moment; then he began to move towards her, smiling oddly.

'You wouldn't shoot me, Jane?' He gave a

nervous laugh. 'What would Morna say if you killed her only brother?'

'Don't come any nearer, Philip.'

'Shoot me, then. Go on, pull the trigger if you dare! You'll be doing me a favour, Jane.'

'Oh, Philip,' Jane caught her breath on a sob, her hand wavering uncertainly. 'Why did you do it?'

She looked up at him, the pistol hanging loosely at her side as she became confused, torn between her anger and her natural affection for Morna's brother. In that instant, Philip reached out and grabbed her wrist, snatching the pistol with one hand while bringing the other back hard across her throat. She cried out in pain, gasping and choking as she staggered back.

'Thank you for bringing my pistol, cousin, you've saved me the trouble of fetching it,' he sneered, looking triumphantly round at the little group of horrified watchers. He waved the pistol in the air, his eyes glittering. 'I ought to kill the lot of you, but why should I bother? You're not worth the trouble of burying.' He gestured towards Jared with the pistol. 'Cut him down and lock him in his cabin – then get on with your work. If any one of you gets in my way, I'll shoot you all!'

With that threat, he strode towards the stables. No one moved for a moment, then Sam took a step towards Jane, who was kneeling in the dry earth.

'Are you all right, Miss Jane?'

'Yes,' she whispered, pressing a hand to her throat. 'I was just winded. I'll be better in a minute. You'd best do as Philip says. In his present mood, there's no telling what he might do. I think he's gone mad.'

At that moment, Philip burst out of the stables, riding his horse furiously towards them. He laughed as they scattered, his eyes wild and shining with a strange excitement.

'He's not mad,' Sam muttered, watching grimly as Philip beat at his horse with a riding-crop to make it run faster. 'Just plain evil.'

'That's as maybe,' Jane said, frowning. 'Cut Jared down, and I'll see to his back. Thank goodness it looks as if his shirt stopped him being cut. We'll lock him in his cabin for now, in case Philip returns – but I'll hide the key. You or Benjamin must go and fetch Morna. She'll know what to do – though what she'll say when she knows what has happened, I daren't think!'

'Here's to you, Morna,' Captain Smithson said, raising his glass of sparkling white wine in a salute. 'Without you, the store would never have been such a success.'

Morna sipped her wine from the delicate, fluted cut glass, one of several dozen the Captain had transported from England.

There were only six left now, and she had decided to keep them for herself.

She smiled at her partner. 'Real champagne, delicious! Still, I think we deserve it. We have done quite well.'

'More than half the cargo has been snapped up already. You'll have nothing left to sell before I even leave for England.'

'Oh, I expect it will last a little longer than that!' She laughed at his enthusiasm. 'Everyone was eager to buy this week because it's so long since most of them have seen luxuries like these. No doubt they will become more choosy now, but I am confident we shall sell most of what you brought by the time you return with another cargo.'

'I have every confidence in you, Morna.' Captain Smithson hesitated. 'I thought I might bring twice as much next time – it's an easier cargo than convicts.'

'And a more humane one,' Morna said, putting down her glass and looking at him with approval. 'A cargo like that would make us both rich, Captain.'

'Ay, I'd thought as much myself.' He set his glass on the table and came round it to gaze down into her face. 'Maybe one more trip or two at the most – then I've a mind to get a grant of land myself. I thought I might resign from the sea and find a pretty lass to give me children before it's too late.'

Morna saw the look in his eyes and

lowered her gaze, her cheeks warm. 'You're not old yet, Captain. I'm sure you've plenty of time to – to find a wife and settle down.'

'I've found the woman I want, Morna – if she'll have me?'

She looked up then, her eyes clouding. 'I'm sorry, Stuart, I can't marry you. I have learned to like and respect you, but I don't love you.'

'It's still Trenwith, I suppose?' Smithson's brows met in a frown. 'Why haven't you married him? Plenty of men have married convict wenches – you could get the Governor's permission if you've a mind to it.'

'Jared is too proud to ask me,' Morna said. 'I've been afraid to ask him because – because I don't want to lose him. Do you understand what I mean?'

'Ay, the man's a fool,' Smithson muttered. 'If you were his bond-servant, he'd marry you. It's being beholden to a woman that sticks in his throat.'

'But he isn't,' Morna said. 'He works harder than anyone else. If the farm is beginning to prosper, it's due to Jared. I am willing to share everything with him. Why does it matter that it was my money that bought the lease to begin with?'

'You said it yourself, lass. It's his pride. He has too much of it for his own good. It was his stubbornness that earned him twenty lashes instead of five.'

'He still resents you for that.' Morna sighed. 'He was angry with me for going into business with you – but the money is for all of us. Why can't he see that?'

Smithson laughed and shook his head. 'It's you that can't see, Morna. The richer you become, the more distance you put between you. Trenwith needs to be the master. He wants to lay the world at the feet of the woman he loves, not to take her bounty – no matter how willingly she gives.'

'So what can I do?'

'That's something only you can decide. Maybe you'll find a way of solving the problem one day... Maybe you'll have to wait until the man's his own master.'

'That can't be for another six years. I can't wait that long. I love him too much.'

'Then maybe you will lose him.' Smithson smiled oddly and picked up his glass. 'I'll be around if you get tired of waiting for Trenwith to realise what a fool he is.'

'I shouldn't burden you with my problems.' Morna gave a shaky laugh. 'Are you coming back to the farm with me? You are welcome to stay until you sail.'

'No, I don't think so. I hope one day Jared Trenwith and I will be able to meet as friends, but until that day I'll not cause more problems for you. If you'll take my advice you'll have it out with him, make him see that his pride is less important than the happiness of two people.'

'Perhaps I shall. I have thought he was becoming less bitter of late.' Morna impulsively leant towards him, kissing his cheek. 'You've been a good friend to me, Stuart Smithson. I shan't forget it.'

'You'll not ride back alone?' he asked, resisting the urge to sweep her into a crushing embrace. She was beautiful, desirable, and the only woman he would ever love, but she was not for him.

'No. Dickon will see me home and then come back.' Morna smiled, unaware of the fierce emotions she had aroused in him. 'I shall see you again before you leave?'

'Of course.'

'I shall give you something to sell for me in England – some jewels my mother left me.'

'You know I will do my best for you.'

'Yes – you did wonders this time. I was afraid you would be too late to buy the horse. I can't wait to see Jared's face when he sees Devil Lad.'

'Devil by name, devil by nature.' Smithson grimaced. 'That brute is the worst-tempered horse I ever had the misfortune to handle. Only for you would I have put up with such a creature on my ship!'

Morna gurgled with laughter, her eyes glowing. 'He's as gentle as a lamb with Jared. He'll own only one master, you see.'

'Like you?' Smithson said softly.

'Yes,' Morna whispered, her eyes suddenly dark with emotion. 'There will only ever be one man for me...'

'I reckon Jared will have the surprise of his life,' Dickon said, grinning at Morna as they approached the homestead. 'He told me about this horse – thinks the world of him, don't he?'

'Yes, he does.' Morna smiled, excitement tingeing her cheeks with a delicate rose. 'When I asked Captain Smithson to buy the stallion I was afraid it might be too late. I knew the bank had foreclosed and the whole Trenwith estate was up for sale – but fortunately, the man who bought Devil Lad couldn't handle him, and he was glad to sell him again.'

'That was a bit of luck. Well, here we are, Miss Hamilton. I'll see you to the door and then I'll get back to...' He broke off as Jane came rushing out of the house.

'Oh Morna, thank goodness you're back,' Jane cried. 'I sent Benjamin to fetch you – did you see him?'

'No. We must have missed him.' Morna slipped from the saddle without waiting for Dickon to help her. 'What's the matter, Jane? What's happened?'

'It was Philip,' Jane said. 'He quarrelled with Jared over that young horse... They fought, and then Philip – Philip had him tied to a tree and – and whipped.'

'He couldn't!' Morna's face went white with shock, and she swayed as the earth whirled round her. 'No, Philip wouldn't do that – he knows I love Jared. Oh, Jane, how could he?'

'I tried to stop him,' Jane said. 'I don't think he knew what he was doing. He looked half out of his mind when he rode off.'

'Where is Jared now?' Morna demanded. 'Why did the others let Philip do it? Why didn't they stop him?'

'Philip threatened to kill them all. They were frightened, Morna, but Sam rebelled. He wouldn't use the whip, so – so Philip did it himself.'

'I'll speak to Philip later.' Morna's eyes were like ice. 'I must see Jared first. Where is he?'

'Locked in his cabin. Philip ordered it, and I thought it best. I've kept the key safe with me.'

She held it out and Morna took it. Turning, she ran across the dividing yard to the men's cabins. Her cheeks were wet with tears and she felt sick. How could Philip do such a wicked thing? She knew he was not the same person she had loved when they were children. Something had changed him when their father sent him away university, but she had not believed him capable of this!

Inserting the key in the lock, Morna's eager fingers fumbled uselessly, delaying her as she tried to open it in a rush. It turned at last and she burst in, calling Jared's name. The words of apology died on her lips as she saw the cabin was empty. The window-frame was broken where Jared had smashed it with a chair. She turned as Dickon and her cousin entered behind her, her face strained and frightened.

'He isn't here,' she whispered, catching a sob. 'Where is he?'

'He has run,' Dickon said, his features grim. 'It was only a matter of time. I knew he was restless – Philip's attack was all it needed to make him go.'

'No...' Morna shook her head, refusing to believe it. 'He was beginning to settle down. I know he was.' She looked at Dickon's face, noticing his odd expression. 'You know something more, don't you? You must tell me – you must!'

'I had a map. Mr Rupert drew it in the earth to show me the route he meant to take. It was the route first discovered in 1813 across the Blue Mountains. I gave it to Jared.'

'He wouldn't try to cross the mountains alone without supplies or even a horse?'

'Desperate men have been known to try anything.'

'Not Jared – he's not a fool.' She frowned,

her eyes narrowing in concentration. 'No, I'm sure he has just gone off in a mood. He'll come back when he's ready.'

'If he does, he's a dead man.'

Philip's voice startled them all. In the confusion, no one had seen him arrive and follow Dickon inside. Morna swung round now, her eyes blazing with anger.

'I'm surprised you dare to come back here after what you did!'

'I came to get that convict you're so fond of,' Philip sneered. 'He attacked me, and I mean to see him hang for it.'

'You will do no such thing. His bond belongs to me. If he needs to be punished, that is my responsibility,' Morna walked out into the sunshine, staring at the young officer who was waiting outside with their horses. 'Why have you come here? I didn't send for you. This is not an escape, merely a small problem I can solve myself.'

'I am sorry, Miss Hamilton,' the officer said, avoiding her angry stare. 'It's out of your hands, now. A complaint has been made to my superiors by your brother. One of your convicts tried to kill him. I am instructed to arrest Jared Trenwith and take him back to Sydney for a hearing.'

'Jared did not attack my brother. That is a lie! I can deal with this myself, I tell you.' Her eyes sparked with anger as she recognised him. 'We've met before, haven't we?'

'Of course you've met Laurence Starr,' Philip said. 'We've been friends for months. If you had ever been interested in what I was doing, you would know that Laurence has been helping me to find a position on the Governor's staff.'

'If that's true, I'm glad of it.' Morna smelt the wine on his breath and knew he had been drinking. Her face was cold as she looked at him. 'If you persist with this farce, Philip, I'm finished with you. I don't want to see you here again.'

'Don't worry, you won't.' Philip's mouth twisted with spite. 'I can't wait to get away from this dump. I didn't want to come here in the first place, and as soon as I've earned my passage, I'm going back to England.'

Morna felt the sting of tears, but she blinked them away. She had not guessed how bitterly Philip resented her, and the look of hatred in his eyes shocked her. She did not know why he had changed so much, or when the gap between them had become a huge chasm that she could not bridge. Despite all their quarrels there had always been a bond of affection tying them together. Now that bond had snapped, and he was a stranger to her.

'Then you had better go, Philip,' she said. 'I'll have your things packed and delivered to Sydney tomorrow.'

Her words seemed to stun Philip with

their finality. He stared at her in silence for a long moment, then turned away and mounted his horse.

Morna watched as he rode out of the yard with his friend, then she glanced at Dickon's anxious face. 'I have to find Jared before they do. You gave him a map – and I know you followed him when he rode out at night sometimes. Where shall I find him?'

'I know where he might be – if you're right and he was planning to come back.'

'Prowther's Rock?' Morna smiled as Dickon looked surprised. 'I followed him once, too. I think he knew I was there, but he never questioned my motives – as I never questioned his. I knew he would come back, but this time it is different. He can't stay here now.'

'You mean...' Dickon stared at her. 'If they catch him, he'll be shipped off to Van Diemen's Land.'

'Philip won't rest until he's dead.' Morna frowned. 'I've known my brother was – was unstable for some time, but I hoped he would get better. Jared will never be safe if he stays here, even if the Governor accepts his story. No, he must cross the mountains – he must find a new life for himself.'

'Yes, if he can hide over the mountains he should be safe.'

'Then I must give him that chance.' Morna raised her head, her eyes a little too bright. 'I'll take him food and a horse. Not Devil Lad; the stallion is too distinctive and might betray him. You select the most suitable, Dickon. Jane, help me pack some food.'

'Shall I come with you?' Dickon asked. 'If I know Jared, he'll still be angry.'

'No – though you can take a package to Captain Smithson for me.' Morna smiled oddly. 'I'll go alone. Jared's been angry before. I've never needed protection from him – and I shan't need it now.'

CHAPTER NINE

Seeing Prowther's Rock just ahead of her, Morna looked back to make sure she had not been followed. The landscape was flat and empty, except for an odd tree here and there. Prowther's Rock was so named because it marked the western boundary of the land which had been granted to Rupert. It stood about twenty feet high, was a pinkish-grey in colour, and there were several cracks and fissures large enough for a man to hide in. At its foot was a small waterhole where the sheep sometimes drank in summer because it never ran dry, and a clump of trees.

Morna dismounted, tethering her horse to a bush and staring up at the rock. There was no sign of Jared, and she felt a sharp disappointment. What if she had been wrong? If Jared had already decided to go on the run, she would have little chance of finding him before her brother and his officer friends. At the moment there were only two of them, but by morning word of the escape would have spread and the whole area would be alerted. Every settler would be on the lookout for an escaped convict.

'Jared...' Morna called, beginning to scramble up the rock to a wide plateau she could see about halfway up. 'Jared, are you there? I have to talk to you.'

There was no answer. She gained the plateau and stood there with her back to the rock, surveying the superb vista below. It was possible to see for miles from here, and she could just make out the tiny shapes of the homestead and barns as a blueish haze on the horizon, while behind her the magnificent dividing range of mountains reared as a seemingly impassable barrier. Suddenly she understood why Jared had come here so often when he was feeling restless. It was like being in another world. The silence was broken only by the sighing of the breeze and the occasional cry of a bird circling overhead.

Hearing a slight sound behind her, Morna

started to turn; but before she could do so, a man's arms enfolded her and she was dragged backwards. Screaming, she began to struggle and kick wildly.

'Let me go!'

'Be quiet, you little witch. If you call for help, I'll have to stop you!'

Jared's hand covered her mouth as he half carried her into the cave. She felt the iron hardness of his body as he held her against him, one arm still round her waist in an imprisoning grip. She had stopped struggling when she heard his voice, but the pressure of his arm was crushing her ribs, and she pushed against it.

'If I let you go, will you behave?'

Morna nodded, and he relaxed his grip. She whirled round on him, her eyes angry.

'Why did you do that? I came to help you... There was no need to attack me.'

'I couldn't be sure you were alone.' His face was cold as he looked at her. 'I've learned to trust no one – not even you.'

Morna saw the contempt stamped into his granite-hard features, and anger flared in her. This was so unfair. She had tried so hard to win his confidence – and still he despised her. He blamed her for Philip's wickedness!

'Will you never believe in me?' she cried, throwing herself at him to beat at his chest in her hurt and frustration. 'You know I would never have let Philip harm you – you know it!'

Jared caught her wrists, holding her while she struggled and sobbed out her pain and rage. After a moment or two, she calmed down, looking up at him with tears running down her cheeks.

'Why don't you let me into your heart, Jared? You know... Oh, you must know how much I love you.'

His eyes flared with a cold flame. 'But you told me you hated me,' he said softly, his breath warm and sweet on her face as he held her imprisoned close to his heart. 'You said one man was as good as another – and you vowed to marry the richest man you could find.'

'I wanted to hurt you when I said those things,' Morna breathed, her heart pounding wildly. 'I never meant any of it! You rejected me. You sent me away from you. I couldn't tell you I loved you then, but you must – you must know it now?'

She gazed up at him, her eyes wide and dark with emotion. Jared's face twisted as if in agony and a groan issued from deep inside him. His hands slid up her arms over her shoulders to catch her face as she lifted it, meeting his kiss with equal desire. Passion flared between them, searing their flesh with the burning urgency of their need for each other.

'I want you so much,' he whispered, burying his face in the softness of the silken valley at the base of her throat. 'I've thought of nothing else for months. You've been driving me mad, my darling girl. To see you and have you near but not to have you was hell on earth.'

She trembled as she heard the tenderness in his voice, pressing her body against his as she slid her arms up around his neck, entwining her fingers in his hair. Clinging so tightly that she was like mistletoe twining itself about the tree that gave it life.

'I want you, Jared,' she murmured, her lips opening slightly as she gazed up at him through love-misted eyes. 'I love you so very much.'

'Morna, my beautiful, passionate woman,' he said, his smile sending a surge of desire washing through her. 'You won't refuse me this time?'

She shook her head, smiling as she lifted her long hair and turned, inviting him to undo the tiny buttons fastening her gown. As his fingers moved at her nape, she shivered and he caught her against him, kissing the hollow between her shoulders.

'Trust me,' he said. 'Don't be nervous.'

'I'm not.'

She moved in the circle of his arms, pushing the gaping bodice of her gown down over her hips so that it slid to the ground. She was naked beneath it save for the white pantaloons that fell away as he pulled their silk ribbons. Morna stepped out of them, smiling up at him with a new confidence as his hungry eyes devoured her. Then she reached out and deliberately unfastened the buckle at his waist.

Jared laughed throatily, not attempting to help her as she pushed impatiently at his breeches. She saw the hot gleam in his eyes as she slid them down over his hips and let her eyes wander to the source of his throbbing passion. He waited for one tantalising, agonising moment, letting her absorb the extent of his desire; then he reached out and drew her against him.

Morna gasped as the touch of his burning flesh seemed to sear her, setting a trail of fire running through her veins, melting her limbs to boneless flesh that had no will but to surrender to the sweet violence of his assault. He lifted her gently in his arms, laying her on their scattered clothing, his mouth hardly leaving hers for an instant as he gathered her to him once more. She moaned softly as his hands moved almost reverently over her body, stroking, kneading, adoring the silken curves they touched. Her head moved restlessly on the sandy floor as he slowly explored her, first with his hands and then with the tip of his teasing tongue. Tiny spasms of sensation exploded inside her, making her arch and writhe. He seemed to know how to set each nerve tingling, playing her with the delicacy of a master violinist, so that her whole body became one singing, glorious flame of desire.

'Oh, Jared... Jared,' she whispered hoarsely. 'Please... I can't bear... Oh!'

She gasped as his body slid over hers suddenly and she felt him thrust into her with an urgency that made her arch wildly towards him. She gripped his shoulders, feeling the dampness of his skin as her fingers slid down over his back. Hearing him groan slightly, she remembered and tried to apologise for hurting his bruised flesh; but he covered her mouth with his own, smothering her words with a tender kiss that went on and on endlessly, like the steady rhythm of his hips grinding against hers.

He was deep inside her, filling her with a throbbing ecstasy that made her cry out again and again. She moaned wildly as the sensation built and built until she thought she would die of pleasure. Then her body shook violently and she curled her legs across his back, clinging to him as she was flung apart by the violence of the spasm that swept her to the edge of death. The earth spiralled as she ascended into paradise. Then all at once she was aware of Jared's weight, and of the sweat trickling between her breasts.

She looked up at him and saw him smile. 'I – I love you,' she whispered.

'I know, my darling.' He kissed the tip of her nose gently, his eyes smouldering still as he saw her slightly dazed look. 'Have I made you happy?'

'Oh yes,' she breathed. 'I've never felt so – so happy. I didn't know it was possible to feel like this.'

'It happens sometimes.'

She frowned. 'For you – with Danielle?'

'Not like this, my jealous little cat.' He smoothed her hair back from her forehead. 'Never quite like this – not with any other woman.'

She sighed, reaching out to touch his face in wonder, her fingers tracing the contours of his brow, nose and cheek until he trapped them between strong teeth.

'We've wasted so much time, Jared.'

'Too much,' he agreed. 'The sooner we're married now, the better. It's time I made an honest woman of you.'

'Oh, Jared.' She gave a little sob, burying her face against the satin hard flesh of his shoulder. 'If only you had said that before – before it was too late.'

He held her away from him, looking down into her tear-drenched eyes. 'Too late, Morna? I thought you wanted marriage?'

'I do. You know I've always wanted to be

307

your wife.' She sat up, her eyes almost too big for her face as the fear swept over her. 'I came here to warn you – to tell you that you must go. Philip and his friends are searching for you. They mean to hunt you down and kill you – or see you hang.'

'For what?' Jared's eyes narrowed. 'He attacked me! I was merely defending myself.'

'I know that – but Philip has reported an attempt on his life. By tomorrow, everyone will be on the alert.' Morna stood up, pulling on her pantaloons. 'You must take my horse, Jared, there's food and money in the saddle-bags. You have to leave now. I have already delayed you.'

'It would be better to wait for another hour or two. I'll have more chance when it's dark – I know the trails at night better than most.' He pulled on his breeches and shirt as she finished dressing, fastening the buttons for her. 'What will you do?'

'I'll walk back to the homestead.'

'I meant, after I've gone?'

'I'll wait for you to send me word – then I'll come to you. I can sell up and we'll start again somewhere else.'

Jared looked at her, his eyes becoming cold and distant as if he were deliberately shutting her out of his mind.

'No,' he said harshly. 'I don't want you to wait for me. Find yourself a rich husband,

Morna, and marry him. Forget you ever knew me.'

She stared at him, her face white with shock. 'You can't mean that, Jared. Not now! Not after what happened between us just now?'

He was silent for a moment, a nerve flicking in his throat as if he were fighting a battle inside himself; then he gave a harsh, bitter laugh.

'Why not?' he asked, a cruel sneer on his lips. 'It was a pleasant way of spending the afternoon, but nothing special. I told you you were a passionate woman, Morna, and you are. You'll find other men to help you forget me.'

'But you said it was special?' Morna looked at him appealingly. 'I thought you loved me, Jared?'

'I lied,' Jared said carelessly. 'I wanted you badly – any man would in my position – but I don't love you. I want to be free – can't you understand that?'

'Yes, I can understand that,' Morna said quietly, brushing the tears from her face. 'But you've always been free. I never wanted to chain you with my love, only to share my life with you. I shan't hold you any longer – and I shan't betray you. Take the horse and go wherever you choose.'

'I'll take the horse and the food, but I don't want your money.'

She shrugged her shoulders, turning away as the pain slashed into her like the blade of a knife.

'As you wish,' she said without looking at him. 'It doesn't matter.'

She walked away, her head high and her back straight. Outside the cave, she paused for a moment, blinking in the bright sunshine, then she began to make her way to the bottom. She stopped beside her horse and took something from the saddle-bag. She looked down at the leather pouch in her hand, then turned and hurled it into the waterhole. Giving a cry of utter despair, she began to run...

'What you need,' Emily said, 'is a proper overseer. Why don't you let Harry find someone for you?'

Morna sighed and shook her head. 'I don't think so, Emily. Sam does his best, and Dickon divides his time between the property and the shop. I expect we shall manage somehow.'

'Meanwhile, you are wearing yourself out trying to be in two places at once.' Emily stifled a groan, pressing a hand to the small of her back. She was nearing the birth of her fourth child and it had not been an easy pregnancy, but looking at Morna's face, she felt herself the stronger of the two. Morna simply did not seem to care any more, and she was worried about her friend. 'You look worn out.'

'I am a little tired, but I need to work. It – it helps me to forget. Besides, I can't really afford to take on an overseer at the moment.'

'But the shop has been doing so well.' Emily frowned. 'Hasn't it?'

'Yes...' Morna bit her lip. 'I gave Captain Smithson my share of the money from the first cargo and the remainder of mother's jewels so that he could buy a bigger cargo this time...'

'Go on,' Emily urged. 'You've more sense than to leave yourself with nothing. What happened?'

'The day I quarrelled with Philip, he – he returned while I was with ... while I was out, and he ransacked my room. He took everything of value he could find.'

'The wretch!' Emily cried, shocked. 'You should have reported it to the Governor.'

'And have my own brother arrested for theft?' Morna shook her head. 'You know I couldn't do that to Philip. No matter what he is – no matter what he has done, I couldn't betray him like that.'

'He deserves to be punished,' Emily said, her gentle face flushed with anger. 'You know he'll simply gamble and drink until the money has gone, don't you?'

'I expect so. I haven't seen him since that

day. He – he spoke of a position on the Governor's staff.'

'A deliberate lie! Philip's reputation would make that impossible – everyone knows he's nothing but a waster and a...' Emily looked at her friend's face, and sighed. 'I'm sorry, my dear. I didn't mean to hurt you. Surely you can't still care what happens to him?'

'I know it must seem foolish,' Morna admitted. 'But he is my brother, and we were once so close. I know he's very unhappy. What he did was unforgivable, but I was angry when I sent him away.'

'You can't be thinking of giving him another chance?'

'I don't know. Now that Jared is not there any more, it might be easier for him...' Morna's face twisted with pain. 'Nothing seems to matter any longer. I can't even hate Philip...'

'You mustn't give up, Morna. You're too young to waste your life regretting a man who did nothing but hurt you.' Emily paused as Morna looked at her sharply. 'Yes, I will say it. You are young and beautiful. I know of several men in the colony who would like to get to know you better. It's time you started to mix with other people – not just your customers, though you must be aware of how many men come to buy when you are there yourself?'

Morna laughed. 'You want me to go to the

Governor's dinner with you, don't you? Well, perhaps I shall, this time.'

'I should think so.' Emily smiled at her affectionately. 'Everyone admires you for what you've done, my dear – especially the men.'

'Philip said I was a source of amusement because I drove about with Pyke.'

'I think people were a little unsure about a woman who dared to cross the world and take up land here without the support of a husband, but now they all admire your independent spirit. It is people like you who will make this country great.' Emily chuckled as Morna shook her head in embarrassment. 'Oh, I know you don't like to be praised, my dear, but you mustn't let Philip's spite mislead you. Everyone is willing to be your friend. Now, what about some more of my special punch?'

'Let me do it.' Morna got up to pour the cool liquid into two tall crystal glasses. 'I think perhaps I shall spend more time in Sydney when Captain Smithson returns. Dickon will be quite happy to devote his time to the farm.'

'What about an overseer in the meantime? If it's a question of money...'

'No, it isn't just that. I feel Sam and Dickon would resent a stranger. Besides, perhaps Philip will come home...'

'So you intend to ask him, then?'

'I'm not sure.' Morna sighed. 'I feel I should at least attempt to see him and make my peace with him – but I shan't try to persuade him to come back.'

'Well, I think you are wrong. He doesn't deserve anything more from you, but I know better than to waste my breath arguing with you.' She sipped her drink again. 'I suppose you haven't heard from Jared?'

'No...' Morna turned away to look out of the window. 'I don't expect to hear from him. I pray that he has managed to find his way across the mountains to safety.'

'It's six months. If he'd been caught, we would have heard by now. I'm sure he must have succeeded.'

'Yes.' Morna blinked hard. She had tried to put the bittersweet memories out of her mind, but they still had the power to wound her. 'If you don't mind, I would rather not talk about it.'

'We'll talk about the Governor's dinner instead,' Emily agreed obligingly. 'Now, you've promised to come, Morna, so what will you wear?'

Morna grimaced as she approached the cluster of shabby wooden buildings near the harbour. It was the roughest part of town, where only the worst elements of Sydney society lived. Sounds of revelry were coming from inside the inn as she paused outside it, still unable to believe that Philip had sunk to this level. Surely Laurence Starr must be mistaken?

She had gone to her brother's friend, expecting Philip to be staying in lodgings near to the officers' quarters, but, to her surprise, the young lieutenant had told her that he had not seen him for several weeks.

'There was a bit of a scene over a gambling debt,' he said, looking awkwardly at her. 'Philip was drunk, and there was a fight. He was thrown out of the mess and I haven't seen him since. I think he's living at an inn down by the waterfront.'

'Thank you.' Morna bit her lip. 'Does my brother owe a great deal? I could perhaps pay his debts in a few months...'

'It wouldn't help him if you did, Miss Hamilton. He won't be welcome in the mess again.'

'I see.' She looked at him coldly. 'Then I shan't waste my money. Thank you, Lieutenant Starr. I shall not take up any more of your time.'

She walked off, her gown swishing angrily over the ground, leaving him staring after her with his mouth open. She was seething with fury inside. Philip's friends had been quick enough to drink with him while he had money in his pocket, but now that he could not pay his debts, they had ostracised him, making him an outcast.

Standing outside the inn, Morna felt a deep reluctance to enter such a foul house. It was the meeting place for ex-convicts who had lost the will to make anything of their lives, and were content to drink and sport with the whores who frequented it. Many expirees had become rich men and an accepted part of colonial society after serving their term, but many more had sunk back into the life of debauchery and depravity which had led them to be transported in the first place. It sickened Morna to think of her brother living among such men and women.

Taking a deep breath, she opened the door and went in. She gasped as the foul stench hit her, making her cover her nose with a scented kerchief. She stood on the threshold, her eyes moving round the room, searching for the man she hoped she would not find here. Seeing him hunched on a bench in a corner at the far side of the room, she began to make her way towards him, uncomfortably aware of the eyes staring at her from all directions. She heard the jeering laughter and the whispers, but ignored them, keeping her eyes on Philip's face.

He saw her before she reached him and scowled, draining his tankard. 'What do you want?' he grunted, as she stood silently in front of him. 'How did you find me?'

'Laurence Starr told me you might be here.' Morna looked at him, and was shocked by his haggard face and hollow eyes. 'Come back, Philip. It isn't fit for you here.'

'Back?' he laughed bitterly. 'You mean to the homestead, I suppose?'

'For now,' Morna agreed. 'When I've sold the next cargo, we'll return to England.'

'To England?' Philip looked up at her, his eyes brightening. 'Do you mean it, Morna?'

'Yes.' Morna's face was white with strain. 'I was wrong to persuade you to come here. I've ruined your life, and I'm sorry. I'll try to make it up to you – if you'll stop drinking and come back with me now.'

Philip covered his face with his hands, his shoulders shaking as deep shudders ran through him. 'I'm sorry, Morna. I've been a damned fool.'

'Yes, perhaps we both have.' She sighed. 'Please come back, Phil, I need you.'

He stared at her in disbelief. 'You need me?'

'Yes. I can't be at the property and the shop. Besides, I miss you.' It was not quite true, but her heart was stirred by pity for him, and what did it matter. 'Come with me now?'

He stood up, his face grey and unshaven. 'I owe ten shillings here – do you think...?'

'Of course.' She took several gold coins from her purse and gave them to him. 'I'll wait outside while you get your things, Phil.'

'Thank you. I'll be there in ten minutes.'

Morna nodded and went outside. She breathed deeply, feeling sick and close to tears. Somehow she had not expected to find Philip looking quite so haggard. She thought he might have been ill, and felt a warm glow inside. A few weeks of Jane's cooking would clear the grey shadows from his skin.

A ship was anchored in the bay, and passengers were coming ashore. Morna watched a family of five children, smiling as she saw them racing about excitedly, their faces revealing the delight they felt in being on dry land again. A rather elegantly dressed man paused for a moment on the jetty, looking around him with interest. Morna stared at him, a cold knot forming in her stomach as she instinctively turned away so that he should not see her face. It couldn't be he! He would never leave London! And yet even as her mind sought to deny it, she knew that the newcomer was Richard Stainton.

Feeling desperate to escape before he saw her, Morna pushed open the inn door, looking impatiently for her brother. She saw him sitting exactly where she had left him, a fresh tankard of ale in his hand. He drained it and then looked at her. For a moment their eyes met and held, then he hunched his shoulders and turned his back on her.

He was not coming with her. Morna closed her eyes for a moment, admitting defeat. Even if she went back there and forced him to leave with her, it would be a waste of time. As soon as he got the chance, he would return to his old ways. There was nothing she could do for him, except give him money from time to time. It was all he wanted from her.

Lifting her chin, Morna walked blindly away. She had lost both the men she had loved. Jared was far away by now, and no doubt he had forgotten her. As for Philip, it was better that she should try to forget him...

'You look beautiful, Morna,' Emily said as the girl came downstairs dressed in a slender gown of rose pink silk, with puffed sleeves and a filled flounce. 'Doesn't she, Harry?'

'She does indeed.' Harry replied, giving her a fond smile. 'Both my ladies look beautiful tonight.'

Emily laughed and shook her head. She patted her bulging stomach complacently. 'I know I look a sight at the moment, but thank you, Harry.'

Morna had moved away to where her cousin was sitting, nursing the youngest member of the Robson family.

'I feel guilty about going to the dinner without you, Jane.'

'Well, you need not be,' Jane replied firmly. 'I shall be much happier here with

Emily's children. You know that's true, so don't look so doubtful, Morna. It's time you went out and enjoyed yourself for a change.'

'And I shall feel so much better knowing Jane is here,' Emily said, glancing nervously over her shoulder. 'With so much talk about a mass breakout, I wouldn't enjoy myself if the children were alone with our servants.'

'You can't think any of them would hurt the children?' Morna looked shocked. 'I know there has been some unrest lately, but you've always been so good to your servants.'

'Well, we must hope you are right,' Emily said. 'It may all come to nothing; there have been rumours before, and it all petered out.'

'Of course nothing will happen,' Harry said, bringing his wife's velvet cloak to drape over her shoulders. 'The convicts know there's nowhere for them to go – so why should they riot?'

'I don't believe your servants would harm you,' Morna said, 'any more than Sam or Benjamin would turn on us.'

'You're a sensible woman,' Harry said approvingly. 'Now, the carriage awaits, ladies.'

Morna kissed her cousin's cheek and followed her impatient host outside. Harry had recently acquired a rather elegant carriage, and she knew he was eager to have it admired on its first real outing. It was both smart and comfortable. The ladies exclaimed over it with delight, and Harry glowed with their praise as he helped them to climb in.

Their journey was far more comfortable than the first one Morna had taken in Harry's wagon. She reminded him of it, and they all laughed together, remembering the day she had arrived in New South Wales. Morna tried not to remember all the disappointments and the pain she had suffered since then.

Her entry into the Governor's salon caused a little stir. Seeing all eyes turned in her direction, Morna wished she could run away, but Emily was clinging on to her arm, and Harry was steering them both towards their host.

'So, we are to have the pleasure of your company at last, Miss Hamilton,' he boomed. She looked up into his stern face, catching her breath, and then he smiled. 'You are very welcome.'

'Thank you, sir.' Morna curtsied gracefully.

Then she was being introduced to everyone present. Many of the faces were well known to her as customers at her shop, others she had seen only at a distance as they passed her in the street, but they all seemed to be smiling at her.

'And now,' the Governor boomed at her side, 'I should like you to meet a newcomer in our midst. Miss Hamilton, this is Sir

Richard Stainton – a gentleman from London we are honoured to have with us tonight.'

Morna had already seen the guest of honour. She froze as he smiled and held out his hand to her.

'This lady is an old friend, sir,' he said as the Governor looked puzzled. 'She is surprised to see me, no doubt. Morna, will you not give me your hand?'

Blushing, Morna held out her hand. It took all her willpower not to snatch it away as he bent his head and kissed it. She looked at him coldly, knowing that she was forced to be polite to him in front of their host.

'I hope you are well, Sir Richard?'

'Thank you, Morna. I am very well.'

'You must have much to say to each other,' the Governor said, smiling benevolently at them. 'I shall leave you together until dinner is served.'

Richard inclined his head as the Governor walked away, his hand fastening possessively on Morna's arm as she would have followed her host.

'You cannot leave me yet, Morna. People will wonder why you are being so impolite.'

She glanced up at him, her eyes scornful. 'If I had known you would be here this evening, I should not have come.'

His mouth twisted in an odd smile. 'Then it is fortunate for me that you did not know, isn't it? I should otherwise have had the trouble of seeking you out.'

'Why should you wish to see me? I think we have nothing to say to each other, Richard?'

'Surely you cannot be so unforgiving?' His brows went up. 'I have made my peace with Philip. We have forgiven each other, and I have undertaken to rescue the poor boy from his foolishness. He is drinking less since we met again, I do assure you.'

'If that is so, you may tell him to come home,' Morna said. 'I still do not believe there is anything for us to say to each other, sir.'

'Morna, my dear girl! You are still so bitter towards me? Yet I was the injured party, I believe? I offered you my heart and my name – and you rejected me so cruelly.' His fingers stroked her wrist and she sensed the menace behind his soft words. 'I wonder what your friends would say if they knew you were a heartless jilt?'

Her face paled. 'What do you want of me?'

'What should I want?' he asked, giving her a hurt look that was so false she felt like screaming. 'I ask nothing of either you or Philip but your forgiveness and your friendship.'

'I don't believe you,' Morna said, her eyes glittering with anger. 'And even if I did, I could never, never forgive you for what you did to Jared! Now, if you will excuse me, I wish to join my friends.'

'What a shame you will not accept my offer of friendship, Morna – and just when you are in such need of friends, too.'

'What do you mean? If you are threatening me...'

'No, I was merely thinking of your terrible loss.' Richard's mouth curved in a triumphant sneer. 'Captain Smithson was your business partner, I believe?'

'Captain Smithson is my partner. Why?' Her heart began to thump as she saw his cruel look.

'It is my unhappy duty to tell you that *Sea-Sprite* has sunk with the loss of all on board...'

'No!' Morna whispered, her hand flying to her throat. 'It can't be true – it can't!'

'I have already informed the Governor. He told me of your involvement with Captain Smithson. I am afraid this must be a shock for you.'

Morna's face was white as she stumbled away from him. Emily came to meet her, looking concerned as she caught her hands.

'So you've heard the news?'

'Yes.' Morna swallowed hard. 'Is it certain everyone was lost?'

'If Sir Richard's information is correct, it seems it must be so.' Emily squeezed her hand. 'Do you want to leave, my dear?'

'No. I – I shall stay.' Morna caught her trembling lower lip between her teeth. 'Captain Smithson was my friend, but he would not want me to run away. He knew the risks involved with a life at sea and wasn't afraid to face them. I have to live my life, and crying won't help me.'

'But you've lost everything, Morna.'

'I have the property – and a few hundred pounds that should belong to my partner. I don't think he would grudge the money to me now.'

Emily shook her head, the sparkle of tears in her eyes. 'You are so brave, Morna – but you know we will help as much as we can.'

'Yes, I know,' Morna said. 'Don't look so anxious, Emily. I shall manage very well.'

The guests were moving into the dining-room, and there was no more time to talk privately. Emily knew how proud her friend was, and her heart contracted with fear for the girl. She would not ask for help no matter how difficult her situation was. If Morna had not already told her that she had invested all her money in *Sea-Sprite*'s cargo, no one'd have guessed it from her behaviour now. She was very calm as she took her place at the dining table, laughing at something another guest said to her as if she had no cares in the world. Only the diamond-bright sparkle of her eyes gave any clue to the emotions she was so determinedly suppressing.

Even Emily could not guess how close to despair her friend was. Nor could she know that it was only pride that kept Morna from giving way to her grief and pain. She alone knew that Richard had hoped to destroy her by disclosing his terrible news so cruelly. Facing him across the dinner table, Morna gave him a scornful smile. If he thought he could break her spirit so easily, he would now see how wrong he was. She had lost the only man she had ever loved, and nothing else could hurt her like that again.

Seeing Richard's frown, Morna laughed and turned to her companion, who leant forward to listen eagerly to what she was saying. Tomorrow she would worry about how they would manage for money. For this evening, she must play out her masquerade!

'Jane, I'm home. Where are you?' Morna looked round the empty kitchen in surprise. She had just returned from Sydney, and had expected to find her cousin busy cooking their evening meal. She turned as Pyke came in. 'Do you know where Jane is?'

'When I went to stable the horses, Sam told me Harry Robson had fetched her an hour or so ago. Mrs Robson has gone into labour, and she asked for Jane to look after the children.'

'Oh, I see.' Morna frowned. 'I wonder if I should ride over to see how Emily is?'

'I'll go myself when I've had a bite to eat, miss. You should stay here and rest. You look exhausted – if you'll forgive me for saying so.'

Morna had spent the day visiting various seamen and asking if they had heard any more news about *Sea-Sprite*, but so far all anyone knew was what Sir Richard had told the Governor.

Seeing Pyke's cheeky look, Morna gave him a reluctant smile. 'You wretch! Oh, Pyke, I don't know what we would do without you these days. Yes, I would like you to go for me, please. I really am very tired, but I must know if Emily's baby has come yet. I've been so worried about the birth.'

'Sit down, and I'll get you some bread and meat,' Pyke said. 'You'll feel better when you've eaten, and there's no sense in worrying about something you can't do anything about.'

Morna sank into her rocking-chair, smiling slightly as she watched her servant fussing about the kitchen, bringing wine and setting the table with bread, cold meat, preserves and cheese.

'A feast fit for a king,' she said as he beckoned her to the table.

'For a queen, perhaps.' Pyke swept her an elegant bow. 'Dinner is served, Your Majesty.'

Morna gave a gurgle of laughter. 'Jared warned me you were a cheeky wretch.' The smile faded swiftly and her eyes clouded. 'I wish he was here! Oh, how I wish he would come back, Pyke.'

'Perhaps he will one day, miss.'

She shook her head. 'No, I know he can't. It would be too dangerous for him, especially now that Richard Stainton is here.'

'Him!' Pyke scoffed. 'The Captain would soon settle the hash of that slimy toad.'

'You don't know how evil he is,' Morna said. 'He nearly destroyed Jared once, and I am afraid of what would happen if they met again.'

'The Captain would kill him – if I didn't do for him first!'

Morna smiled at him. 'I believe you would, too! I never did ask you why you were transported, did I, Pyke?'

'Best you don't ask now,' Pyke said grinning at her. 'Not if you want me to ride over to the Robsons' tonight?'

'It doesn't matter.' Morna shook her head. 'I don't care what you did, Pyke. You were Jared's friend, and you've been loyal to me.'

'I'd give my life for you, miss,' Pyke said gruffly. 'Now I'd best go before I embarrass you.'

He went out quickly and Morna stared after him in surprise. She was used to Pyke's jokes, and to hear him speak so fervently was rather touching. It eased a little of the ache inside her. But she was not completely alone. She still had Jane, Emily – and Pyke.

Morna was smiling to herself as she washed the dishes. No matter how hard the next few years were, she would manage somehow. Suddenly realising that neither Sam nor Benjamin had come in for their supper, she frowned. Had they eaten earlier, before Jane left?

Looking out of the window, she thought the yard seemed oddly empty. There were no lights in the cabins, and no sign of the men. It was a little strange, and she decided to go and investigate. They would hardly still be working this late in the evening.

Pulling a shawl round her shoulders, Morna left the house and walked across the yard. She knocked at Sam's door and then at Benjamin's; there was no answer in either case. Noticing that the stable door was wide open, she hurried across to look inside. It was empty: all of the horses were gone.

'No...' she whispered. 'Oh, Sam ... Benjamin...You couldn't.You couldn't...'

She stared in disbelief at the empty stalls, shivering as the full horror of what had happened hit her. The two convicts she had trusted so completely had run away, and they had stolen all her horses – except those Pyke and Jane had taken.

Morna felt sick at their betrayal. She had felt so confident when she had told Emily that her convicts would never harm her. She shivered, realising that she was probably lucky to be still alive. If it was to be a mass breakout, as many colonists feared, she was in terrible danger, alone, and the horses gone. She was trapped, and she had no hope of escaping if the rampaging convicts should come this way.

Morna ran quickly back to the house, bolting the door behind her. She leaned against it for a moment, her heart beating wildly. Then she remembered that the windows were open and she rushed to secure them. Coming back to the little front parlour, she looked for a weapon, wishing Philip's pistol were still in the house. Finally, she fetched the carving-knife from the kitchen. It had a long wicked-looking blade, and it made her feel a little easier. At least she could fight for her life if need be.

She glanced at the little silver watch pinned to her silk blouse. It was nearly nine o'clock. How long ago had Pyke left, and how soon would he be back – if he ever came back? Now she was doubting everyone! Morna chided herself mentally: she must not lose all hope. But the house was so silent, and every creak set her nerves jangling. What time was it now?

Five minutes had passed, and she laughed at herself. She was being foolish. The convicts would probably not come here, and even if they did, she had no reason to fear them. She had never done anything to harm any of them. Yet even as she tried to reassure herself, she knew that they would loot and burn every property they passed through. Many of their number had old scores to settle, and in their bitterness they would not care whom they destroyed.

Morna picked up a shirt from a pile of mending, and forced herself to concentrate on patching it neatly. Sam would probably never wear the garment again, but it did not matter. She needed something to do – anything to keep her from jumping at her own shadow!

Suddenly she heard the sound of a horse's hooves, and listened intently. Yes, it was just one horse. It must be Pyke at last! He had come back to her, and she had been wrong to doubt him. She jumped to her feet with a cry of relief, letting the shirt fall to the floor. Running to the door, she unbolted it, flinging it open just as a man came up the veranda steps.

'Pyke – is that you?'

Morna halted as she saw the man clearly in the moonlight her heart missing its beat for one terrible moment. 'Richard?' she gasped. 'Why have you come here?'

He moved purposefully towards her, an odd, gloating smile on his lips. 'I have some news for you, Morna. Won't you ask me to come in?'

CHAPTER TEN

'You have news – about the convicts?' Morna moved back, unwilling to let him enter, yet eager to learn more of what was going on. 'Has there been a mass break-out as some of the colonists feared?'

Richard pressed home his advantage, moving inside and closing the door behind him. 'Wild rumours have been flying about the town for most of the day, though no one knows for sure. It is probable that some of the outlying homesteads will be attacked.'

'Did you come here to warn us?' Morna looked at him curiously, wondering that he should show such concern.

'The Governor was anxious about you and your cousin. Two women living alone this far from town are naturally more vulnerable than those who have their menfolk to protect them.' Richard glanced around the small parlour. 'I saw no sign of your convicts as I rode up, and the stables are empty – have they deserted you?'

Morna hesitated, instinctively distrusting him. 'I'm not sure where they are. They've probably ridden out to check on the flocks.'

'Don't lie to me, Morna, I know you are

alone. Your cousin is at the Robsons' – I saw her arrive as I left for town – and your trusted servants have joined the revolt. I saw it in your face when I arrived. You are alone and frightened!'

'You didn't ride out here to warn me about the revolt, did you?' Morna stared at him suspiciously. 'Just why did you come, Richard?'

'I told you, I have some news for you. I heard something when I returned to town that concerns you – and, naturally, I thought it my duty to tell you in person.'

'I thought you meant...' Her heart raced as she looked into his eyes and saw the cold gleam of triumph there. 'But I should have known you did not come out of concern for my safety. You want revenge, don't you?'

'I told you I would make you sorry for crossing me, Morna. You and your poor, foolish brother.'

She gave a gasp of horror. 'What have you done to Philip?'

'It was not necessary for me to do anything.' His lips twisted cruelly. 'Philip was destroying himself. I merely helped him to do it more quickly. It was an act of kindness. At least his suffering is over.'

'Philip is dead!' Morna felt the certainty of it as she looked into his face. 'You murderer!'

'Your brother was a drunken sot, and he died in a brawl with the scum he lived with.

I merely gave him the money to buy rum. I did not force him to quarrel with the dregs of humanity who slit his throat. They were ex-convicts and they will hang for their crime when they are caught, of course.'

'For a crime you masterminded,' Morna accused, her eyes flashing angrily. 'Oh, I'm sure you have been very clever about it, but I know you had him killed. I know it, and I shan't rest until you are brought to justice!'

'How beautiful you look when you are angry,' he murmured. 'Indeed, I think the life here suits you. You are no longer a girl, but a woman – a very desirable woman.'

Morna recoiled as she heard the note of menace in his words. 'Don't you dare to come any nearer! If you touch me, I'll...'

'There is no one to hear you scream, Morna – and I shall enjoy your resistance. Do you know your eyes are almost purple when you are frightened? It is such a pity that you would not marry me. We should have made a striking couple, and it would have amused me to teach you to obey your master.'

'You would never have been my master.' She took a step backwards as he moved towards her. 'I am not afraid of you, Richard. I despise you! You are evil and cruel, and I would die before I surrendered to you.'

'Oh, but you will surrender to me, Morna. I mean to have what you denied me.' His eyes flared with a hateful lust as he saw the shock run through her. 'Yes, now you have begun to understand. I shall have my revenge... A complete, satisfying revenge.'

'If you touch me, I shall have you arrested for rape.'

'But you will not be able to tell your tales, Morna.' He smiled as he heard her gasp of horror. 'I came too late, you see. The convicts had been here before me...'

'No...' she whispered, backing away from him in fear. 'Even you could not be that evil!'

'You call me evil,' he growled, moving towards her menacingly as she retreated. 'Yet you led me on with your false smiles. You promised to wed me even as you betrayed me with your lover – and then you jilted me. You left me, and I could see them all laughing behind my back, wondering why you ran away – and so far away. I swore I would make you pay one day.'

Morna felt the table at her back. Her fingers ran along the edge of it until they touched something hard and cold. She seized the handle of the carving-knife, lunging at him as he reached out for her. Her attack surprised him, and the blade of her knife ripped through the. velvet sleeve of his jacket. She saw the shock in his eyes as he felt a stab of pain, and blood seeped through the slashed material.

'You viper!' he snarled, seizing her wrist and twisting it hard so that she cried out. The knife dropped from her hand as he exerted more pressure. 'You'll pay for that, you bitch!'

He struck her across the face, the force of the blow sending her spinning into the table. She screamed as he came at her again, grasping her long hair and twisting her head towards him. His mouth came down to cover hers, but she spat in his face defiantly. He pulled her hair again, bringing tears of pain to her eyes, holding her head so that she could not avoid his greedy mouth as it ground against hers so hard that she tasted blood. She went for his face with her nails, drawing deep lines across his cheek. He cursed, and thrust her roughly back so that she stumbled and fell. As she struggled to rise, he was on top of her, bearing her to the ground as he ripped at the bodice of her gown. She heard the fine material tear, and shuddered as his hands clutched at her breast.

'Leave her alone, you filthy beast!'

Morna heard Pyke's cry and gave a sob of relief. She saw him dart across the room and bend down to pick up the carving-knife.

'No, Pyke, you mustn't!' she screamed as he raised his arm to plunge the vicious blade into Richard's back.

But Richard had become aware of the

danger. He sprang away from her and turned to meet the little man's attack with a muffled curse. Pyke lunged at him desperately with the knife; the blade narrowly missed his throat, but before Pyke could steady himself to strike again, Richard grabbed his forearm, forcing it back so that he shouted in agony. They struggled fiercely for possession of the weapon, and then they were on the floor, rolling over and over as they crashed into the furniture.

Morna got to her feet, watching in horrified fascination as the two figures locked in a fierce combat. She heard a terrible scream and gasped, shrinking back as Richard got to his feet and turned to look at her. There was blood on his face and hands, blood on his shirt and breeches. On the floor, Pyke's body twitched horribly and then lay still.

'You killed him,' Morna whispered. 'You killed poor little Pyke. You wicked, evil man! I hope you burn in Hell...'

'If I burn, I'll take you with me.'

Richard took hold of the handle of the knife as he started towards her. Morna screamed wildly, looking for a way of escape, but the door was behind him and there was no way past. He was like a rabid dog, his eyes full of an insane hatred as he raised his arm to slash at her face with the knife – and then the shot rang out.

Morna saw Richard jerk as the ball embedded itself deep into his back. A look of surprise entered his eyes as he seemed to crumble at the knees and sink slowly to a kneeling position, still looking at her until he fell forward on the ground at her feet.

Only then could Morna tear her eyes from him. She looked across at the door, seeing the man who stood there for the first time, the pistol still smoking in his hand. She drew a deep, sobbing breath, calling his name as she ran towards him.

'Oh, Jared...' she cried as he dropped the pistol and caught her in his arms. 'You came back to me – you came back to me...'

'My darling girl,' he whispered hoarsely, stroking the nape of her neck as she wept against his shoulder. 'I stopped to check the barns. Thank God I was in time.'

He held her tightly until she stopped shivering, and then she drew away from him, gazing up into his face in wonder. 'But how – how did you get here? How did you know I needed you?'

He touched her cheek, brushing away a tear with his thumb. 'Pyke came to fetch me. He was on his way to the Robsons' when he saw a group of escaping convicts. They called to him to join them, but instead he came to fetch me.'

'How did he know where to find you? I thought you must be safe across the mountains by now. Oh, why did you come back, Jared? You know how dangerous it is for you – especially now. You could be shot on sight by the militia.'

'I've been hiding out at Prowther's Rock for a couple of weeks, waiting for an opportunity to see you. Pyke and the others knew I was there – they've all brought me food.'

'Oh, Jared, if only you knew how much I've needed you!' Morna caught her breath on a sob. 'So Pyke knew you were here all the time. Why didn't he tell me?'

'I warned him not to.' Jared frowned. 'I wasn't sure you would want to see me after what I said to you before I left.'

'Of course I wanted to see you! I've thought of you constantly since that day – praying always that you would reach safety and be free.'

'Then you don't hate me, Morna?'

'You know I don't! I have always loved you – nothing you could do will ever change that.'

'What a fool I've been,' Jared said, his voice husky with emotion. 'What a blind, stupid fool, not to see that your love was the most precious gift a man could possess.

'Oh, Jared...' she whispered. 'You do care for me...'

'Morna, my sweet girl...'

They gazed into each other's eyes, caught up in the wonder of their love, bound by invisible ties. For the first time there were no barriers between them, no lies or mis-understandings. It might have been eternity or merely seconds before the spell was broken.

'Pyke...' Morna said at last. 'He was trying to defend me...'

They moved as of one accord to bend over the man who had been such a good friend to them both. Any hopes that Morna might have had were stilled as she saw the blood staining the ground where he lay. Tears sprang to her eyes, and Jared caught her hand tightly.

'He died almost instantly, my love. Remember he was your friend, and don't weep for him. He always liked to see you laugh. He worshipped you from the moment you rescued him, did you know that?'

'Tonight he said something...' Morna brushed away her tears. 'Richard is dead, isn't he?'

'You can be sure of that,' Jared said, his face grim. 'I aimed to kill, and my shot went home.'

'Then it is my duty to arrest you for the murder of Sir Richard Stainton...'

Morna and Jared swung round as the officer advanced into the room. He was armed with a pistol, which he was aiming at Jared, and followed by two uniformed soldiers.

Morna gasped as she recognised Philip's friend. 'It was not murder, Lieutenant Starr. Richard Stainton killed my servant and attacked me. Jared shot him to save my life!'

Laurence Starr looked down at the baronet's lifeless body. 'A ball in the back – that's murder to my way of thinking, Miss Hamilton.'

'If Jared had not fired instantly, he would have killed me,' Morna said. 'Why won't you believe me?'

'It's not up to me to believe or disbelieve your story, Miss Hamilton, though I've reason to suspect that you would lie to protect this man. He was already wanted for an assault on your brother and for trying to escape. It will be up to the Governor to decide whether or not he is guilty.' He turned to the soldiers behind him. 'Put the chains on him – he's dangerous.'

'No!' Morna cried. 'I won't let you take him.'

She darted forward, intending to pick up the pistol Jared had dropped, but he guessed her motives and caught her arm, restraining her as she struggled against him.

'No, Morna, you will not be implicated in this more than you are already.' She looked up at him imploringly, and he smiled. 'I know, my darling, I know – but this time you must let me decide what is best.'

'Oh, Jared,' she whispered. 'If I should lose

you now…'

'Don't be foolish, my love,' he chided, glancing towards the lieutenant. 'I am not armed, sir. May I give something I have in my pocket to Miss Hamilton?'

'Yes – but don't try to trick me.' Laurence Starr's finger moved uneasily on the trigger.

'If anything should happen to me, this is yours.' Jared took a small oilskin packet from the pocket of his coat and pressed it into her hand.

'Jared… No!' she cried, her face white with agony.

He touched his fingers to her lips. 'Keep it for me, then?'

She nodded, the tears streaming down her cheeks as Jared smiled. He walked away from her, standing calmly as the soldiers fastened a chain around his wrists.

'I am ready,' he said.

'Miss Hamilton, I am afraid I must ask you to come, too,' Lieutenant Starr said, looking at her awkwardly. 'I think the Governor may want to question your part in all this.'

'No!' Jared strained at his chains, suddenly racked with anger as he realised she also was to be accused. 'She had nothing to do with it. I killed him. Hang me if you will, but leave her alone.'

Morna ran to him, catching his hands before the soldiers could turn on him. 'I want to come with you, Jared. I know the truth – I am sure the Governor will listen to me.'

'You have more faith in British justice than I,' he said bitterly.

'I have faith in God,' Morna replied quietly. 'He brought you back to me when I needed you so desperately. Surely He will help us now?'

'So Emily has another daughter,' Morna said, looking at Dickon as he brought the news to her in the little parlour behind the shop. 'She is well? They are all safe – there was no trouble with the convicts?'

'Emily is as well as can be expected after a hard birth.' Dickon frowned. 'A few barns were burnt at a neighbouring farm, but the Robsons were lucky. The revolt has been squashed and the Governor has decided to be merciful. Some of the ringleaders will be flogged, but there will be no executions. In William Bligh's day they would not have got away with it so lightly, but our present Governor is a reasonable man.'

'That remains to be seen,' Morna said. 'Have you heard from Sam and Benjamin?'

'They are at the farm as usual.' Dickon shook his head at her. 'You should have known they would not join the revolt, lass. Sam has asked me to explain about the horses. He knew something was going on, and his first thought was to hide them. He didn't realise you were alone in the house. He wasn't there when Pyke left for the Robsons', and he assumed you must have gone with him. When he and Benjamin came back to find Pyke dead and you gone, he was half out of his mind with worry. Anyway, he wants you to know he's sorry he wasn't there when you needed help.'

'It was not his fault,' Morna said. 'Even if he had been there, he could not have prevented what happened – he might even now be imprisoned with Jared.'

'You've heard nothing yet?'

'No.' Morna got up to pace the room restlessly. 'As you know, the Governor ordered my release, provided I stayed here in town, but he has refused to grant me an interview.'

'Could you not ask Harry Robson to intercede for you?'

'I do not think it would help, Dickon. The Governor says I must be patient while he examines the evidence – but how can I be patient while Jared is a prisoner? He is innocent of murder. If he had not fired when he did, Richard would have killed me!'

'If only there were witnesses,' Dickon said, his face grave. 'Jared and Richard Stainton were old enemies – you can understand why the Governor feels he needs to examine the evidence carefully.'

'No, I cannot!' Morna cried, stamping her

foot. 'Do you think I would lie about what happened?'

'Yes, you would if it meant saving Jared's life.'

'Dickon – are you against me, too?'

'You know I'm not, lass. I'd swear black was white myself if it would help him,' Dickon smiled. 'Anyway, I thought you would want to know that Mrs Robson is recovering, though she had a bad time, and Miss Jane is staying to look after the children for a few days. I didn't tell her what had happened, as you asked me not to.'

'Jane thought a lot of Pyke,' Morna said. 'There's no point in upsetting her while she's at Emily's. She would feel it her duty to come to me, and the children need her more at the moment.'

'That's as maybe,' Dickon said doubtfully. 'But you'll have your own way as usual.'

Morna laughed ruefully. 'Now, don't scold! I need all my friends about me.' She caught his hand. 'What am I going to do, Dickon? What am I going to do?'

'There's nothing you can do, lass, except be patient.'

'I shall not sit here idly while Jared's future is in doubt,' Morna said, a militant gleam in her eyes. 'I am going to the Governor's house now, and I shall demand to see him. If he won't see me, I shall go every day until he gets tired of hearing my name!'

'If you will wait for one moment, Miss Hamilton, I shall ask if the Governor will see you.'

The Governor's aide-de-camp ushered her into a small salon, which was elegantly furnished in various shades of green, leaving her to pace impatiently up and down. This was the tenth day she had called, and on each of the previous nine her reception had always been the same. She turned hopefully as someone came into the room, frowning as she saw it was not the aide but a rather large, pleasant-faced, civilian.

'I beg your pardon,' he said. 'I came to recover my cane. I left it here, I'm sure. Ah yes, there it is.'

He walked across the room to pick up an ebony walking-stick with a gold top. Turning, he half bowed to Morna and went out, closing the door behind him.

Morna frowned as she tried to remember where she had seen the man before. It was some time ago, and in England, she thought. Before she could recall just where they had met, the door opened again and the aide returned.

'If you will please follow me, Miss Hamilton, His Excellency will see you now.'

Morna smoothed an imaginary crease from her lilac muslin gown, worn today over a silk slip of a slightly deeper shade. She had draped a delicate lace fichu round her shoulders, and her hair was tucked neatly beneath a cottage bonnet with wide ribbons of velvet to match her gown. Settling her face into a suitably demure expression, Morna followed her guide along the hall to the Governor's study.

He stood up as she entered, coming round from behind the large mahogany desk to set a chair for her himself.

'It is fortunate that you should call this morning, Miss Hamilton,' he said with a bland smile – as if he did not know that she called every day! 'I was about to write to you, requesting the pleasure of your company.'

Morna looked at him suspiciously. There was something a little unexpected in his manner. She thought she detected a twinkle in his eyes, and wondered what he could possibly find amusing in the situation.

'You must let me tell you what happened the other night, sir. Captain Trenwith saved my life. Had he not arrived when he did, Sir Richard would have murdered me.'

'That is a very serious accusation, Miss Hamilton. Why should Sir Richard wish to deprive us all of the company of one of our most beautiful ladies?'

'Because – because I jilted him a week before our wedding.'

The Governor's brows went up. 'Dear me, how very uncivilised of him! Surely a lady must be allowed to change her mind sometimes?'

Morna frowned, certain now that he was teasing her. 'I think you are unkind to mock me, sir. Jared is innocent of murder. He has suffered enough for the mistake he made. He does not deserve to be punished any more.'

'As it happens, I tend to agree with you.' The Governor smiled and shuffled a small pile of documents in front of him. 'I have some exciting news for you, Miss Hamilton. Captain Trenwith has received a full pardon from His Majesty King William IV...'

'A pardon?' Morna cried, her eyes flying to his face in astonishment. 'But I don't understand. How? Why? Oh, this is too wonderful to believe!'

She half rose from her chair and then sank back, bursting into tears. The Governor handed her a large white kerchief; and she thanked him, wiping her cheeks with trembling hands.

'You should thank Lord Edward Marston,' the Governor said. 'He arrived in Sydney only this morning, and he came straight to see me. It seems that a few months after Captain Trenwith's trial, Sir Richard Stainton was exposed as a cheat at the gaming tables. He killed the man who had accused him of cheating in a duel, and was obliged to leave London in a hurry, leaving behind a very incriminating document.'

'Incriminating...?' Morna stared at him. 'I don't understand – how could that help Jared?'

'Sir Richard was in the habit of keeping a journal. In it he described in great detail the people he had blackmailed and cheated out of their fortunes. Mr William Trenwith was among them. He also wrote of his intention to lure Captain Trenwith into a trap by encouraging him to hold up his coach. Lord Marston took this new evidence to the King, with whom he is apparently intimate, and His Majesty was gracious enough to grant Captain Trenwith a royal pardon.'

Morna gazed at him in wonder, still unable to believe what she was hearing. 'Then Jared is free at last?'

'There is still the little matter of the other evening.'

'But I told you what happened,' Morna cried. 'You must believe me?'

'I should not dream of doubting the word of such a lovely – and determined – young lady. If you will sign a statement exonerating Captain Trenwith, I think the matter can be closed.' He pushed a paper towards her. 'Lieutenant Starr may have exceeded his duty, Miss Hamilton, but he is an honest young man. He told me your story – I believe you will find it is all in order.'

Morna's eyes scanned the script eagerly,

taking the slender gold quill from his hand to sign her name with a flourish.

'When will Jared be free?' she asked. 'When can I see him?'

'Lord Marston went to secure his release a few moments ago. Perhaps you may have seen his lordship?'

'Yes, I did. He came to recover his cane. I could not recall his name – but now I remember where I first saw him. It was at Jared's trial.'

'He spoke in his defence, I believe? It is justice, then, that he should carry the good news to Captain Trenwith. I asked him to bring the captain to see me... Ah, I think this must be them now.' He looked up as his aide knocked and entered. 'Please show the gentlemen in.'

Morna rose as the two men entered, running to greet her lover. He smiled and caught her to him, holding her for one precious moment before taking her hand and turning to his companion.

'Teddy, I want you to meet Morna – the lady I hope will do me the honour of becoming my wife very soon.'

'Jared has told me a little about you, Morna. I hope we shall be friends?'

'I don't know how to thank you for what you have done,' she said, taking the hand he offered and smiling warmly. 'You must know how much this means to Jared ... to all of us.'

'It was nothing,' Teddy said. 'It was deuced boring at home without this rascal! I considered it an adventure.'

The Governor got up and came to join them. He handed Jared an important-looking document, and smiled.

'I wanted to give you this myself, Captain Trenwith, and to tell you that I believe justice has been done at last. I hope your experiences in the colony have not given you a distaste for the country. We need men of determination and stamina – and we need courageous young ladies like Miss Hamilton. Now that you are a free man, I shall be happy to do whatever I can to help you if you should choose to settle here.'

Jared took his hand without hesitation, grasping it firmly. 'The happiness of my future wife is my only concern, sir. I think you may be aware that she left England for my sake. It will be for Morna to decide whether we stay here or return.'

'You will at least be married here, I hope? If Miss Hamilton will permit me, I should like to give a reception for you. It is the least we can do in the circumstances.'

'We shall be married as soon as it can be arranged,' Jared said, looking down at her with a question in his eyes. 'If that is Morna's wish?'

She blushed as three pairs of male eyes turned on her expectantly. 'I'll marry you today if you wish it, Jared.'

'Perhaps we should wait until I've shaved and bought some decent clothes?'

They all laughed and Morna shook her head at him mock reproof.

'If you will let me know the details, my aide will arrange everything. Now, Captain Trenwith, I shall keep you no longer. I am sure you and Miss Hamilton must have much to say to one another.'

They all shook hands once more; then Jared took Morna's arm and led her outside. Once the door had closed behind them, he reached out and drew her into his arms, brushing her lips lightly with his own.

'If Teddy wasn't such a delicate soul, I would show you just how much I want to marry you, my darling,' he said, grinning at his friend's indignant look. 'But perhaps it would be better if I shaved first.'

'I brought your clothes with me,' Teddy said. 'My man will have secured lodgings for us by now, and a hot bath for you would not come amiss, my friend.'

'You brought your valet all this way? By God, that beats everything!' Jared threw back his head and roared with laughter. 'Forgive me, Teddy – but a valet?'

His friend smiled, understanding the cause of Jared's high spirits. 'You may mock me if you will, but James is invaluable to my comfort on a sea voyage.'

'Oh – if only Pyke could hear you say that!' The smile faded from his eyes, and Morna's hand reached out for his. 'God rest his soul.'

'He has been decently buried, Jared,' she whispered. 'He is at peace now.'

'Amen.' Jared carried her hand to his lips, kissing it. 'You will excuse me, my love. I must leave you for a little while.'

'I shall be at the homestead. Jane will have returned by now and I must tell her the good news.' She looked at Lord Marston. 'You will both dine with us tonight, I hope?'

'I shall be delighted, Morna.'

'Then I shall see you later.' She glanced up at Jared, her heart skipping as she saw the look in his eyes. 'Do not be late, Jared – you know my cousin does not like to be kept waiting.'

'I shall try not to disappoint you, Miss Hamilton.'

He laughed as her eyes took fire, watching as she turned and walked away from them.

'That was a delicious meal, Jane,' Jared said. 'I believe you have excelled yourself this evening.'

Jane smiled across the table at him. 'I could do no less for such a special occasion.' She got to her feet and looked round at the expectant faces: Emily and Harry; Sam, Benjamin, Dickon and his Mary – and in the place of honour, Lord Marston. 'I should like to propose a toast to the man who made this all possible.'

'I shall drink to that,' Jared said at once, saluting his friend with his glass. 'To you, Teddy – the best of comrades.'

'Dash it all, old fellow.' Teddy Marston's skin was brick red. 'Only repaying a favour, what?'

Morna was sitting at his right-hand side, and she turned to salute him with her own glass. 'We owe you a debt we can never repay, Teddy.'

'The pardon was a small thing. As for the other charge against Jared, well, my dear, the Governor was about to release the fellow into your custody when I arrived. He told me he was convinced of his innocence, and that even if he had believed him guilty, he would have been obliged to give way before your persistence.'

His eyes were gleaming with mischief, and everyone laughed. Morna had wondered if the elegant lord from London would object to dining with her bond-servants, but she need not have worried; he was completely at ease and had spent most of the evening entertaining everyone with stories of military life in India.

She glanced across the table, letting her eyes dwell on the handsome face of the man she loved. All trace of bitterness had gone from those masterly features, yet the pride and the strength remained. He was not the youth who had captured her heart so many years ago, nor was he the bitter, resentful soldier who had returned home after his father's suicide. This was another man, one who had suffered terribly and survived. He was perhaps a better, stronger person for all that had happened to him over the last two years, more capable of showing compassion and love.

Tonight, dressed in an immaculate white shirt and black breeches, with a velvet coat that fitted his broad shoulders like a second skin, he was a man that any woman would be proud to wed. Morna's heart was filled to the brim with love and pride, and the happiness shone from her like a beacon.

'I propose a toast to Jared and his future wife,' Teddy said, and everyone murmured agreement.

Then Jared got to his feet, his eyes bright with sincerity and deep emotion as he looked at Morna. 'Now, my friends, I want you to lift your glasses in a very special toast. I am grateful to Teddy for securing the pardon and for coming all this way to help me – but without one special person it would have been too late.' He smiled at Morna, his eyes gazing into hers as he lifted his glass to sip the wine. 'To you, my darling – for without your love and devotion, I could not have borne it.'

Morna blushed as everyone got to their feet to toast her. She looked across at Jared, suddenly wanting desperately to be alone with him.

'There is someone who must be feeling very left out in all this,' she said.

'Oh?' His brows went up. 'I thought all our friends were here tonight?'

'I'm talking about Devil Lad.'

Jared looked puzzled. 'I don't understand you.'

She looked at Jane and her servants, laughing as they shook their heads. 'He doesn't know – so you all kept the secret?' She rose as they nodded and grinned, holding out her hand to Jared. 'Come, I have a surprise for you...'

'What made you buy him, Morna? And how on earth did you persuade Smithson to ship him out here? I know what a vicious brute he can be.' Jared stroked the stallion's velvet nose, laughing as the horse snorted and shook his head. 'Yes, it's me, old fellow – and I've missed you, too.'

'I knew you always planned to breed from him,' Morna said with a little smile. 'It was my intention to be your partner when I offered to buy him.'

'Only my partner?'

Jared's eyes glinted with amusement as he

looked at her in the shadowed dimness of the stables, and Morna laughed. 'You wretch! Must you remind me of my foolishness? I was a child then – a wilful child who thought she could have anything she wanted.'

'I was the fool, not you, Morna.' Jared reached out and drew her against him, so that she could feel the warmth of his body through the fine lawn of his shirt. He held her close to his heart, possessively, as if even now he could not quite believe that he was free at last – free to touch and love the woman he had wanted so desperately for so long. 'I was so blinded by my bitterness and my desire for revenge that I could not see the happiness you were offering me. When I came back from India, Naomi begged me to punish the man who had destroyed my father. In my heart I knew that his own grief and unhappiness had led him into Stainton's trap, but I allowed myself to follow the same path he had taken. When Naomi tried to keep you from seeing me that day, it was because she was afraid I might fall in love with you and so be swayed from my purpose. I think it was her thirst for revenge that made me act as I did.'

'She must have loved your father very much?'

'I believe she did. That is why I asked Teddy to provide her with a cottage and a pension when the estate was sold. Now that it seems I may be able to recover at least some of the money my father was cheated of, I shall be able to repay him. You should be entitled to reclaim Philip's estate, too.'

'Poor Philip,' she said, looking up at him with sadness in her eyes. 'Why did he quarrel with you, Jared? He never would tell me.'

'Does it matter now?' Jared frowned as she was silent. 'Philip was my friend once, but when he came back from university he had changed. He asked more than friendship from me. I showed my revulsion too plainly, and he forced a fight on me.'

'You rejected his love, and so it turned to hatred. Poor, unhappy Philip.'

'An unnatural love, Morna.'

'Yes. He could not help his nature although he struggled against it – and so it destroyed him.' She turned away as tears stung her eyes.

Jared's hands slipped round her waist, his lips moving softly on her hair. 'Philip was weak, Morna. I sent you away with cruel words, but you followed me into exile. You saved my life – and my soul.'

Behind them the stallion snickered softly, and Morna swung round to face her lover, her eyes bright. 'Let's go to Prowther's Rock, Jared. I watched you ride out alone so many nights from my window – tonight I want to go with you.'

Jared nodded, understanding her restless mood. He saddled her horse and Devil Lad, leading them outside and helping Morna to mount. They rode out of the yard, away from the house and the lights and the laughter of their friends. The night sky was lit by a pale moon that cast a silver-white light over trees, fields and the dark, forbidding mountains, giving them a magical air of mystery. The horses seemed to sense the mood of their riders, carrying them at a gentle pace so that their spirits were lulled by the silence and beauty of the night.

Helping her to dismount at the foot of the rock, Jared took Morna's hand as they climbed to the plateau. She stood looking out over the land, seeing it as Jared must have seen it on so many nights, feeling the peace and tranquillity enter her soul. As Jared's arms went round her, she trembled, leaning back against his warm body, sighing her content.

'I used to stand here and look at the mountains,' he said, his voice soft and husky in her ear. 'Sometimes I wanted to go on – to find the freedom I thought I needed. Then I would look back at the house and I knew I could never leave you. Sometimes I almost hated you because you held me here, yet even while I chaffed at those invisible bonds, I wanted you so desperately.'

Morna turned her face so that his lips brushed hers. 'Yet when I sent you away, you came back. Why?'

'I found the trail across the mountains easily, Morna. I intended to go for ever when I drove you away with those cruel lies. I knew I could never come back, and I didn't want you to waste your life waiting for me when I might never have anything to offer. You were already such a success.'

Morna moved within the circle of his arms, so that she could see his face. 'I wanted nothing from you but your love.'

'I know that, my darling.' He smiled ruefully. 'I was too proud to take all you offered without being able to give in return.'

'But you worked so hard for me.' Morna sighed. 'Well, I have nothing but the property now. Everything else I had was lost when *Sea-Sprite* went down.'

'I am sorry, Morna. I mean that. If I could turn back the clock and restore everything to you, I would. I was wrong to resent your success. I know that now. When it seemed that I had lost you for ever, I realised that, without love, nothing else is worth having. Money, property, power – they are useless if you have no one to share them with.'

'I lost a friend when that ship sank,' Morna said, smiling up at him mistily. 'The rest doesn't matter – especially now that I have you. We can sell up and go back to

England if you wish, Jared.'

'Only if that is what would make you happy. If we wish it, Teddy will settle our affairs in England.' He paused for a moment, looking at her thoughtfully. 'There is another alternative.'

'I don't understand?'

'Did you open the packet I gave you when I was arrested for Stainton's murder?'

'No, why should I?'

'Because it was yours. I gave it to you.'

'I kept it for you,' Morna said. 'What would I have found if I had opened it?'

'You asked me why I came back. The most important reason was that I found my life was worthless without you, but...' Jared paused, an odd look in his eyes. 'When I was imprisoned in the holds of *Sea-Sprite*, I tried to help one of my fellow convicts. He was an old man, and he died before we reached land, but before he died he gave me something. He said it was the lease of a thousand acres north of here in the Hunter valley. He had been there some years before and had been granted this land. When his wife died, he went back to England expecting to live out his days on his old family estate; but his cousin, who he had left in charge as his steward, had been cheating him for years. They quarrelled violently over it and the cousin was killed in the struggle. He was charged with murder and sentenced to transportation, but he had managed to keep the packet hidden on him while he was in prison. I suppose he had some hope of escaping and going back to his land.'

'So you had the lease all this time?' Morna gazed up at him enquiringly.

'Yes, but I didn't really believe it was genuine. I thought someone else would have settled it long ago, even if it had once belonged to my friend.' Jared's eyes gleamed with sudden excitement. 'But it is there, Morna, just as he said. There's a house, barns – everything. The land is fertile, and there's so much of it...'

Morna saw the gleam in his eyes and smiled. 'You want to go back again, don't you?'

'I think we could make a good life for ourselves by the Hunter, Morna. There are no penal settlements, and it is an area where a man could feel free – but it depends on you. I want you to be happy. I know your friends are here, and...'

She pressed her fingers to his lips, silencing him. 'My life is with you, Jared. I followed you half across the world; I'll follow you to the Hunter River if it's what you want.'

He looked down at her, his eyes lighting with a deep, fierce love. 'You have a wild, brave heart, my darling,' he said. 'What other woman would have had the courage to do what you did?'

'Every week women give up the comfort and safety of their homes to accompany the men they love to a new life, Jared. I am no different from any of the other women who come here.'

'But you had to do it alone, Morna.' He touched her cheek with a kind of reverence, feeling the certainty of his love for her. She was his woman, his love and his friend. He realised now that he had known it always, but he had fought against the chains, believing that he needed freedom more. Now he saw that there was all the freedom he could ever desire in a love that gave more, much more, than it took. A glorious, wonderful love that made his insides melt as he looked at her. 'You sacrificed so much for me, and in future I intend to do whatever pleases you.'

A wave of happiness swept over her, bringing her close to tears. She had waited so long for this moment and now she felt so full of emotion that she could scarcely bear it. To cover her intense feelings, she lifted her head, looking at him with a teasing smile.

'Do you know what would please me most just now, Jared?'

He saw the wicked gleam in her eyes and laughed softly as the flame of desire surged in him. She was his woman – and what a woman! She was not afraid to let him see that she wanted his love, and he gloried in it, knowing that her hunger would match his own.

'Your wish is my command,' he whispered huskily, taking her hand to lead her inside the cave.

With a sigh of content, Morna moved into his arms as his mouth came down to brush hers with the softest of kisses. She felt the familiar tingle of desire inside her as she strained against him, her pulses beginning to race madly.

Her fingers pushed impatiently at the thin material of his shirt, wanting to explore his gleaming skin, and he laughed exultantly as he heard her moan of frustration.

'Patience, my wild one,' he murmured, his voice throaty with desire. 'I'll have you know that this garment you have so little respect for is fashioned of the finest lawn!'

But he was as eager as she, and soon their clothes were scattered heedlessly on the sandy floor of the cave. Her skin was like pale silk in the moonlight as he gathered her to him, his hungry cry lost as their lips met in a passionate kiss and their straining bodies fused. Then there was nothing but the soft sound of their breathing and the sweet murmurings of love. A love that would last for all eternity.

Overhead, the moon smiled benevolently on a shadowed earth, rising high above the mountains.

This Large Print Book, for people
who cannot read normal print,
is published under the auspices of

THE ULVERSCROFT FOUNDATION

L W
St. M
GP
WP
Wat
Wh P
IOOF
MM
R.P.
MR.S